HIDDEN VALLEY
THE AWAKENING
2nd Edition

JON MORGAN WOODWARD

"*Hidden Valley: The Awakening* is more than a story, it's an experience. Inclusive of *young love*, terrifying horror, and **suspense** that will leave you at the edge of your seat; *Hidden Valley: The Awakening* can only be defined as such. I was never a big fan of horror/thriller flicks, but this book, and the script, left me **smiling, tearing,** and **fearing**."

~ Amir Villani, Executive Producer,

"With *Hidden Valley: The Awakening*, the actor and filmmaker Jon Woodward emerges as a fresh young literary talent. **Addictive** like crack-cocaine; sleek, **sexy**, and vivid. I devoured this book with an insatiable hunger; my compliments to the chef! **Move over** *Twilight, True Blood*, and *Hemlock Grove!*"

~ Chris Berube, Writer, Chicago

"Reading *Hidden Valley: The Awakening* was certainly an awakening to me! A horror/thriller has never been in my selected genre of reading. I found the book **eye-opening** about what truly transpires in high school these days, from the secrets of young love, to sexuality amongst teens, corruption between adults and children, law enforcement and the schools they protect, and even a flashback to the simplicity of **small town America** gone horribly and horrifyingly wrong. This book has it all, and then some. Thanks for waking me up Jon Woodward. I could hardly fall sleep at night! Can't wait to learn more from your **next book!**"

~ Denise O'Brien, Publicist & Author

"*Hidden Valley: The Awakening* is **fresh**! It's more than your average horror/love story. Jon Woodward hits audiences on all levels of life and makes the story **relatable to anyone** who reads it, from teens to adults. This is going to be the next best-selling book series with a great new flavor."

~ Hassan Mahmoud, Actor &Write

"*Hidden Valley: The Awakening* was an **awesome read**. It kept me coming back for more. I had a hard time putting it down. The story line kept adding things in at just the right time. It was like a soap opera in book form. Good **plot twists**, and in-depth characters. I look forward to the movie."

~ Kevin Pappin

"It's *Friday Nights Live* meets *The Lost Boys* via *Werewolf in Paris*. **Jon Woodward** does in one book what *Twilight* couldn't do in four movies."
~ Chris Berube, Film Editor, Sherman Oaks, CA

"*Hidden Valley* promises to be a saga beloved by youth and adults alike. **Raunchy** and **raw**, Jon Morgan Woodward perfectly captures the **passion** and **tomfoolery** that is part of the adolescent experience. What appears to be a simple story of young love and **old friendships** unfolds with **chilling complexities** to a tale that will leave your mouth wide open. You won't be able to set the book down for fear **the story will come alive** in your absence."
~Kali L. Findley
Ohio Northern University '13

"A **captivating** story encompassing several genres – teen angst, horror, fantasy and a touch of **comedy** to relieve the suspense. It delves into relationships intimately and from all angles. A fascinating look at **a small town with a terrifying secret**."
~ Kat B., Avid Reader

HIDDEN VALLEY

THE AWAKENING

Jon Morgan Woodward

Adapted from the screenplay Hidden Valley: The Awakening

Copyright © 2013 Jon Morgan Woodward

2nd Edition 2015

ISBN-13: 978-1-935795-36-0

Printed in the United States of America by

DEDICATION

To my children,

For pushing me to go back to the industry that I truly love.

Shane and Desiree

Josh

Christopher and Anna

Miranda and Eric

and my inspiration, Jacob!

ACKNOWLEDGEMENTS

I would like to thank four people in my life that have inspired me. They kept me going through the good and the very difficult times of my life.

First, my sister's, Judy and Kathy who has always been there for me, come hell or high water.

Then, the inspiration in my life, Teresa Donovan-Cotter.

Kathleen Buchholz, who, without her, my life would never be what it is today.

Denise O'Brien, for her steadfast support and belief in my dream.

FOREWORD

It is rare indeed that a story concept in an early draft of an uncompleted screenplay can knock you out of your seat. Imagine my surprise when it happened to me.

I've known Jon Morgan Woodward for many years, and I knew him to be a talented and accomplished actor, a man of letters, a PhD in Naturopathy with specialization in Forensic Profiling, and a darn good friend. We had been talking about making a film together for quite some time, so he emailed me some twenty odd pages of a screenplay that he had started to write, and he wanted my opinion.

I was busy writing my own films, putting together film projects, so I received the pages and printed them out, anticipating that I would take a look later that evening after I could come up for air from my day's activities.

As the pages spat out of my printer, I found myself compelled to read the damn thing. I got hooked. I could not put the pages down. I had to read it all, then and there.   When I had finished, I realized that I wanted more. It kept me hanging. I wanted to know what happened next. I called Jon and asked him, "Where are you going with this?" He said, "You'll have to wait until I'm done."

Some weeks later the screenplay was finished, and I hungrily consumed it. The story and the characters were compelling and so vividly described that it was an easy read. What struck me the most was the surprise throughout the overall story. I could never anticipate what would happen next. There were harder left hand turns and shocks than I had seen in any script, EVER!

I have been in the business for better than 35 years, and I had read many screenplays, but I knew that this was something rare indeed! Jon had created a well-constructed horror film with shocking revelations and deeply human characters with a unique twist.

My somewhat checkered past led me to become involved with many successful horror film franchises including *Friday the 13th*, *Nightmare on Elm Street*, and *Halloween*. I could recognize when someone had caught lightning in a bottle. Jon Morgan Woodward had done it. It was an amazing screenplay.

We immediately set to work with getting the movie produced because I KNEW this film HAD to be made! It was during this process that Jon announced that he was writing a series of books, based on the screenplay. I was skeptical to say the least. The screenplay was so right from a cinematic standpoint that I was concerned that it would not translate as viscerally, and dynamically, to the page as it would play on the screen.

Damned if the son-of-a-bitch didn't succeed again!

You hold in your hands one of the most entertaining books that I have read in the genre. It is a coming of age story, filled with laughter and tears, violent and brutal murders, unbridled sex, and of course, werewolves. . .

Things just don't get better than that!

~ John Carl Buechler, Sherman Oaks, CA

Director, Producer, Writer, and Special Effects Artist
Director, Empire Pictures' *Ragewar* (1984)
Director, Empire Pictures' *Cellar Dweller* (1988)
Director, Paramount Pictures' *Friday the 13th Part VII: The New Blood* (1988)
Designer & Director of Special Effects *Troll* (1986)

HIDDEN VALLEY

THE

AWAKENING

CHAPTER 1

The branches of wet pine trees sag along the path at head level forcing me to crawl beneath them in order to avoid a shower of frigid water drops from falling onto my neck, chilling me to the bone. The moonlight, filtering through the gaps in the leaves and gnarled branches that loom above me, barely light the trail. Along with the fantastic spectacle of the leaves, I see the light piercing through the fog in little rays of luminescence. They shift and dance around the earthen floor, quite a beautiful sight. With every breath I take, an accompanying puff of steam surrounds my face and blends into the rolling fog.

As I climb up the hill, the forest starts to thicken along the path and I am left in total darkness. An incredible pressure forms in my head, and with it, the realization of something strange. It is already 4:00 a.m. and the sun has not risen. The only light I have is that of my cell phone, which barely illuminates the world around me; and the moon, which cannot penetrate through the thick brush. Continuing up the rocky, wet slope, I am praying the forest will open up into a clearing.

Proceeding on the trail, I realize that along with the heavy darkness pressing in on me, the sounds of wildlife in the area are diminished. The pounding in my head increases with each step I take. The throbbing in my head is the only noise I can hear other than a faint echo of water dripping down from the trees and rocks scattered throughout the terrain. I don't think I've ever been this high in my life.

Finally, I have arrived at a clearing and I perch my body upon a cliff ledge that overlooks a small canyon a few miles outside of town. This has become my new ritual, finding a place for me to alleviate my stress and start the morning on a good foot. Maybe . . . maybe, that's what I'm really looking for, the feeling of starting my life anew, yet this thought was only a friend of my imagination, and not my reality.

I'm happy, I think to myself, as I watch the fog roll mysteriously through the trees, falling just short of their peaks. The moon is now glowing brightly through the light rain clouds and it illuminates my way along the forest trail. The woods, this morning, feel empty. Absent are the usual scurrying sounds of animals. The birds are silent and the wind has died. The only sound I hear is the echoed hoot of an owl in the distance distorted by the tall pines and the light drizzle that is turning into a fine mist.

As I light my second bowl, the sun breaks the horizon. The dark blue sky turns a bright yellow and I watch the forest go from near black to a beautiful monochromatic blue, and finally to warmer colors as the sun pierces through the atmosphere. When it shines across the valley, the sun appears to be a massive explosion on the horizon, frozen in time. Rays of light now illuminate what the nighttime shadows once covered completely. The birds, however, do not chirp as usual . . . the morning remains silent. The most evident sound is the chattering of my teeth induced by the cool, damp air.

I was a fool to walk barefoot down the old path, and next to naked. All I am wearing is my now soaked-through bright red running shorts, which barely cover my legs, with no shirt to accompany them. The raindrops on

3

my body glisten in the rising sun. I'm sure it looks picturesque; everybody always says I should be a model, I myself am probably not tall enough for it, nor do I care to be a "Glitter-boy" as they call them. My abs are "perfectly refined" along with the rest of my body . . . or so they tell me. I can't picture myself being one of those perfect guys out in Hollywood or somewhere else; the thought seems so strange to me. I'm fine staying in my small town, smoking my weed, loving the girls, and living life in the moment. Sure, I could do all of that in Hollywood, party with models and what not . . . but I'm not theirs to be a fucking puppet, that's all they would want me for.

The feeling of the sun rising and its rays beating upon my face and chest is phenomenal. Perhaps even to the point of overwhelming me now, but my ass and legs remain chilled as the rock is still wet. My weight is squeezing every ounce of moisture from pockets of rain-soaked moss. God damn, it is freezing! I was going to keep moving to stay warm, but now it is 6:10 a.m. in the morning. I don't think those edibles are going to let up soon. I am feeling way too fucking lazy, and this view is just awesome. Life is always better after a bowl. Sure, sure . . . I don't need it, but it makes me feel fucking great!

The bathroom filled with steam for a good five minutes this morning before I got into the shower. As badly as I wanted to hop in there as soon as possible, my high was wearing off, and I needed to get perked up again before school. Well . . . no, I didn't need it, I just wanted it. I just made it sound as though marijuana was an issue. The thought of that makes me crack a smile all by itself.

For me, the school day always flows by fast; it's so simple! I half-ass the work they give me and finish it before the day is up, so I never have homework to waste my time. Somehow, I always get an "A" even though I don't pay attention to the assignments. It's ridiculous. I suppose it's because I God damn near own the fucking place. Nobody questions me, and what I say goes, for both teachers and students alike. I don't know how I got to be in charge of this stupid school, but I enjoy it. I do feel a bit of guilt over it though. I can do whatever the hell I want and everybody follows. No questions asked and no consequences. When I do something bad, it just means I get a slap on the wrist. Hell, even the football team doesn't get that kind of respect.

My buddy Jeremy likes to think he's in charge, even though he's been following my lead. He's a great kid though. I'm kind of going to miss this place in a month when I launch myself into the "adult" world . . . oh the fun that will be. I hope I get a fun job; whatever I end up doing, I can tell you that being a teacher or office assistant or some shit like that would just kill me inside. I guess I'll let things work themselves out, they always have for me.

"Zach! Hellooo?" A female voice is speaking to me as harshly as she can, which ironically, isn't threatening in the tiniest bit, as hard as she tries. Looking up from my desk, I see a beautiful face surrounded by flowing blonde hair coupled with brilliant blue eyes that always seem to glow. Ah, Brittany, along with her personality she always has a smile on her face for everyone. She's one of those people that will reach out and help anyone she can. She is a straight A student who doesn't only get A's on her exams, but truly and honestly understands everything she studies. She's a remarkable, talented and brilliant young woman and if anybody could run off to Hollywood from this school, it's her. But, she has bigger plans for the both of us. She has us going off to college together, maybe to Princeton or UCLA - her studying law and me studying to

5

be a doctor. I think this is very comical especially when my father is the lawyer and with her wanting to study law. The only thing I can really imagine me doing is becoming a doctor.

"Yeah, what's up?" I say with a dazed smile, and she giggles like she always does when she talks to me. Looking around at the small classroom I see empty rows of desks with papers scattered beneath them on the floor. I glance back at the girl. The teacher is sitting at his desk with his head in his hands, smiling at me in a mocking fashion. I must have been lost in thought for at least five minutes.

"I was wondering when you were going to come out of that daze, Zachy."

The teacher just shakes his head at me some more as he jots down a few notes on some class papers. Man, I hate that guy . . . it seems the more I insult him or blow him off, the better he likes me. He's nothing but a creep.

"He's awake now, Mr. Andrews!" Brittany tells him in this cute, high-pitched voice. She turns back around to talk to me, and I can see him sneak a look at her ass as she bends over my desk to talk to me a little more. I flash him an angry look and like a puppet on a string he quickly buries his nose in a teacher's book, and his cheeks shine red with embarrassment. The class is empty, and the halls near vacant except for a few kids I can hear at their lockers. I guess I really had zoned out for a while.

"Zachy, it seems like you've been in your own little world forever now! Come on silly, class is over. You're not going to let a lady walk to her car all by herself are you?"

There she goes, playing her games again. It was cute, though; how could I resist?

"Of course not, hun, we have some of the best fucking walks! Let's go!" I said all too enthusiastically and jumping out of my chair, I wrap my arm around her and we head out of the classroom.

"See ya, Mr. Andrews!" Brittany shouts in a preppy, high-pitched voice before turning back to me. "Oh, and Jeremy is out on the track, so maybe before he goes off," abruptly stopping in the middle of the hall she leans up to my ear and softly whispers into it, "maybe . . . you can kiss me goodbye again, Zachy?"

She looks so seductive and beautiful in her tight pink sweatshirt and pre-ripped skinny jeans and yet at the same time she seems to be frightened. I can't help but smile when she acts cautious about us . . . it's so cute in such a strange way.

Crossing my arms and shaking my head no with the most ridiculous smile on my face, I look right into her eyes and harshly reject her. "NEVER!" I turn away from her in disgust, and before I know it, my cheek meets the palm of her hand, along with a loud "SMACK!"

"Ow! What did ya do that for, babe?"

It was actually much louder than it felt. I readily had my hand up playfully, as if I was about to smack her right back. Somebody would have to be blind and stupid if they couldn't tell I was kidding around. "Watch out! You asked for it girly!"

I extend my arm so my hand was on the back of her neck and placed my other hand on her side, attacking her with a flurry of tickles. Her giggle is so cute . . . something I absolutely love hearing. Whenever she smiles at me, her eyes become even more brilliant and just seem to sparkle. I can't think of any reason somebody wouldn't fall to their knees over her, she's absolutely beautiful in every regard and seems so innocent. Although, it's quite obvious to those who know her, that innocence does not play a role here. In fact, the more I think about it, pure becomes a very hard thing to picture her being.

She raises her hands onto my chest and pushes her body into mine, throwing my torso against the lockers behind me. Her tiny body squeezes me tightly, and very quickly our legs become locked - her eyes light up with hot passion. The top of my thigh moves back and forth slightly between her legs and I can feel her starting to get very, very warm. She looks at me like she wants to wrap herself around me and go at it like a couple of wild animals. As quickly as that look of desire flashed on her face, it disappears, and is replaced with a look of fear.

Brittany pushes herself away from me and frantically starts looking around for prying eyes. Even though I know why, the simple fact that she has it in her mind that we can't be seen together at all still angers me. I like this girl, and there are times that I just want to hug her and hold her in my arms, just cuddle with her. Yet I realize that wouldn't be prudent or acceptable to her.

Not seeing another person in the hallway, she giggles a little and looks relieved yet I sense she feels some indecision about her actions and our playing around together. It's obvious this is bothering her a great deal.

"I'm . . . I'm sorry. Hey, I'll see you around, okay babe?" Not waiting for an answer, Brittany walks away from me, leaving me hanging in the hall. Even though there were no other people watching, I still felt like the entire school saw our interaction and I'm pretty sure she felt the same way.

It was chilly in the afternoon, but going with tradition, I put my school bags in my locker, rip off my shirt and head down the stairs outside. Running across the field toward the track, the cool air hits my lungs invigorating me. As I'm running, I think how odd it is that the weather is so cold and gloomy at this time of year. I notice that there are quite a few students on the track, but it isn't hard to find Jeremy. It's funny, when I was a freshman, I could barely run TO the track, my lungs would be hurting and my skinny legs aching after only a few minutes of running. Now I can go for hours around the thing, with almost no consequences. I'm glad I'm no longer out of shape like I was four years ago. My legs swiftly carry me around the track. Jeremy is jogging ahead of me, but after looking back, he darts out as far and as fast as his legs can carry him, knowing I'm trying to catch up.

It won't be a problem, as I pick up speed too; Jeremy is now only a few feet ahead of me. The track is still wet from the night's rain, and I constantly have to look down to avoid deep puddles on the school's underfunded track. While my eyes are fixated on the ground, I yell out to Jeremy between breaths, "Are you ready for me, ya bastard?" I cracked a smile and looked back up, but the guy was already on the other side of the track! God damn, he's fast!

"Oh! Slow down, Zach! I'm so far behind!" he hastily says, pushing a group of freshmen out of the way as he looks at me with a grim smile. Before I could even finish the top of the track, he is already about 10 feet behind me, and he caught up to me in a hurry. He looks as ridiculous as I do, wearing bright red running shorts straight from the 70's to match mine with his manhood bulging out like a porn-star's. He's not wearing another God damn thing besides his running shoes.

It is obvious we don't fit in with the other students running their laps. Most are wearing sweatshirts or tank tops and basketball shorts. They stare at us while we run passing judgment of us, but we know they are staring with jealousy and even with a tad bit of lust in their eyes. Yet, as with anybody who stands out, the bratty 14 and 15 year olds will try and mock us to our faces. Some of them would anyway; some just didn't have the guts. It was so fun messing with them. I like to think that I slowed down a little bit and allowed Jeremy to catch up with me, but the fact is, he slowed down when he reached me. Kid should be in the Olympics.

"Dude! Can you believe we only have a month left before we graduate?" Jeremy spoke as he came up behind me. "Man, it's really hard to believe . . ."

The truth of his statement blew its way into my mind. In a few short weeks, everything that I know will change. I mean, I've been thinking about this for a while now, but it never felt as real as it did now. Funny how things hit you at the last minute sometimes, what am I going to do in the future?

"We're graduating man," I said with disbelief. A few quiet moments went by and finally, like a light bulb, excitement spread throughout our bodies and smiles sprang to our faces.

"We're graduating man!" I yelled out at the top of my lungs. It was exciting, riveting! I would soon be free from this school. It seems like I would be free forever. We exchanged a powerful high five as we turned the corner on the track.

"It's our last four day weekend, Zach! What are we going to do?" He glared at me with anticipation.

"We gotta go out with a bang whatever the hell it is," I half-heartedly replied, thoughts of how things are going to change still filled my head. My thoughts were abruptly interrupted by an annoying voice.

"Why do you two always have to be such faggots all the time? Can't you put on some normal fucking shorts for once?"

All of a sudden, my right arm felt like it was being ripped off and I halted to a stop, as did the kid who just came up to us, Donovan Gray, a low-life of the school. Jeremy had yanked us both to a stop on the track.

"Wow, dude, those tighty-whities you're sporting got you all up in knots? Let the freedom flow baby!" Jeremy said sarcastically as he started thrusting his hips at Donovan, his dick swinging obnoxiously far. Donovan's face became so overwhelmed and disgusted it was almost cartoonish, but his eyes were locked on Jeremy's bulge. A smile crossed my face and before I knew it, my arms were around Jeremy. Donovan's eyes, after about 10 seconds, finally broke away as he ran off yelling, "FAGGOTS!" A few freshmen, mainly girls, stopped on the track to watch. Laughter exploded out of me and we continued running.

"Man, we've been fucking with these jocks for years, and I really don't think they know whether we're straight, gay or anything at all! It's God damn hilarious," I said with excitement.

"Yeah, well there is one person who knows we're straight, one very hot lady frie - FUCK! I got it! Oh man, oh man! I know what we're going to do now! Let's take Brit and go camping behind the old Hidden Valley Bed & Breakfast!"

The second Jeremy said it my body felt like it was hit by a rock square in the chest. My heart started racing along with my breathing. Did my friend really come up with such a stupid idea? Was he joking? I started to breathe heavily and sweat profusely, and it was obvious he was fully aware of my thoughts right now.

"Oh come on, Zach, don't be such a pussy!" he said in a cocky manner.

I shot back with anger, "Dude! Come on! You know we can't go up there! I mean, yeah, that would be cool and all, but I also don't want Brittany and us torn apart by some rabid fucking animals!"

Jeremy snapped his fingers at me and shot back in an all-too-confident manner, "Relax man, the only thing that's gonna get torn up is Brittany, and that'll be by me!"

For some reason, I still felt a little jealous when he said things like that about Brittany. He's such an idiot. "Come on, Jeremy, you know what happened to those people up there . . . and there were two of them . . ." I paused.

"We can take a few angry raccoons, Zachy boy!" He started throwing punches at the air while intently looking into my eyes. "Well. I don't know about you, but I can. Hell, why don't you stay in your room and maybe I'll just go up with Brittany alone. I'm sure we'll have tons of fun together."

He pulled out his cell phone and held it up to his face in an obnoxious manner and started pressing away at the keys. "Whoops! That's her right now; she says she'll go without a problem. Guess it really will be just us. Sorry bro."

"Come the fuck on Jeremy. No, I'll go along on this stupid trip," I said testily. There was a moment of silence between us as I gave him an angry glare. "I'm sure that the bear or whatever it was has moved on to a new spot by now anyway."

I think I am buying what just came out of my own mouth, but there's a strong underlying thought that screams at me in the back of my head, telling myself that I only said the dangerous threat was gone to try and convince myself. I started fiddling around in my short's tiny pockets, feeling the round edges of my pipe and stroking my fingers around its glassy curves to try and calm my nerves. This kid was really starting to piss me off. Best friends can be good at that sort of thing.

Jeremy saw I was getting a little irritated and decided to stop kidding around. His face even got a bit red and he

12

stepped a little closer to me. I wonder what this kid is up to now. Out of his mouth comes a barely audible sentence, he whispers, "So, you know that thing we talked about with all of us?"

I'm confused, "What thing? What are you talking about?"

Jeremy stopped and looked around to make sure nobody was watching or listening to us, and then he leaned into my ear once again. "The thing man! I mean, you and I are already both fucking her."

My eyes grew wide in amazement over him remembering such a drunken conversation we had last year.

"And she already thinks she's cheating on us with each other, we might as well take it to the next step, man!"

I cracked a smile, but started to melt down on the inside. "Man, we were wasted. Are you serious? Have sex . . . with you and her? I was drunk as hell when I said that," I said in a hushed tone to Jeremy.

"FAGGOTS!" Donovan yelled as he passed by us on the track. We returned an appropriate gesture and, as soon as possible, Jeremy tried to continue with our conversation. I slapped him on the back reassuringly.

"We'll talk about that later man. But yeah, I agree with a couple things, we should def go up there and party, and tell Brittany. This whole secrecy thing has really been bugging me lately." Before he could ask why, and I'm sure he would question me, I chuckled and took off running laps.

CHAPTER 2

The lights from the far bottom of the pool reflected on the surface of the water, casting an amazing array of spectacular shapes and odd concentrations of light shining onto the pool walls.

Looking up, the atmosphere was complimented by the alluring array of stars looming above us. I was still with Jeremy, as usual. I just sat there, high as fuck, while Jeremy swam his laps in the water. Life is just so dull, unless you're high all the time, it seems . . .

"Come on man! It's gonna be a blast camping with Brittany! We'll get stoned and fuck our brains out. She'll love it!" he said as he pushed his way through the water and propped his face up over the side of the pool. Part of me wanted to listen to Jeremy, but at the same time, I worried about Brittany, too . . . this whole trip feels kind of wrong to me.

"I don't know man, she's probably gonna get bitchy when she finds out that for the past four years, we both have known that each of us has been having sex with her, not to mention the other girls you got with," I said to Jeremy.

"Yeah, I fucked 'em! So what? What's that gotta do with this trip?"

"Shit man, I don't want her to stop having sex with me. I mean, I'm not having sex with other girls, and I never have. I kind of wanna keep it that way." Jeremy looked at me with a cocky, shit-eating grin and chuckled a bit.

14

"Zach, do you actually think Brittany is going to get pissed when she finds out? She actually thinks she's been keeping it from us dude!" declared Jeremy.

My hands start sweating and my chest begins thumping. As much as I know that, it still hurt to hear. I don't think I want to share her anymore, but at the same time do I really want somebody who would run off and cheat on me with somebody else? I don't want to share her at all - I felt I had to speak up, but how? For as confident as I make myself out to be, I was being such 'a little bitch' as he would put it.

"I know man, but still, I don't think it's a good idea," I said somberly.

The same look I had crossed Jeremy's face, and he pushed himself out of the pool, strangely synchronized with a cold breeze blowing through the yard. The water rippled violently as the wind blew across the surface. Looking chilled as hell, he stood upon the edge of the pool naked, appearing as a silhouette against the porch lights. I could see the water glistening on his skin, and it wasn't until that moment that I realized he was actually a good looking guy. I also took note of what great shape he was in, perhaps even better shape than me!

Thinking back to the prior conversation, maybe I did like him as more than a friend. The thought startled me - yet, I felt a strange calming sensation; maybe, just maybe, I was happy to admit that to myself. I'm not sure, but I know that I needed a topic change, and quickly. Jeremy seemed to read my mind.

"Dude, you and me go back a long way. I've known you since your dick was smaller than my pinky," he said looking at my dick. "Well, I mean, there's not much of a difference now,
but . . ."

"Fuck you man!" I shouted back at him.

"Dude, my point is we've been the best of best friends. There's nobody else who can relate to each other the way we do. Point is, dude, we've had some great times."

15

I couldn't help but smile at him. I knew exactly what he was doing, trying to cheer me up and still get his way. He's a manipulative bastard, but I allow myself to fall into it anyway, I always do. "Yeah man, we've had the best fucking times together," I add.

A real smile came over my face thinking of our past. I may get irritated at the guy sometimes, but he's my best friend, and we have such a deep relationship together. It's so odd, my head was pounding a while ago in pain and frustration. Despite appreciating the stars above, the entire day has been depressing for me. But, being with Jeremy wasn't depressing. In fact, he always has a way of lifting me back up.

At that moment Jeremy came over and sat down beside me and looked me right in the eyes like he's done so many times in the past. With that look in his eyes, I knew what was about to happen. As much as I knew that I was unsure about it, I knew I could never resist him. Jeremy reached over and kissed me ever so lightly. I sat there frozen. He was so tender as he placed his hand on my face and touched it gently. I am sure I had that very stoned, seductive look in my eyes that both Jeremy and Brittany have told me scream's out "take me to bed." One part of me wants to quit because we are talking about Brittany, but the other part of me, the part I always give in to, wanted more. I leaned in and looked into his beautiful blue eyes. Jeremy kissed me again and followed that kiss down onto my neck, which sent a chill running up my spine. It's amazing how passionate and caring Jeremy can be, especially for someone who loves their sex to be fast, hard and hot. He whispered in my ear, "The pleasure is all yours." He always takes me to another space and time and gives me the most incredible stress relieving moments. Jeremy smiles at me and I laugh a little bit as he reaches over and gives me another light kiss. "Are you feeling better now . . . my very best friend?" he asked.

I smiled at Jeremy and handed him the towel from the cold cement. It was a bit damp in the corner from the pool, but I don't think he minded. The temperature was quickly becoming frigid and his eyes lit up as he wrapped the towel around his body.

I knew that what just happened was to be forgotten and was never to be talked about. It was our secret, a secret that we shared for years. Along with all of the other wonderful secrets and moments we have had throughout the years of our undying friendship with each other. A friendship that most people could never understand it was so deep, so caring. We had some of the most amazing moments that anyone could ever imagine. We have laughed so hard our bellies ached, we have smiled so much that our faces hurt. It was all about the great moments in time that we have had together.

He was always there for me as I was for him. Those were some of the roughest moments and they almost always revolved around his father who was such an asshole. I remember once when Jeremy couldn't have been more than nine and a half and he came to my house and had a bloody nose and a black and blue eye. My father was extremely concerned and asked him what had happened. Jeremy, as usual, played it off as though he had just been clumsy and done something stupid until my father left the room, then he told me the truth. His father had gotten drunk again and beat the crap out of him because he spilled some cornflakes on the floor. I could never understand that type of punishment, that a father could do that to their kid. My father is so incredibly awesome, so understanding and loving. I think that's the episode when my father basically accepted Jeremy into our family. He knew there was more than just the bond of friendship between Jeremy and me.

I sat there and looked at Jeremy, smiled and thought to myself, "We are so stoned right now." Lost in my thoughts for a few more minutes, I then smiled and told Jeremy, "You know, my dad told me that he wishes he had friends like you when he was growing up. He actually told me that he's jealous of the good times we've had together."

"You know, your dad is really the coolest dude. I remember the time you got all dressed up in your prep clothes in the ninth grade and headed down to the brand-fucking-new Hidden Valley Community Bank and convinced them that you were the chairman of the God damn board. You almost pulled that shit off for a week!"

Again, his plan was working. I was feeling confident and happy again, especially after remembering that stunt.

"Yeah, Jeremy, it was definitely one of my greatest deceptive achievements," I agreed.

He raised his finger at me for emphasis as he said, "And, it was your dad that bailed your ass out of that one."

Feeling shy, I wanted to divert the attention toward him. I guess it wasn't just the feeling of being shy. As I have said, Jeremy and his father were never really close at all. I didn't want to say how awesome my father was in front of him. I thought back to something he did, something funny that slightly related, but didn't go back to the father issue. But, what was something deceptive he had done? I can't remember too much, as he's gotten so blunt with his feelings in the past couple of years, he really hasn't had the need to lie or scheme.

"A ha!" and then it hit me. "What about the time you convinced Mrs. Beach you were so aroused by her that she was gonna switch classes for the entire year!"

We both doubled over with laughter.

"My dad bailed your ass out of that one, didn't he?" I laughed, but then a feeling of paranoia came over me the instant I let loose that sentence. I had every intention of swinging away from the topic of my dad because I could see Jeremy becoming a tad emotionally down thinking about my dad.

He smiled, regardless of what I just said. Sometimes pretending to be oblivious is perhaps the best way to stop yourself from getting hurt.

18

"Her gray hair just turned me on so much, man!" Jeremy joked. I cracked a smile, and he burst out laughing at his own joke like he always did no matter if it was good or bad. With his laughter, he gained a little confidence and threw off the towel.

"See man! We do have the best times! We deserve one more great time to remember for the rest of our lives! I'm not trying to push it, but God damn it!"

He threw his fists up in the air and yelled out to the stars above. "I want to have a fucking blast!" he cried into the night.

He stopped his dramatics and came to sit next to me on the edge of the pool and said sincerely, "Honestly dude, before I graduate high school I want to celebrate with the two most important people in my life. You know, we will go off on our separate paths and Brittany is going off to New Hampshire next year to study."

His upper lip began to quiver slightly and he looked worried, "This may be the last time we ever get to do things our way."

There was a pause between us for a moment. The sound of the crickets in the distance filled the air. I'm not quite sure what he was thinking at this point in time, but I could tell this meant a lot to him, and he did have a point. Personally I wish we could hang out for once without the alcohol and all that shit, but Jeremy gets a look on his face where his eyes shine and I can't help but say yes to him. And, it's not because there is an attraction, but simply because I just feel for this guy and want him to be happy, even if it means having to compromise my own feelings. Against my better judgment, I went on to support the idea.

"Oh . . . uh," I stuttered for a moment, as I realized I may have been spacing out again. I was probably just being paranoid because of the weed. We were still stoned because we had smoked at least three bowls of this incredible weed I had gotten earlier today. I wonder how many things I can blame on the drugs.

"Uh, yeah!" I said, shaking my head a little. "That would be the greatest of all times! Just think . . . we may be able to do it again ten years from now when we all come back to our reunion." Smiling, I laughed and so did he.

"You know, Zach, all of these fucking idiots that we've fucked with over the years . . ."

Forcing a laugh I looked at him and spoke with confidence, "Yeah! We'll be the kings of that reunion . . . and for all those guys, we'll show them that Brittany is our queen!"

At that moment it was as though we simultaneously realized how untrue that statement was, and all went quiet. We did not speak, or even acknowledge to each other that we knew how one another felt. It was an odd moment. I quickly changed the topic to something a bit more comfortable.

"Okay man, you got to let me do the talking to Brittany. I know you're not stupid man, you know how I feel about her," I shared.

"Yeah, Zach, I do and I think it's really cool man. She's great, and sure, sure, you can say all of the smooth words Mr. Stud!"

CHAPTER 3

The main lamp that usually fills the living room with light had burned out, making the interior a rather dark area in which to walk. A dim lamp sat in the corner, illuminating part of the room and casting long shadows across the area. Sitting on the couch was Mark Gooden, my father.

He is a tall, muscular guy. I honestly always hoped that I could reach his height, but here I stand, 5 feet 7 inches and not a damn bit taller than I was sophomore year. Before heading out, I donned the t-shirt I had thrown on top of the coffee table earlier. I was rather cold after being out by the pool in the nude.

I admired dad a lot. He has always been there for me, and has never turned his back on me like the parents of some people I know. I think it's horrible when a parent turns on a child.

"Well I see at least one of you has the brains to put on something," he laughs as he gestures toward me while I finish getting dressed. Before I could say a word to him, Jeremy threw out his classic line, which dad could see coming from a mile away.

"You just gotta let the freedom flow Mr. G.!" Jeremy jostled as he thrust his hips toward my dad and waved his arms in the air like an intoxicated fool. I hated when Jeremy did this. I felt embarrassed, yet I couldn't keep a smile off my face the entire time.

"Alright ya little prick! I like letting the freedom flow too, but someday you kids are really going to have to learn that wearing clothes around people is just something that you do. You're gonna have to cover that tiny pecker of yours up ya know."

"Well, daddy," I said loud as hell to cut through the room's laughter, "Hopefully that day comes much, much later."

Suddenly, there was a change in the atmosphere of the room. Jeremy's face became serious and for the first time that I remembered, there was no little twinkle in his eyes and no cocky grin. He said something that made the room go from a bunch of loud guys laughing and yelling to dead silence. With a trembling voice, he spoke and the moment he opened his mouth, we listened intently.

"Hey Mr. G., I understand that you're a little jealous of the relationship between your son and me . . ."

I instantly start to blush. I didn't expect him to bring up such a topic with me in the room.

". . . Well, I just wanted to say that I'm a whole lot jealous of the relationship that you have with Zach."

Jeremy's eyes looked vacant, almost dead-like. Something was going on in his head lately and it just now was starting to come together and make some sense to me. The increase in partying, wanting to get intoxicated all the time and escape his thoughts, I really felt for him. I suddenly wish I could somehow change the way he and his father get along. I know that sort of thing is out of my, or anybody's, ability to control. It's so sad.

His facial features hardened; he was fighting the tears back as much as he could, yet one rolled down his cheek anyway. This boy really felt that nearly everything he did was wrong. He was a "fuck up" in the words of his father and I'm sure, in the back of his mind, he repeated those words to himself on a second-by-second basis.

Dad was totally caught off-guard by what just came out of Jeremy's mouth. So much so that it took him a good thirty seconds to conjure up a word.

"Well," he replied as he put down his newspaper, stood up and crossed his arms with his head pointed down toward the ground. The silence was thick around the room; I'm not sure a car crashing into the side of the house could even break his concentration . . . or the moment.

Looking up at Jeremy he smiled and taking off his glasses he handed Jeremy a tissue as I stood by, silent and watching. I didn't know what else to do.

"Jeremy, that's right. I am a bit jealous of you and Zach's relationship, as I never had a friend like that growing up. And, honestly, the closest thing I have to him is you, Jeremy."

I hated when he complimented me. It's not that I don't like the spotlight, but it's so much different when a friend does it, than when it's my father. I shuffled my feet a bit against the carpet and crossed my arms tighter. I decided I wasn't going to say a word back. Thank God, he shifted his attention back to Jeremy.

"You two live life like it's all going to end tomorrow and I wish I would have done that when I was your age. Now I have too many responsibilities for that . . . but I wanted to let you know that you mean a lot to me too, Jeremy. If you and Zach looked more alike, I would think most people would confuse you for twins, which I really like."

Jeremy's tears now flowed more freely, yet on his face was a smile. He wasn't fighting that back at all. I couldn't help but smile myself. In fact, I probably looked goofy as hell, but I didn't care. I was so proud of my dad and happy that Jeremy had a father figure to look up to even if it wasn't his own dad.

23

"Wow, Mr. G.! That's really cool of you, and I would absolutely love to have you as my father. You're an awesome guy who's always supportive of Zachy-boy over there and me, too, even though you don't have to be. You're the best. Zach is so lucky to have you as a father . . . I am too."

Jeremy, the person who tries the hardest to hide his flaws, his weaknesses, and his softer side was now being himself. It was amazing to see, because when it did come out, he became the most amazing person anybody could have the honor of knowing. He's just too low on confidence at times. It would really show people how brave he was if he could show that vulnerability all the time. Wow, I should be taking notes for myself. I wonder if that's what Brittany sees in Jeremy.

"Thank you, Jeremy. That's a really nice thing for you to say," dad replied with a small tear in his eye. "I can honestly tell you, Jeremy, I love you like a son. I really do, and I would be very proud to have you under our family name."

The old man let out a chuckle and then yelled at the top of his lungs in a playfully angry manner, "Jesus Christ! What the hell is going on here? Would you get out of here before we all start to have a crying fest!"

With a new-found confidence Jeremy spoke out loudly, "All right! It's party time Zach! We're outta here!"

He grabbed his dick through his pants as he headed out the door and let out a scream. "I'll be in the car boy! Don't keep me waiting!"

Laughing, I yelled back to the bastard, "I will, don't worry. Just gimme a sec man!"

I felt a strong need to address my father about what had just happened. "Dad, have I told you lately how awesome you are? Thank you for saying that to Jeremy and for being here for me man. I love you, Dad."

Now, I couldn't help it either, I lost it. My eyes were red and tears were flowing down my cheeks onto his shirt as I hugged him tightly. "I'm very lucky to have you dad, so is Jeremy."

He looked at me and not just a look, but an acknowledgement. It seemed he actually understood everything I was feeling and I think, at that moment, just how deeply I cared about Jeremy. He smiled and I looked into his eyes and nodded slightly, then walked away.

"Good night, Dad," I said walking out of the room. I didn't look back at him either; no, instead I put a smile on my face and diverted my attention to what I was going to tell Brittany. I really wish there was a way to get out of this. I mean Jeremy just wants Brittany for sex, that's all. Even though Brittany is using both of us with our knowledge, I feel bad for her being with somebody like that.

"Get in fucker!" Jeremy barked at me as he slammed the passenger door shut. My car was brand new, yet I've put enough scratches on it to make it look as though it had been around for nearly a decade. I'm not exactly a safe driver when I am by myself, partly because I don't care too much for regulations. Also, if I crash and burn the car it would be my own damn fault. I would be the only one around to get hurt, funny how that's acceptable thinking in my mind. Jeremy likes to be reckless all of the time, whether there are family and friends in the car, or just himself. That's exactly why he is getting into the passenger seat of my car. The good thing about it is I don't have to worry about my car getting wrecked. The bad thing about it is I have to listen to his bitching the entire way about me following the speed limit. He is in a different mood though today, so perhaps it might be better. Preparing for the worst stunt-devilish, back-seat driving possible, I open the door and slide on in.

Something strange is happening with Jeremy tonight. He is being honest and open about everything, I wonder what happened. With that in mind, I wonder if Brittany, after all of these years, did start to make him happy. Maybe he liked her too now. If that happened, I'm not sure what I would do. Of course, the choice would be up to her. It's hard to watch somebody you really like, maybe even love, be in the hands of another as well, especially when that other person is your best friend. And, she thinks she's cheating on both of us. For four years I have had to wonder if she really was worth my time. A deep weight sank over my heart and a frown appeared on my face.

It was a quick drive, and Jeremy was surprisingly quiet the entire time. I believe we were both so wrapped up in thoughts over everything, that we had plenty to keep our minds occupied without having to talk to one another. Not even the radio was of interest, though I am sure if it was playing it would be tuned out by the questions raging throughout my mind. What if my dad knew I was questioning myself? Why was Jeremy so emotional tonight? Does it have something to do with his father trying shit with him again? I really, really hope that is not the case.

"Whoa, dude! Slow down! Her house is right here!" Jeremy screamed in my ear, obstructing my view of the road momentarily with his outstretched finger.

"Relax, Jeremy! It's fine, it's all fine," I retorted in an annoyed tone as I quickly slowed to a near stop and sharply turned into her driveway. We came upon her house, a rickety, old, two-story building with flaked white paint all along the siding. It was a very old house and was not kept up to any standard.

As I slowed to a stop, I couldn't help but yell, "See! Look, Jeremy! We're alive! What a miracle!" I glared at him for doing what he always does.

He met me with a smile and an annoying laugh, "Ha ha, I love fuckin' with ya!"

Looking away, still slightly annoyed, I pressed both of my hands against the horn a few times to let her know we had arrived. Almost immediately, I could see her shadow dance across the curtains in the house and we followed the sweet moment by proceeding to get out of the car. It was little things like her running out to see me that make me love her so much . . . but then I realize that this time it wasn't just me she was coming to see. I dreaded her treating me like just a friend one more time, because her other man was present. All the more reason we should invite her up for this weekend and tell her, right? I hated the idea, but it does sound a little fun. It's interesting how jealousy can ruin a wonderful thing.

I glanced over at Jeremy. *He doesn't love her like I do*, I thought to myself. *He just wants to use her for sex.* Almost as soon as this thought entered my mind, I saw a discrepancy in what I was telling myself. He opened up his wallet to look for something, and I spied dead center in his tri-fold wallet, behind his driver's license, there was a high-school picture of Brittany. He took it out while trying to find a card or something and feelings of guilt started to come over me. Whether he will admit it to me or not, Jeremy did like Brittany. But, I love her! I sat there wondering who she loves more, me or Jeremy.

The old wooden screen door to her house slammed shut and she hurried down the porch stairs with a gorgeous smile on her face. As soon as I saw her, I felt at ease and relaxed. Brittany had apparently gone shopping, because she came out in a new, beautiful, form-fitting dress that showed off her every curve and stopped about an inch short of the bottom of her hips. She honestly looked as though she was ready to walk the red carpet or go to a photo shoot. She gracefully ran up to the car and charged into me giving me a quick kiss on the cheek and wrapping her arms tightly around me. It made me get this fuckin', goofy smile on my face.

"Well, hello to you, too, Britt! You look incredible, as usual."

She flashed me a smile and stroked a finger across the tip of my nose, "Oh, Zachy! You're so cute!"

Her interest immediately shifted as her eyes landed on Jeremy. She didn't hug him, but daintily pushed him on the chest with her hand, "Hey, Jeremy! How's my sexy boy?"

Just shrug it off, Zach, I kept thinking to myself over and over. Jeremy smiled and shrugged his shoulders with that classic, charming grin of his.

"So," Jeremy said, "What are your plans for this weekend?"

I think it was obvious to both of them I was kind of stressed at this point in time as I instantly blurted out to him, "Jeremy! Remember?"

Jeremy looked down at his feet and spoke in a disappointed voice while Brittany got a look of confusion over her face, "Yeah, yeah! I remember the stupid rule you set. Go ahead."

"Go ahead with what?" Brittany asked.

I looked at her and became lost in her eyes for a moment.

"Well? Go ahead big man. Speak."

"Yeah, Brit, we came up with this really awesome, fucking incredible plan for this last big weekend before we graduate," I said enthusiastically. I was trying to hype her up and myself as well, but she stood there with the

28

kind of smile one gets when you know somebody is throwing you some bullshit.

"Oh, yeah? What's this awesome plan Zach?" she said sarcastically while crossing her arms, expecting us to pull some joke on her again. As a matter of fact, I couldn't fault her for thinking this as this is actually how our jokes always seemed to start.

"Okay! So here it is. We want you to come camping with us behind the old Hidden Valley Bed & Breakfast."

She looked at me and then Jeremy. She appeared excited, yet slightly concerned, "You mean for the weekend?"

Jeremy interjected in a joyous tone, "Yeah! Isn't it great?"

There he goes again! "Jeremy! I told you to be quiet man. I got this," and I gave him a light punch on the shoulder.

"Yeah, Brittany, for the whole weekend just you, me, and Jeremy."

Her eyes widened even more while trying to avert the obvious concern she had about all of us going camping together. "Well, I don't know if that's really a good idea. I mean, I don't want to sound like I'm overly concerned, but, ya know, ah . . . what about all of those murders up there just like two months ago?"

"You really don't think anything can happen again, do you? I mean that seems like a one-time thing," Jeremy stated, as he had already pointed out to me earlier in the day. The bastard was starting to annoy me again, but he just gets so excited over things. It's rather hilarious.

"Look, hun, it was just a crazy thing that happened up there. It's not gonna happen aga - "

"Look, Jeremy," I interrupted, "I am talking. We agreed that I would be doing the talking, so let me do the God damn talking man!"

Brittany was looking at Jeremy. It was obvious she was wrapped up in his charming smile and calming, deep voice. Women are so artificial.

"Okay my cute poster boy," he said in a seductive voice.

This made me angry, of course. Even though I may have regrets later, I felt bad right now and lashed out at him, "Fuck you!" It was out of pure jealousy and I realized what was strange about it is that it was resentment both ways. I was jealous of Brittany showing affection to Jeremy, and I guess, maybe a little of the opposite too. I'm not sure what this means. Maybe I said yes to this trip for more reasons than just pleasing him. Maybe I wanted to have a threesome with them. Several thoughts filled my mind and I became so confused . . . but I had to stay focused. I turned back to Brittany who looked like she was waiting for me to lash out at her as well. I took a breath and spoke in the calmest tone I could muster at that moment, "Look, Brittany, I really think it will be a great time. Think about it, just you, me and Jeremy. There'll be marshmallows, weed, a lot of vodka and beer, and . . . "I paused for a moment, hesitating to finish my sentence, "Well, you know the rest."

Brittany crossed her arms tighter and took a step back from both of us, not looking either of us in the eye. "I just . . . " her lips started to quiver and her skin became pale as she looked away from us and spoke in a softer tone, "I don't want anybody to get hurt . . . and that may happen - especially you, Zachy."

It was obvious the poor girl was uncomfortable, and she looked really, really ashamed. Even though she looked so down, I couldn't help but smile. She was worried about me; maybe she did like me more than Jeremy. Now was the time to hide all of my emotions from her because you can't include sincerity with this situation.

"Brittany, I'm not going to get hurt, babe."

Now in utter confusion, Brittany looked at me for a good two seconds and then shifted her eyes over to Jeremy who greeted her with an all-knowing smile. She returned his expression with utter shock.

"You didn't . . . are you guys mess -" she was completely lost for words. "Are you two telling me that you both know what's been going on?"

I, simultaneously with Jeremy, nodded my head yes. It wasn't until now that I realized just how angry I had been that the girl I cared for and thought the world of, was cheating on me. Denial helped me get through the four-year relationship, I guess, and maybe that's why I find him so annoying. Jealousy! The thought scared me, but it was also exceptionally pleasing to let her know we knew we have both been fucking her and she's not the smart, conniving girl she thinks she is. I guess that's a little fucked up to think, but this whole God damn situation has been unconventional so I guess there are no rules here that I should feel obliged to follow.

"Oh my God, you guys! How long have you both known?" Britt was now hyperventilating and profoundly shocked. I felt the need to go over and calm her down, but I wasn't sure how that would make her feel.

"And . . . neither of you is hurt . . . or mad?" She shifted her eyes between both of us and took a deep breath, smile, and disbelievingly giggled.

"I definitely have the two coolest boyfriends in the world," she said exhaling a long breath.

"So, does that mean you will come with us, Brittany?" Jeremy inquired.

I was so eager for the answer I couldn't help but to chime in, "Yeah! Brittany, you'll come with us?"

She hesitated for a split second, and then her face became a giant smile and her voice perked back up to its normal state, "Of course I'll go guys! It'll be the best, greatest time I think we'll ever have!"

I was still nervous over the whole thing, but a bunch of stress dropped away from my shoulders and my mind stopped worrying. I knew that I was going to have sex with her first when we got up there. With no justifiable reason, I feel like she belongs to me more than ever. Maybe I just don't feel so guilty with all of this secrecy out of the way and I'm allowing myself to be freer about it all.

Jeremy and I exchange a high-five and scream together at the top of our lungs, "FUCKING AWESOME!"

Maybe this trip won't be so bad.

CHAPTER 4

Finally the weekend has arrived. After we load up Jeremy's car with everything we could possibly want or need, we bring out the most important ingredient to a successful camping trip, and I'm not talking about the tents. On the road we leave the highway behind and head down the old dirt road to the campsite behind the bed and breakfast. We could have taken the normal way to the B&B and been right there, but you can't drive a car back to the camping site and we didn't want to hike the mile or so into the area with all of our gear, so we opted to take the old trail even though it is bumpy with ruts.

The car is already completely filled with smoke and we are a trio of jolly, fucking people. I'm waving a joint around between my lips to Jeremy and it's about three minutes before he finally realizes what I want. We're lighting up what must be our eighth joint so far this morning. In the process of handing it to him, a hand starts to grab at it and claws it out of my fingertips. It was just after I removed the joint from my lips. I feel an amazing sensation on my thigh. Reaching over from the back seat, Brittany starts dragging her pink nails along my thigh, growing closer and closer to my crotch, but stopping just short of it.

"Thank you, Zachy baby!" she says in a seductive tone as she gives me a passionate look. She proceeds to take a long, seductive drag off of the joint and hands it back to me, but pushes my hand away from my lips as soon as I try to take a drag. She puckers her lips and softly blows out the smoke into my mouth and meets me for a kiss while she drags her dress right over her head to reveal a tiny bikini. No matter how many times I've seen her body, it always seems to get better. She has perfect curves, a finely toned torso, a cute round ass and perfect breasts, which the bikini does an excellent job of showcasing.

"Yeah, now this is what I'm talking about right here! It is party time right here!" Jeremy is staring at her body through the rearview mirror and I don't blame him; she's fucking phenomenal!

"Oh, God," I shout at the top of my lungs. "I can't believe we are really doing this, guys! This is going to be the best fucking time of our fucking lives, so let's get fucking crazy!" I guess I am simply caught up in the moment and while yelling, I start pumping my fist in the air.

"You know what I can't believe?" asks Brittany, "Just how in the fuck you guys have known for the last four years and have never let on!"

My laugh bellows out of me while I give Jeremy a shot since his hands are on the wheel. Slamming one down and taking a hit from a joint.

"And why would we," his speech is slurred, "ruin . . . such a perfectly good thing?"

He may be drunk, but he is driving well and he had a point and I silently agreed with him. He laughed and looked very charming at the moment. Suddenly, I thought back a few mornings to when we were running on the track and started to get very angry.

"So Britt, you know what that douche bag, Donovan Gray, did the other day?"

She rears her head in disgust.

"We were running on the track strutting our shit like we always do when he starts screaming in our face outta the blue and asking why, apparently, we always look like faggots."

Jeremy chimed in, sounding much more sober than before, "He's such an idiot, and I don't know why he said that shit because if anyone is a faggot, it's that son of a bitch and we all know it!"

Brittany kills the last joint and brings out a pipe and starts to pack it in the bowl. We had at least an ounce and a half of weed with us and we had barely touched the bag.

"For some reason it felt really good to dig on Donovan for being gay. I was totally enjoying bullying somebody for their sexual preference. That sounds so wrong me getting such a kick out of it, but at least I wasn't doing it to his face. That is really, really scary for me though, it was too exhilarating for me to stop."

"Yeah, and when he went back down to the rest of those football players, he looked back, and I saw you both smile at each other. I think he likes you," I laughed.

The car became very, very quiet. The song on the radio faded out at the same time, making the car empty of all noise but the humming of the engine. The silence lasted for at least ten seconds and I could tell it was a very uncomfortable time for Jeremy. His face was filled with worry.

"Fuck that," he finally retorted as 'Party like a Rock Star' came on the radio. "I'm all yours and Brittany's," and he let out a loud scream, accentuating his excitement.

By the time we reached the campsite, it was all simply a blur. I remember setting up the tents, and drinking a hell of a lot of beer and vodka. By the time we had our tents set up, almost half of our drinks were gone. When the campfire was lit we only had a tiny bit left in a few scattered bottles. Any smart and sane person would probably realize at this point we could get alcohol poisoning, but we kept on drinking bottle after bottle, puff after puff. We didn't give a fuck! It was great. The thing on our minds the most though, was the threesome. Brittany sure wanted it, and Jeremy seemed ready for anything with us. Brittany's excitement of being open and having sex with the two people that meant the most to her was fantastic. I, however, was unsure about my own stance on the act.

I can't believe how warm the campfire feels to my touch. It's a wondrous source of warmth, which is very welcome amongst the cool forest air. Thinking we needed something to digest some of the intoxication, we pulled out marshmallows and the sticks we had cut from the dead trees earlier and started to set them over the rising flame. Across the dim firelight and through my intoxication, I am entranced by Brittany's beautiful look. She is in her silk bra and lace panties perched on a log next to the fire directly across from me. Amusingly, my mind travels to a bad place as she starts to wave around a very long, thick stick with a marshmallow on the end.

"Quit it, girl! You're supposed to put it in the fire," I yell, as she pushes the stick into the flames. The raging flame wraps around the marshmallow, which turns a soft yellow followed by a deep black. The sugar boils on the surface, and it appears to re-crystallize as a flame engulfs the whole marshmallow. Brittany starts shaking the stick, "Oh! It's on fire! I-I can't put it out!"

I don't think she said it in a joking manner. Jeremy gets up from his seat and leans seductively over to the marshmallow while staring straight into my eyes; he gives me his hot bedroom eyes look and blows out almost all of the tiny flames before Brittany yanks it away from him.

"Now, Jeremy! Don't get rid of it all! I like them 'hot' if you know what I'm saying." With the flames extinguished she licks her lips and in a very sensual manner, starts to lick the top of the marshmallow, staring directly into my eyes after she noticed Jeremy staring at me. I felt myself getting very, very aroused.

"Oh, my, God! That was so hot," Jeremy yells and takes a deep breath while staring into Britt's eyes. Brittany turns her attention away from me and starts focusing on Jeremy. I felt like I should be jealous, but we had been fucking each other all day, so I guess it was his turn to have her. The thought of sharing her with him sent a shot of anger through my spine straight up to my head which resonated in pain. I'm not sure if these feelings are being created by the weed and drinks we have had, or if the drugs had just let me glimpse a part of myself I normally guard against. She started to touch herself on her inner thighs dragging her fingers closer and closer to her panties and looking at Jeremy with a sense of intensity.

"Oh, you have no idea how hot it is," Brittany said, as she bent over in a Marilyn Monroe sort of way, her breasts dangling in front of his eyes.

Knowing she was ready for him he speaks up, "Oh, Brittany! I think I hear something in the tent calling my name! What do you think, Brittany?"

She seems to ignore him though, contrary to my original thoughts. I just sit here rolling the last of the joints like as a factory worker who would run his part in an assembly line. I suppose occupying myself with work was my defense mechanism to take my mind off the attention she was showing Jeremy. I hate these feelings of jealousy. I'm a crazy bastard, I think to myself.

"Zach, for the preppiest, straight-A boy I've ever known, you sure love your weed don't you?" asked Brittany.

It was obvious why she started talking to me. She felt guilty for showing him attention in front of me, but at the same time, she's ready for more sex. Although Brittany felt a little guilt, the choice became simple to her after another chug on her beer bottle. She quickly started her seduction games again.

Looking down at her marshmallow, she shouts out, "Oh no, Jeremy! My marshmallow isn't hot and hard again! What am I to do?"

With a look of excitement and a giant grin across his face, Jeremy throws down his own stick and leads her away from the light of the fire and into the tent, "Come on! I'll show you!"

Well, that couldn't get any more obvious, could it? I started chuckling to myself more and more as I realized how much fun she was to toss around earlier. She's not exactly a short and petite girl, but she is very fit and very light. It made the ride all the more enjoyable for sure.

After they stepped away, only the crackle of the fire greeted my ears, with the occasional cricket off in the distance. I was surprised how far away from the tents we ended setting up the fire pit, but I guess we did it for privacy. If, you know, we really cared about such things. Zach and I were always naked around each other and the same with Brittany around us both. We were all totally comfortable naked. Well, maybe not all the time, but it was often just underwear or something. We were never fully dressed.

A soft snap and a strange deep pitched groaning noise sounds out of the darkness of the forest, not even 15 feet away from me. Snapping my head back, my eyes must look like they are bulging out of their sockets. Staring at where the sound came from, listening intently, I start to hear Brittany and Jeremy ruffling around in the tent and a slight moan as he pushes himself inside of her.

BOOM!

Another one! My legs instinctively rise to the ferocious sound. This time the sound is followed by a slight growl. This noise is louder and closer than before. My heart beats faster and faster as I lose control of my body. My legs move at a rapid rate to the tent. I was starting to panic. Thoughts are flooding my mind about the couple that was ripped apart at this same location a few months back, and I suspected that whatever I just heard must be related to that incident. Maybe it was just the marijuana talking, but I have a high suspicion that whatever is out in those woods is watching us. I'm ready to burst into the tent and tell them that something is out there, but for some reason I stop short of the tent.

"Hey, uh . . . Jeremy?" A sigh is what I hear in return, followed by another small crackle much closer to me. I scan the dark bowels of the forest that I can see from my position, but I can't see anything but darkness and the small area of forest illuminated by the now dying, flickering light produced by the campfire.

"JEREMY! Man, did you hear that noise out here?" I yelled.

"Dude! What noise?" he groaned, his voice muffled by Brittany's stomach or breasts. I could hear kissing sounds coming from inside the tent and friction amongst the blankets.

"I don't know man!" I shot back in fear and a little bit of frustration. "This noise I just heard, it's really freaky as shit man!"

"It's just the sound of great sex, Zach."

SNAP!

"JEREMY!"

My head is pounding.

"You gotta come out here right now! There is something out here Jeremy! And I don't think it's good!"

My warnings are worthless! He's so preoccupied with MY girlfriend, whom he considers a piece of meat, that his best friend doesn't matter. All I can hear from the tent is thrusting and him softly whispering to her. "I'm almost fucking there . . . oh, baby! This is so fucking good!"

You could hear my presence of mind falling apart. "JEREMY!" I screamed at the top of my lungs in total irritation, "Get your fucking ass out here right now!"

Finally, Jeremy emerges from the tent naked with sweat dripping down his rock hard body, still half-erect and looking very satisfied. With a stoner's smile on his face, he looks at me and laughs.

"Dude, you have smoked way too much weed," he accuses.

"No man! There is something out here!" I'm so irritated and wound up with frustration that I can actually feel my arm start to lift itself up, ready to hit the guy square in the dick.   Thankfully, a soft voice from the tent said my name in such a calming manner my heart rate slowed down and a sense of calm befell me.

"Zach, it's okay, really. The noise you heard was just probably me and Jeremy babe. Come in the tent and talk to me for a minute."

Taking a deep breath while looking at Jeremy's exhausted face, I could tell he was expecting an apology from me, but I wouldn't give him one, not this time.

"Okay Jeremy, you gotta keep an eye open and listen. I'm sure there's something out here."

He said something as I walked off, but I have no idea what it is, nor do I really even care. I kneel down and climb into the tent, zipping it back up so that we are concealed in darkness. I hadn't been staring at the campfire for a while and my eyes adjusted slowly to the total darkness inside the tent. Again, tonight, I was being met by Brittany's beautiful naked body. With my eyes barely able to make out the shapes in front of me, one would think that absence of light would leave a lot to the imagination but I already know her body so well that I can recall every detail of its perfection. She really is class "A." I didn't need to use my imagination either. I lay my naked self next to her naked body and wrap her tightly in my arms for a few moments before loosening my grip and laying my head on her shoulder.

She looks at me through the darkness and I can see the outline of her face as the little bit of moonlight that's seeping through the tent illuminates her beauty. I want to kiss her.

"Zach, it's okay. There is nothing out there, really, babe."

Her eyes shift from me and she looks up out of the center hole in the tent at the sky. "It's a beautiful night, Zachy. Did you see the moon tonight? It's just awesome."

Her voice is so relaxed and sweet.

"Yeah, I did. But Brittany, I heard something out there and it sounded and felt like it was right over my shoulder, breathing on my neck with an icy breath. It was scary and I know I'm not crazy. I did hear it!"

Brittany just stares into my eyes again and puts her finger to her lips, "Shhh . . . it's okay. You didn't hear anything sweetie."

She places her hand on my hip and grips it tightly. "Maybe it's time for Jeremy to hear something, babe."

Just like that, her lips press against mine and I start to kiss her passionately. My teeth bite her lower lip lightly and I pull it down, opening her mouth for our tongues to meet. She lets out a soft whimper as I run my hands up and down her side, sensually scratching at her back and pulling her body closer to mine. I'm starting to get hard. How could I not with a body as beautiful as hers? I love being this close to the girl, and while I wish I was the only one, at least I can enjoy it now. I try to pull away for a moment, but she keeps kissing me, pressing her lips gently against mine for a period of time and looking into my eyes until finally, she retracts.

"You really do care about me Brittany . . . don't you? Because you know," I'm so dreading these next few words, but I have to say them anyway. I have this doubt that they don't mean as much to her, as they do to me, but I have to say it.

"I, I love you Brittany. I love you so . . . so much." Tears start to form in my eyes as I caress her body gently and she looks away in a moment of hesitation. Luckily, she turns back to me and presses her nose against mine.

"Yes, I know. It sounds crazy, doesn't it? To be having sex with two guys, knowing that one loves me and with the other it's just sex? Well . . . I love you too, Zach. You're an amazingly passionate person and I love you. You're so caring and handsome."

My heart starts to pulsate strongly and I'm sure if it was not for the damn darkness, you would see my chest move with every thud. What a feeling. When she tells me she loves me it's like somebody hit me in the head and I became disoriented. The sound of the world around me fades away and I just can't get over the feeling, or think of anything else but those words.

"I love you too . . . " I whisper to her softly.

"Zach?" she said with a tad of concern.

"Yeah, Brittany," I answer.

"You know it's just sex with Jeremy, right?" she asked, her voice quivering and falling apart toward the end of her sentence. She knew she was hurting me.

"Yeah," I sighed back. "I know. I'm the one that's full of passion and loving, caring emotions. Jeremy is just the best damn sex we've ever had."

"Oh and it is!" she exclaimed with enthusiasm. "It's hard and hot, but there is no connection there. Slow, loving, passionate sex - that's all you, sweetie."

All of a sudden she pushes herself on top of me, her breasts pressed firmly against my chest. Once again her lips meet mine and we kiss. It's so soft, her body, the way that she touches me. It's caring. I'm glad I have this connection at least. I wonder if she really means it. Part of me doesn't really care, but I want it to be true.

She clenches her teeth on my lower lip delicately and pulls away carefully and then she covers me in kisses. Her soft lips start pressing against my cheek, then my ear where she bites and tugs in a playful manner. Giggling a little in my ear she whispers, "You mean so much to me, Zach."

I tighten my grip on her as she rains kisses down my neck and runs her tongue along it down to my chest, where she kisses and bites my nipple gently, teasing me. As hot as this is, I can't help but think that if she seeks hot sex from Jeremy, she must want it. It's something I'm not giving her. I need to step up to the plate and be there for her . . . in all areas.

By surprise, even to me, I grab her by her shoulders and flip her around, putting her underneath me, as I pounce on her neck with my teeth, biting her and sucking on her neck with a newfound passion. My manhood pulsating, ready to penetrate her I push in just the head, with no warning and she gasps loudly and starts to breathe heavily. I was teasing her.

"Oh my God, you animal, what's gotten into you?" she exclaims between breaths of shock and pleasure.

I put my finger to her lips hushing her and bury my face into her chest. Biting her collarbone hard enough to leave light marks on her skin, I glide my fingers along her back. My lips navigate to her breasts, where my hand cups one breast tightly, massaging it, and my mouth sucks on the nipple of her other breast. I put my arms around her back and grab her shoulders from behind, then I thrust.

"Oh, my God!" she screams in pleasure. "This is so . . ." and she screams again with another thrust. I keep going, relatively slow at first, and then faster and faster, increasing with the power.

The feeling of her tight lips wrapped around my cock is almost orgasmic in itself, and this rough sex is a whole new experience I never even thought about. I was starting to love it though. Maybe I will satisfy all of her needs!

"Zach? Hey man! I think you're right! There's something out here!" Jeremy yells from outside the tent.

"No man!" I said between breaths in an animalistic fashion. "YOU are right - it's just the . . . sound . . . of great sex!"

I sat up for a moment and held Britt's hips up in the air while fucking her furiously, her legs bent over my shoulders and her whimpering increased dramatically.

"No! DUDE! LISTEN to me! There really is something out here! I'm coming in the tent!" he cried out.

I want to stop; I do believe him, but quickly after thinking it the thought vanishes from my head. This just feels too good and means too much to me.

"Me too! Oh my, God! Me too!" Brittany squeals out between a series of moans.

Suddenly, a bit more light pours into the tent and her face is lit up by the faint moonlight. She is in pure ecstasy . . . I don't think I've ever seen her feeling this good before . . . and it was me doing it! My body covered in sweat, makes our bodies more slippery and easier to fuck her.

The light floods into the tent as Jeremy rushes in and sits down inside. "Hey! You need to pull your little wiener out of there and listen for a minute. There really is something outside. I don't think it's safe here, we need to go, NOW!"

"Don't you dare fucking stop, Zach! I'm coming so hard right now! Ohhhhhhhhh!" She screams out in pleasure. A surge of it fills the tip of my penis, an incredibly warm feeling that makes my body quiver and throb all over. It's so much better than it ever has been before.

"You're crazy, Jeremy! I'm almost ready to . . . to . . . oh, my God! I'm coming!"

An inconceivable feeling of pain and at the same time, serious numbness covers my pubic area. It is an unimaginably sickening feeling that fills my entire body. An incredible amount of liquid runs down my leg and my vision turns sepia and the noise suddenly stops . . .

It wasn't that I could no longer feel my dick, it wasn't there. I feel so numb, I can't possibly fix this, or even comprehend what I'm seeing, but some sort of hairy mass comes into the corner of my eye, and throws a dark, bloody blob against the tent wall. I could see Brittany's mouth moving, her eyes in complete fear . . . and tears. I don't understand what is happening; I am fading away, my vision darkening. She's pushing me off of her, and I am completely at her mercy. What happened?

As my sight fades away, I can hear a variety of different, incredibly powerful and moving sounds. I'm afraid. Crying! This was a mistake! Why am I being pushed along by these events? Everything is a blur. Brittany appears in front of me with a blank expression on her face. Her long hair is shining and is almost washed out by the bright light. She waves to me while her pearly white teeth are shown off as her mouth gapes open. It shifts into a slight smile as her eyes gaze at me. They are not looking at my face, not into my eyes, but at me. Almost like she just found out I was going to be happy. I was going to be okay! The white light is becoming much more intense at the moment and her precious face bleeds and blurs into the light.

I'm going away now, my arms growing heavy and worthless. I try and reach out to her, to wrap her in my arms in desperation. Brittany frowns and looks at me . . . disappointed, wishing she could help. I yell out to her, begging her to hold me as the tears begin to fall down my cheeks. She turns around with a fearful look upon her face. She screams as her neck is torn by an invisible force. Her head tilts back, her vocals chords severed into a mass of blood that pours down her body. There is a look of surprise on her face, frozen in time. Falling, her head is falling backwards, being ripped from the rest of her body until it is finally removed. The headless corpse now filled with light, vanishes completely from my sight.

A final scream echoes in the distance as the white void surrounding me fades . . . Jeremy . . .

I'm fading . . .

I'm . . .

CHAPTER 5

A large, older man stands in front of a group of raging, frustrated townspeople. Flanking each side of this man are officers, they stand still and silent for intimidation purposes. The man dons a classic sheriff's hat; the brim is curled in an almost comical fashion.

"People, I am telling you that until that area is not a crime scene, I cannot allow this bonfire to happen!"

You can see the fear in his eyes, and frustration. You have a few hundred people up in arms about a particular topic and you're the only voice of reason, you would succumb to a little fear and worry yourself. He is desperately trying to make them understand his reasoning, but there is no swaying them, it seems.

An interesting man stands out amongst the crowd. He is wearing a button up shirt with an accompanying red tie and small glasses are perched on his nose, making his eyes appear to be small beady dots. His round face is bright red with no hair on his head, but if it was there, it would be gray.

"Jesus Christ, Sheriff! This bonfire has been a tradition at Hidden Valley High School since I went there! And, that was 35 years ago! We can't stop it now just because we don't know what the hell happened out there."

As soon as the sheriff starts to address his concern, another voice erupts from the crowd over all of the others. A brown-haired teen, Donovan Gray, and his friend, Tommy, stand up to speak. They are part of the local high school and members of the football team, which wasn't obvious by their height and small build. Donovan is a tiny kid, not even reaching 5 feet 8 inches. Tommy is 5 feet 7 inches. In this town you take what you can get for sports, no room to pick and choose, although the football team was doing exceptionally well this year, oddly enough. Donovan's eyes were piercing. In making eye contact with him it felt as if he were practically reaching right through your eyes and groping around the inside of your skull. His eyes are definitely his strongest feature. His other outstanding features include a well defined chin and thick eyebrows that correlate well with his eyes.

"Come on Sheriff!" he yells out, and the crowd grows quiet over his sudden outcry. Donovan puffs out his chest and stares right into the sheriff's eyes.

"It's going to be fine! The whole team is going to be there. Nobody is going to try to take us on when the football team is around! We'll protect everybody, and anybody who tries to hurt our friends will get the hell torn out of em!" Tommy gives Donovan a high five.

His eyes were lit with excitement and aggression, which on its own brought out even more charm. The sheriff adjusted his belt buckle as a dispatch officer voiced some code over the channel. Pulling up his belt and locking his eyes on the young man, he said fiercely, "Now, you understand me boy! It's a crime scene."

Turning his head around to address the whole crowd for a moment, he added, "People! This is an ongoing crime scene! We have no idea what happened up there, and until that crime scene is officially done, there will be no bonfire up there."

"Sheriff, It has been six months since that horrific night!"

On the other side of the crowd, a woman in her mid-40's jumps up. Her eyes are tired and she is wearing conservative clothes. She holds her hands to her hips with attitude. It is Susan, Donovan's mother. Perhaps this is where her child learned the art of intimidation.

She has a list to share and continues droning on in a generally bitchy voice, ". . . and if you can't figure it out - number one," she flings her right hand out in front of her with her index finger held high. "Maybe it shouldn't be a crime scene anymore! And - number two!" She follows this with the accompanying gesture. "Maybe it's time we got ourselves a new sheriff in town! You've been here for 23 years and I think that's plenty enough!"

A small agreement roars from the crowd and with it a general feeling of relief from those who didn't cheer, as though everybody was glad somebody finally said what was on all of their minds. Though a few are disagreeing, they are small in numbers.

"It's time to get somebody who can do the job right!" shouts a voice deep from the crowd.

"He doesn't care about anything," an elderly bitter voice yells.

The sheriff's face becomes a maddening red, with a deadly look upon it. He raises his hands after keeping his cool for a long period of time. "May I remind all of you that it was my daughter up there! If anybody wants to know the truth about what the hell happened up there, I can guarantee you, it's me God dammit!"

Silence falls upon the room. Many faces, which were once full of energy and anger, are now solemn or blank. One thing is constant though, all eyes are fixed upon the sheriff. The sheriff's eyes are heavy, and between his lashes tears well up. He fights the tears and his lips form a frown. Taking a deep breath, the large man walks away from the crowd silently. The silence maintains itself . . . everybody is completely stunned that the young girl who was brutally murdered in the campground was his daughter, Brittany Thompson.

CHAPTER 6

"I know there's a clue here somewhere; they had to have missed something." The young boy mutters to himself in anger as his footsteps crunch on the fallen leaves on the forest floor. The small campground is next to silent besides his presence. Suddenly it is disrupted by heavy footsteps and breathing.

His barely functioning flashlight casts its light upon the forest trees, their bark shines back as they are dampened from the light rain. The beam is readily visible as it illuminates the moisture in the air and creates a beautiful effect. The area seems unnatural, almost devoid of life. The plants are brittle and light brown, complete shells of what they once were, expanding a good 10 to 20 feet away from the campfire. With every step he takes the leaves under his feet loudly crackle and fall apart under the pressure of his weight.

With his next step, a boom bellows in the distance, as though a tree was pushed out of the way by some extreme force. A deep gargle, almost like an angered whimper comes from the same direction . . . directly in front of him.

"Oh, shit," Jordan whispers stressfully under his breath. He starts to run frantically in the other direction, his head turning sporadically to look behind him. He doesn't want to see whatever made that noise, but curiosity forces him to investigate. His face is sweating furiously and pale as snow. He looks behind him once more, not a quick glance as the others were, but for two or three seconds he desperately scouts the area behind him that he is leaving at a fast pace. There is nothing unusual he can see in the distance, yet a sound still looms around him.

His feet, not rising far above the ground due to the speed at which he is running, slide on some leaves in an area where a puddle must have previously resided. He falls flat on his ass in a matter of seconds, twisting his leg as he falls; he now faces the direction from which he was running. This, however, was actually the least jarring in his mind at the moment. Jordan screams out in pain as his kneecap peaks through his skin. The large rock he landed on forced it out of place, leaving him screaming on the ground in excruciating pain and misery. Disoriented, he gets up, knowing only that he is moving forward, not that he has turned around. He somehow manages to force himself up off the ground and hobbles away from the jarring rock.

A pressure suddenly appears on his chest, and in a flash he is back down on the ground, this time on his back. Looking up with half-open, barely conscious eyes, he sees thick black matted hair of a very large, muscular creature. The creature, a wolf reared on its hind legs drops down on all fours with its muscular legs stepping over him. It snorts and snarls at the boy, and his chest becomes wet with saliva dripping from the animal hovering above him.

In a final attempt of desperation, he shakes his head back and forth in disbelief while mustering all of his strength to crabwalk backwards, his injured leg dragging along. The creature's massive claws slash into Jordan's forehead and cheek as the creature lets out a noise almost as painful to hear as his injuries are feeling. It is a screeching, yet deeply pitched bellow reminiscent of a laugh.

Jordan's face is covered in blood. Somehow he somehow stands up on one leg screaming in agony and hobbles but ten feet before stopping to wipe blood out of his eyes. He is coughing and choking on his own blood. His cheek is cut all the way through, giving him a ghastly smile on his right side. His skin flaps loosely against his jawline, blood reflecting visibly in the dark from the light of the moon, flowing into his eyes and soaking his shirt.

An earsplitting howling sound is heard once again and in a purely instinctual manner, he jolts his head back to look for the creature. Seeing nothing, he turns back and runs into a broken tree branch. It goes directly through his right shoulder, impaling him. The branch punctures through the front of his shoulder, but doesn't break through the skin on his back; however, it lifted him up about two inches off the ground.

Weeping dramatically, Jordan is feeling every bit of pain; his body is shaking and he is unable to move due to the pure torture he is experiencing. He cries in complete dismay as in an act of total desperation, tries to remove himself from the tree, but once again a massive claw presses upon his back. He is pushed farther onto the tree as the sound of his cries and the tree's bark rips the muscle tissue of his body. The rain picks up and the ground below him turns to a thick mud. Through his haze of pain he tries to pull himself from his impalement.

"No . . . no . . . no," Jordan gurgles out of his throat through the blood. This thing is just messing with him, having a great time simply using him as his toy.

Another impact lands upon his face. This one is so hard that it literally knocks him back; the tree branch breaks off and moves along with his body as it topples to the ground. His body sloshes in the mud below, which at this point is almost a liquid floor. Jordan, drowning in his own blood, opens his eyes to raindrops pouring into them. His cheek is flapping with his desperate movements; the muscular creature stands over him.

CHAPTER 7

A bright hallway illuminated in sickly fluorescent lighting is filled with people shouting and moving around frantically. The sheriff, the most recognizable figure, bursts into the hallway from a pair of adjacent swinging doors. A nurse runs behind him, shouting for him to come back into the waiting room at the front of the hospital.

"No! Let me see him!" he shouts out to the young intern behind him. Not wanting to restrain the lawman of the town, she stands there with a worried look and an open mouth; arms crossed not knowing what to say.

He runs past the hallway full of people, barely noticing the rest due to the high amount of energy in the room. Everybody is focused on an assigned task, or lost in thought over what has happened to the young man. Tripping over his own feet, his body leaning ahead of him as if it were making him go faster, the sheriff moves forward, shoving a couple of orderlies out of the way until one finally steps in front of him, forcing him to stop.

"Where is he? Is he alive? Please, tell me he's alive!" he yells with raw emotion.

Seeing his face in such desperation, the nurse yells back under the pressure. "Yes, Sheriff," taking a breath, the nurse calms himself as a doctor steps between them for a moment, and exits into another part of the hospital. "Sheriff, the boy is alive, but right now he's in critical condition. I'll get the doctor so he can explain it to you when things calm down."

About four hours pass and it seems like an eternity to him as the sheriff sits in the waiting room. He has sat there with his head in his hands, completely without motion. His hands cover his face completely. You don't need to see his face to know that he is totally distressed.

Finally, the nurse who had talked to him previously enters the room with the doctor who is responsible for taking care of his son.

"Doctor," the sheriff said with a sigh, expecting the absolute worst. No one had given him any more information, but with the look in the staffs' eyes during his wait, he expected the news to be bad.

"Your son is alive, Sheriff."

A heavy pause, during which not a sound is made lasts momentarily, followed by a half smile that appears on both of their faces.

"Can I see him?" the sheriff asks in a quivering and mentally exhausted voice.

"Yes," the doctor sighs. "Yes, you can see the boy in just a minute. He's lost a lot of blood, Tom. If that dog hadn't found him, he'd be dead right now. He severed one of the main arteries in his shoulder and has severe gashes over his eyes and down his face. His cheek was ripped open and we had to stitch one half to the other . . . he's going to be in the hospital for a few weeks. It depends on him and how fast his body can recover."

With a look of shock and disbelief on his face, Sheriff Tom asks him slowly, "Doc, what the hell happened? Have you been able to talk to him at all? Can he talk? Did you ask him anything?"

"No, Sheriff . . . he's been unconscious since he came in; he was barely alive when we found him and as soon as they pulled his body from the ambulance he slipped away and I had to defib him. All I can say is thank God he's got a common blood type."

"God, this can't happen again. I lost Maggie two years ago, Brittany was torn to shreds six months ago, and now I've almost lost Jordan."

They both take a big breath and sigh deeply. In a tired voice the doctor replies, "'Almost' is the word, Tom; but you didn't. And, you need to remember that. He's here. He's alive. Now, I'm not saying he's out of the woods; he's going to spend a long time recovering from this one, but he'll make it. Consider this a gift, rather than a curse."

An orderly came through the door into the room, and said not a word. Instead, the girl simply nods to both of them, giving her condolences and letting the doctor know her job was done. Sheriff Tom motions his head to the door the orderly just disappeared into.

"Now go see him . . . and tell him you love him."

A look of confusion, but mostly relief is the most prominent thing about Tom at this moment. "Does that mean I can see him now, Doc?" he asks in a fearful manner.

"Of course you can."

"Thank you, Dr. Marcus."

The sheriff shakes his head in disbelief and looks Dr. Marcus straight in the eyes for a moment and then looks down at his feet. He shakes the doctor's hand and walks toward the door as Dr. Marcus walks with him, giving him a reassuring pat on the back.

Jordan lies in his bed motionless and with a swollen face. There is still dye on his skin from whatever medical procedure they performed on him. He is barely recognizable. The periodic beating of his heart is highlighted by the monitor he is hooked up to. An oxygen mask is on his face and an I.V. is in his arm.

Dr. Marcus closes the door behind the sheriff and stays out in the hallway. Jordan was almost dead. He lies in front of his father without motion as he is unable to recognize his father is with him in his room. Sheriff Tom turns off the light, and sits in an uncomfortable chair propped against the room's wall.

He's holding Jordan's hand. "Oh my God," he exhales. "Jordan, what the hell were you doing up there? I don't know what I would have done if I had lost you, too. I love you son . . . I love you so much."

CHAPTER 8

A pile of cars is lit up by the noon sun, surrounded by several other piles of junk such as loose ties mixed in with cardboard boxes and amongst the mess, a young, handsome male in his early twenties walks through all the junk.

Stepping past an old stove, long since removed from its home, he is wearing a red flannel shirt with a backpack on his back. The man stops for a moment to survey his surroundings. A blue car about 10 years old sits lopsided, it's front end on the back of another car. Another car, rusting with its paint peeling had obviously been sitting there for years. A small building peaks his interest and he starts to make his way toward it with caution. Before he reaches it, the sound of an empty tin can falling to the ground makes him turn his head in confusion as he continued to approach the building slowly.

A grumbling sound is heard, barely audible in the distance, followed by a crow squawking. He takes a cautious step backwards and turns his body in the direction of the sound. Another growl is heard, this one much louder than before. He sees a shadow dart behind one of the cars, moving in a blur. With a wary, yet curious expression upon his face, he steps closer to the car, cocking his head at an angle as he makes his way to the back of the blue car. The growling grows louder and louder as the man comes closer to the source of the sound.

BAM!

A mangy and underfed brown dog leaps out at him with a bloodied side, ribs exposed under the dog's skin. It leaps toward him with a snap of its jowls.

"Jesus Christ!" he exclaims as he falls backwards onto the ground, putting his arm up to protect his face. The dog is stopped in midair by the chain around his neck, which is attached to the car. The man's back is now covered in orange dirt. He drops his guard momentarily and smiles, getting back up.

As soon as he looks away, another dog runs up and lunges at him, but this one also falls just short of his body. Caught completely off guard, he falls back onto the first dog that approached him. The dog squeals out in pain, and the man, once again, is fearful for his life and gets back on his feet. The dogs continue to snap at him, blocking the way where he came into the junkyard. He stares at the dogs with his back hunched, motioning nervously to them with his hands to calm down. It is obvious the dogs would tear the flesh off of him in an instant if they were loose.

His back meets the body of a male in his mid-thirties, dirty, though not toothless as would be fitting for his character. His teeth are yellowed and unkempt. Jason's one-piece mechanic-style jumpsuit is dirty and stained with grease and oil. For the third time in the last minute or so, the man is scared shitless again, but regains his composure in a matter of seconds and laughs at the situation.

"Didn't you read the God damn sign?" Jason shouts with a slur as he points to the distance.

"No, I-I'm sorry. I didn't see a sign here anywhere."

The mechanic spits chewing tobacco at him and it spatters onto his shoe. "It says no trespassing!"

His voice is clearer than before, but still covered in a thick accent and he wears a look of sheer animosity on his face that is unmatched by anything the man has ever seen. "You're lucky my dogs here didn't eat your balls for lunch!"

"Yeah . . . sorry about that, uh . . . my name's Curt." Curt extends a hand and a warm smile to the man, but Jason doesn't accept his handshake. The dogs have quieted down.

"I'm just . . . just wandering through, uh . . . ." Curt pauses.

The angered man crosses his arms, "Jason. And you can wander your ass on outta here before I let 'em eat you. You are breakin' the law ya know, and if my dogs get to you, well . . . that's not gonna be my fault."

"Okay," Curt offered. "I don't want any trouble now," Curt stammers with a little worry in his voice as he starts to walk away. However, about five steps into his retreat, he turns around and addresses Jason once more.

"Jason, I don't suppose you can tell me how to get to the high school, can you?"

Jason moans in disgust and reaches into his pocket to grab more of his chewing tobacco. Before putting it in his mouth he extends his hand to the old rusted pair of gates, one has rusted off of its hinges. "Just keep walking out that there gate and take a right onto the road. Ya can't miss it, it's just that way."

Curt, maintaining his respectable presence, nods his head at him, "Okay, thanks, Jason."

As Curt turns to walk away, Jason simply stares at him with a look of anger.

Curt continues walking through the junkyard and just before he walks out the gate, the dogs start to bark again in an aggressive manner, he barely hears the words muttered by the red-neck Jason, "Fuckin' Hobo."

Curt is actually much closer to town than he had thought. The old road is beaten and torn down due to lack of proper maintenance, as is typical in smaller towns. The road has several off-shoots leading to small trailer parks or to smaller roads that bend out of sight in the distance. These are of no particular interest to Curt. As he walks further into town, it becomes more civilized but not more populated. It is a typical town and once he gets past a few blocks of houses with perfectly manicured trees, he sees a set of shops, which perk up his interest. The town is very rustic and unusually quiet; populated, yet barely.

He walks over to the shops with titles such as "Ken's Barber Shop" and "Books of the Trade." The most eye catching to Curt is "Katie's Pasta and Baked Goods," which has a large glass window facing the street. When he first glances through the shop window, his sees a bright, newly furnished shop and on its display case are a few cookbooks. In the display case is an assortment of sweets including chocolate pies and apple Danishes. The glass is so clean it looks as though he could reach out and grab the goodies. For a moment he licks his lips as his body starts to sway toward the entrance to the shop; however, he swerves away and backs right into a beautiful female, the shop's owner, Katie Parker, in her early fifties.

"Woah!" he yells in surprise as he turns around and sees her beautiful smiling face. He notices there are fine lines around her mouth and eyes, but her aging face does not at all detract from her cute essence.

"Oh, dear, I didn't mean to give you a jump there. I just saw you looking in and thought I would come over and say hello."

"Oh, no," Curt said with delight. "I should have been watching where I was going."

Realizing his eyes are fixed on hers, he looks away and turns around quickly back to the shop window with enthusiasm, "I was just so mesmerized by those pies!"

Turning back to her, he sees a wider smile than before across her beautiful face. "Thank you," she said proudly as she takes a drag off of her cigarette.

"Wait a second; did you bake all of these?"

Putting her cigarette down by her hips and exhaling deliberately facing away from Curt, she takes a prideful stance. "Yes, I did." Her eyes light up and her face leans into Curt's a little bit, "From scratch, too!"

She lets out a small giggle with a southern twist, "You know, they've been voted the best darn pies in six counties."

"Well, from the looks of them, I certainly believe it," he said with a twinkle in his eye, inflating her ego even more and using some of his charm at the same time.

"Oh, I'm sorry! Look at me forgetting my manners and all," she extends her hand with a smile that just seems to grow larger by the second.

Curt cocks his head for a moment, and looks directly into her beautiful green eyes, "Curt Bloom," he says with confidence.

After the shake, Katie doesn't let go. "Oh, you just wait until you get a whiff!"

The resistance he had felt toward going into the shop earlier fades as Curt allows Katie to lead him through the open door. As soon as he steps into the shop, his eyes close with sheer delight and a fantastic calm comes over him. Sniffing the air and closing his eyes for a good five seconds, the smell of baked delights pours into his nostrils and he becomes handicapped by the delicious scents. Almost like a fantastic high, he becomes lost in the scent that brings back memories of his mother's kitchen from his early childhood.

"So?" Katie says in her perky voice with a small southern twang.

Curt's eyes slowly open and they get very serious for a moment. He maintains a slight smirk on his face, even though his mouth is as straight as can be.

"Well," he pauses once again, inhaling the wonderful, almost sensual smells that fill the bakery. His nerves are calmed and all the stress from his earlier encounters with Jason and his dogs simply dissipate into the back of his mind. "If they taste even half as good as they smell, sweetie, then I guarantee it'll be the best God damn pie I've ever eaten," he said as Katie stood there twirling her hips with her hands clasped tightly, her cheeks now a bright red.

CRASH!

The sound of a glass rolling around is heard in another room. Katie's feeling of admiration quickly changes as her mouth flies open and her head snaps to the right, looking further into the store's kitchen. As they rush into the adjoining room, they are greeted by a very large, burly man who hops up from behind the counter with a disgustingly red, thick liquid all across his thick beard and pudgy cheeks. He smiles like a 5-year-old boy caught doing something wrong.

"Har, har, har," he laughs out in a hillbilly-like tone. "Shucks, sorry, I couldn't help myself." The large man bends down and scoops up the remnants of pasta sauce from the floor. When he smiles there are parts of the sauce adhered to his teeth. Laughing to himself he said, "I spilt the damn thing all over the counter. Figured it was wasted anyways so I might as well have a few bites, right?"

Curt has a large smirk on his face; he is amused by this strange man and most of all, this entire town, which has offered him several surprises since his arrival in the junkyard.

"Curt," Katie said with slight disapproval on her face, followed by an exhale, "This is my husband, Bob."

A smile still upon his face Curt walks over to him with an extended hand. Bob flinches, realizing his hands are filthy with what looks like a coat of somewhat clotted blood. Grabbing a rag he wipes off the mess and turns back to Curt and shakes his hand firmly. Bob feels somewhat intimidated by Curt. It is though he is trying too hard to act proper for this new guest although it is hard to hide his true nature.

"You have a great bakery here," Curt praises in his distinguished voice.

"Aw . . . har, har!" Bob blushes, matching Katie's red cheeks earlier. "It's all her bakery. I just stand around here and pretend to run the place."

Bob leans over to Curt and says in a hushed, goofy voice, "Truth be told, I can't even microwave a bowl of spaghetti!" He laughs and gives Curt a heavy pat on the shoulder, not realizing his own strength. The man is a brute, as even Curt's tough build swayed with his pat.

Although he feels badly for thinking such a thing, Curt is hoping that he is underestimating the intelligence of Katie's husband, Bob. Curt forces a smile, trying to look comfortable. Once again Bob bellows a hillbilly-like laugh. He looks at Curt with arms outstretched due to his laughter, "The bastards just explode all over the damn place!"

"Bob!" Katie says harshly as she gives the man a light push, "Quit your jabbering. He's a customer!"

Trying to distract himself from the situation at hand, Curt turns back into the display area and asks for permission to look at the pies more closely, even though he is going to do it anyway. "May I?"

"Yes! Feel free darlin'!" Katie nods with a delightfully heart-warming smile. Before he reaches the pies he turns around with a firm smile of acknowledgement.

"You look hungry," Katie said.

"I'm starving!" he exclaims without a pause.

"My favorite is the Banana Crème Puff!" yelled Bob.

Slightly irritated, Katie turns around to Bob and waves her hand to him, hushing him away. His face grows sad with disappointment as he starts to realize he is being a pest. Katie sneers at him with disgust, "Let him pick it out, Bob!"

Feeling dignified Curt smiles without hesitation and readjusts his stance. "No ma'am, it's fine. I'll take his advice," Curt agrees as he points his finger in the direction of the big oaf, who smiles pleasantly. Curt then makes soft eye contact with Katie.

"Banana Crème Puff sounds just fine." She meets his gesture with a warm smile and for a moment . . . it is more of a connection. After this tender moment of appreciation, not knowing quite how to react, Curt simply smiles back at her beautiful face.

"You got it!" she exclaims as she begins to put a delicious looking Banana Crème Puff pie into a box. "So, I know you're not from around here, what brings you to Hidden Valley, you a relative of someone?" Katie asked Curt.

Curt looks at the pasta sauce mess back in the kitchen, which is now running down onto the floor, and back at Bob, who seems much calmer than before. His mind can't help but wonder what else has happened in the store. "I'm the new coach at the high school."

Bob's eyes grow curious and he starts to pay attention to him, "Oh yeah?" he questioned in an unbelieving fashion. "What happened to that feller who was runnin' the team before . . . Ol' Bob Miller?"

Curt smiles suspiciously as though he has been asking himself this question over and over again. "I haven't figured that one out yet."

Ignoring the conversation between them previously, Katie now turns around and cocks her head to the side in thought. Practically before Curt finishes his sentence she interjects, "Well, I say! That's weird! He was just in here last week and he didn't say anything about quitting his job."

She pauses in thought, "But now that I think about it, I have not seen him around since then and I don't think anyone else has mentioned him either."

"I have no idea what's going on either, Katie. All I know is I got a phone call a few days ago and was asked to finish out coaching the school year. I know my grandfather used to visit this town many years ago, so I jumped at the opportunity to see one of the places he had spent so much of his time. I don't know much about this town except what he told me when I was just a kid."

Her light chuckle, in reply, was absolutely adorable and any man would be falling over backwards for her, which begs the question . . . what was she doing with Bob? Struck by curiosity, he started to open his mouth to ask such a question, but realizing it would be extremely rude, he shut his mouth and remained silent, letting Katie have the next word.

"Aw, well I hope you like the place darlin'. It's small, but there are a lot of mysteries to this place, and a lot of magic. "So, hmm," she began to stroke her chin, deep in thought and then looked at him. Her eyebrows cocked curiously, "So Curt, or Coach, I guess, where did you park?" she asked, motioning to the front of the store, indicating that there was no car out there where his should be.

Curt crossed his arms, slightly embarrassed to answer the question, "Well, I took the bus up from Bakersfield and here I am."

"Oh, sweetie, where are you staying?"

Curt chuckled and with a wide grin said, "I really have no idea!"

Katie walks over to the counter with his boxed Banana Crème Puff pie and looks at him with an unforgiving expression, as though she was thinking, 'You idiot, typical man.'

"Well, you best be careful around here. The woods ain't safe. Ya know a few kids have been killed up here in the past few months," shared Bob.

The mood in the room shifted from positive to one of heaviness and foreboding. Curt's eyes grew wide and then returned to normal, as though he must have misheard what Bob said.

"Killed?" he questioned after a profound silence.

"Yes, a young couple from the city was killed while camping and then some months later the sheriff's daughter and two boys from the high school were also killed while camping. All three were quite popular kids. It's been about five, six months now . . . still not the place I'd want to be after dark though," Katie stated. Maybe the expression she gave him was more worry than what he initially thought.

"Yeah, it was pretty gruesome. The daughter had her head torn clean off, and the boys were butchered really badly. All evidence is pointing to some wild animals, but nobody knows for sure," Bob chimed in. Realizing this conversation was a bit startling, Katie, once again, changed the topic.

"You know, if you're interested, my sister owns the only nice place to stay in the whole area."

Curt perked up with interest, "Oh, yeah?" Finally, he thought, a lighter topic.

"Yeah, it's pretty nice! We're going out there to visit; it's a really beautiful place ya know," her voice was so soft and sweet, and the southern accent was exceptional. Curt almost became lost in it.

Realizing Curt wasn't answering, Katie continued, and took it as a rejection. "Let me get you directions, you know, just in case. It's sort of out in the middle of nowhere."

"Yeah, that would be great!" Curt stated as he sprang back into the conversation with a warm voice. Katie returned his smile.

"And, probably safe," Bob said as he wiped some more pasta sauce from the counter and put it in his mouth.

CHAPTER 9

Silence and tension fill a small office crowded with aerial photos of the town and several legal documents are pinned on a board with thumb tacks. Sitting at the desk is the sheriff accompanied by two men, Sheriff Tom's longtime friend and co-worker, Deputy Bodie Cooper to his left and on the opposite side of the desk, Dr. Hyde.

"Well, Sheriff, I know this is something you are not going to want to hear, I mean with your boy in the hospital and the town in a damn uproar an-"

He was immediately cut off by Sheriff Tom. "Yeah, yeah, I got everybody screaming in my ear wanting to know what the hell is going on with this thing," he says as his face turns beet red and he buries his face into his hands momentarily, then clasps them together in a sarcastically peaceful manner.

"And really, Doc, with all due respect, it has been long enough . . . so, what the hell do ya got?"

"Tom, I am pretty sure it was an animal. I can't be sure without more testing, but there was most certainly saliva present on both of the boys, especially Jeremy. He had animal saliva all over his lower torso."

Stressed out and with a long sigh, Tom asks the doctor with a concerned look, "Do you have any idea what kind of animal we're talking about?" Tom's face is lit with exhaustion. He felt helpless and wanted to do so much more than he was able.

"You see, Sheriff, that's where it gets strange." The doctor takes a long sigh and has a puzzled look on his face. He sees the exhaustion on Tom's face and wants to help but, unfortunately, has little information to offer. What he does have is uncertainty, nothing positive. The truth is many people have turned up dead. They keep showing up brutally murdered, while officials are no closer to the light at the end of the tunnel.

"There are two components to it, Tom," he continued. "I mean, it's got some human DNA and it has dog, or maybe wolf . . . or something like that. I'm saying it's probably wolf."

The sheriff is completely in disbelief of what he is hearing and so is the deputy. Cooper bursts out in laughter as Tom shakes his head. Cooper, with a smirk of disapproval says, "Well, isn't that the damndest thing I've ever heard! Maybe we've got ourselves one of them werewolves!"

He sees the glaring eye of the sheriff who is thoroughly angry, and he stops laughing. "It's probably just like I said. It's that God damn wolf pack that has been around here for years - used to kill all of the livestock around here a good number of years ago, you remember that, don't ya, Sheriff?"

The sheriff meets Cooper's eyes with the same glare as before as Dr. Hyde starts speaking, remaining composed and professional. "I do know this is the same makeup of the saliva found on the young couple from the city. But, there's another thing, Sheriff. This is a little hard for me to tell you about right now . . . "

He motioned with his eyes to Deputy Bodie Cooper, and then looked back at Sheriff Tom.

"It's alright, Doc. Just tell me. I'm sure I know exactly what you're about to say."

The Doctor takes a long breath, looks back at the deputy and then to Tom, "Okay Sheriff."

The Sheriff shakes his head, in disbelief, preparing for the worst.

The Doctor explains, "If you're thinking Brittany and Zach were having sex, you're right, they were. But, well . . ." he makes another dramatic pause followed by a deep breath. "There's no easy way for me to tell you this, but evidently Brittany was having sexual relations with both of the boys. She had a large amount of semen in her vaginal and anal area."

The deputy looks away with widened eyes and puts his head in the palm of his hand. The sheriff stares, emotionally distraught. The doctor stops talking . . .

"Don't stop; just tell me!" the sheriff says to Dr. Hyde.

"Well . . . from the amount of semen we found, not only in her, but on all of the sleeping bags, they were having a lot of sex, Sheriff. I don't know if you are going to be the one to tell their parents or not, but you know the rumors and speculation surrounding those boys? It wasn't just speculation; they were definitely in a sexual relationship. They had each other's semen all over themselves and well . . . let's just say they were lovers, Sheriff."

Tom instantly tried to get himself into career mode, removing his emotions from the situation at hand to avoid showing the pain and disappointment he felt. As a matter of a fact, his face became stone and was void of any emotion on it whatsoever. Yet, his words said otherwise. "I really, really don't think we have to make that public, do we?"

Seeing his serious face, Deputy Bodie pulled himself together as well.

"Sheriff, the law says that everything found in a crime scene has to be made public once the investigation is completed."

"Bodie, the investigation will not be completed then, until I say it is."

"There's more, Sheriff." Dr. Hyde continues, "As I was saying, I do believe it's some type of animal - probably wolves, and I say this because . . . well, evidently Jeremy got close enough to whatever it was and in his hand, he had some fur that is definitely consistent with wolf or dog fur."

At that moment the door opens partially, and the head surgeon of the hospital, Dr. Marcus, peers in at the group. He appears stressed and tired. This night has not gone well for anybody investigating the crime. Tom jumps out of his seat worried as he feels the information Dr. Marcus is bringing has to do with his son.

"Sheriff, I need to talk to you," Dr. Marcus says in a depressed manner.

"Is my son okay?" Tom eagerly questions him with a wild look upon his face.

"Yes, Sheriff, he's doing fine, but some of the lab reports have come back and there are some very interesting findings."

Dr. Marcus looks around at Bodie and Dr. Hyde. "Can I come in Doc?"

The Sheriff nods his approval to Dr. Hyde, and Dr. Marcus enters the room quietly, realizing he just interrupted a serious discussion.

"Okay, here it is, the first thing is we've found animal saliva mixed in with the wound on your son's shoulder. Secondly, there was animal fur, dog or something, in the gashes on his face. And, it's strange . . . I mean, I can imagine the dog licked some of the blood, but there was a lot of saliva. The fur was matted and even embedded into the gashes, which doesn't make sense. The only way the dog that found him could have gotten his fur in there was if it was the aggressor."

"Actually it makes a hell of a lot of sense," surmised the sheriff as he sat back down.

"Dr. Hyde here was just giving me the toxicology report on the boys and Brittany. We have the same elements in the report you're giving us right now."

Deputy Bodie looks seriously spooked, "Okay!" he says as his lips quiver and his eyes are wide with concern. "I was just making a joke about this maybe being a werewolf, but now I'm starting to get a bit concerned . . ."

"Jesus Christ, Bodie," Sheriff Tom states with a forced smile. "How about we throw in the towel to logic and just say it was an army of them, and they did it with the help of vampires and ghosts and all that other bullshit." He gets very serious and looks directly at Dr. Hyde. "Did these toxicology reports from the couple have semen in them, too? I mean, was it obvious they were having sex also?"

The doctor looked at him perplexed, "Yes, now that you ask, yes, there was. I think they were in the same sex position that Zach and Brittany were in when they were killed."

There was a pause in the conversation, and finally a light arrived in the sheriff's eyes. He was on to something. "Okay! I want you to go back over that report, and I want it looked at with a fine tooth comb. Every single irregularity needs to be put together for me, alright?"

Dr. Hyde grins a little, feeling relief, and also feeling a new found energy and reason to work on the case. "I certainly will," he said with enthusiasm. "You know, now that I'm thinking about it, Sheriff, other than the situation with Zach and Jeremy this could be a copycat kill. There was animal saliva, that's why we were pretty sure it was animals that killed them. I don't recall if there was any fur involved in the other case or not, but I'll go back over it for you, Sheriff, and get my report to you tomorrow."

Dr. Hyde quickly and excitedly leaves the room, off to work. He would love to take credit for the breakthrough in the case. They all would; too many people have been lost and torn away from their families.

Dr. Marcus, who is leaning against a wall in the far corner of the room, steps forth and clears his throat, making his presence known again. "To me, it looks like you've got a herd of wild dogs out there. Probably a combination of German shepherds of some kind or another. By the way, Tom, I'm starting to take Jordan out of the induced coma. Perhaps tomorrow when he's a little more able, you should come by and ask him a few questions, Sheriff.

A tear wells up in Tom's eye, "Jordan," he whispers to himself. It was all the more reason to drive as hard as he could to solve this crime. "You're not doing things too soon? He's going to be okay?" he asked with some hesitation, not wanting a bad answer.

"No, Sheriff, he will be okay. His vitals are stable and have been since we got him under control. I've just been keeping him in the coma to help with the pain management. He's suffered a lot, Tom."

Once again there is an interruption at the door. Sandy Goodwin, the sheriff's secretary, comes into the room not even a second after knocking, nearly defeating the purpose of a knock. Sandy is a very friendly woman in her early fifties with short brown hair and a gorgeous, glowing smile. It isn't showing today though, because it is covered with layers of exhaustion and stress.

Her voice is raspy and tired; she addresses Sheriff Tom, "Sheriff that was Ken Hall from the City Council.

They are very persistent about having a meeting with you tomorrow morning along with the school board, regarding the annual bonfire. It's not going to go away, Sheriff. Sadly, I think you have to give into this one."

"Shit!" he yells out in anger, looking away for a moment, then back to her. The sheriff feels bad for talking to her in that fashion, but he is not a man to apologize for his behavior when it is related to work. Instead, he regains his composure and speaks in a calming voice. "Okay, well, we will see about that. You call Ken back and tell him that I will not be there for any meeting until after one o'clock tomorrow afternoon. I'm going to spend time with my son in the morning."

CHAPTER 10

The interior of the truck is barely illuminated by the light of the clock on the radio and the accelerometer, along with its accompanying gadgets. Katie sits comfortably in the passenger seat with a mound of pastries on her lap. The old pickup truck rocks back and forth as its suspension takes a beating during the drive along the old road to the Hidden Valley Bed & Breakfast.

"It's pretty late for us to be going out here," Bob comments, trying to stay awake on the road after a long day.

"I know. I just got into the baking mode and I was up all night!" Katie states as she lets out a small, high pitched yawn. She is exhausted, but still perky and excited. "You know how I am when I get into a groove, sweetie."

This causes him to bellow out a frustrated grunt, "So why then, Katie, didn't we just come up tomorrow?"

She looks towards her husband who is sitting sloppily in the driver's seat, slightly irritated. "Well, Judy called and she told me that the handsome new coach at the high school, Curt Bloom, came by and rented one of her rooms! She said he raved for close to 20 minutes about how good my pie was."

Her eyes are met with Bob looking over at her and batting a jealous eye. "Oh stop it, you!" she stammers as she lightly hits him on the shoulder. He wanted to say something back, but his lips remained sealed. "Anyway, she also said that he was unpacking all his stuff and he was walking around in his fucking boxers . . . and that . . . oh my

God, Bob, he was fucking gorgeous!" she exclaims, her feet tapping at the bottom of the floor boards, shaking in excitement.

Then she laughs, covering her mouth with her hand. "Did I just say that? Oh my, God," she pauses for a few moments knowing Bob is not pleased, and then she cries out again, "But you have to admit he is! I mean, I can just imagine him without a shirt on! Oh, God! And Bobby, you know how picky my little sister is! I mean if she is all over this guy, then he must be absolutely gorgeous!"

"Grrrr," Bob groaned out to her, but it was obvious she was either completely oblivious to this or she simply didn't care.

"So anyway, I told her that I would make some pasta sauce for him, so she could serve it to him tomorrow! She really, really likes him, even though she's about fifteen years older than he is."

Her face lit up with excitement and she looked as though she was eight years old again, seeing something really shocking. "Oh my, God, does that make her one of those cougar women?" She gasped in excitement, much to Bob's dismay.

"Oh my God, my sister's a cougar, Bobby!"

"Yes, Katie," he replied while gritting his teeth. It was obvious Bob would much rather be at home sleeping than listening to his wife drone on and on about somebody she finds so much more attractive than himself. If he so much as batted his eye at another girl, Katie would make sure it was not forgotten. She continues to laugh; her energy seemingly endless.

"So, if I don't show up late tonight with that pasta, you know how my little sis will worry about me! She's turned off her phone as she always does, and hasn't turned it back on so she's probably worried sick right now!"

"Oh," he frowned, shaking his head, "I'm sure right now we're the last thing on her mind. You know - HOLY SHIT!" His eyes widen as a bloody mass is thrown into the windshield of the truck. It is the chest of a man without the attached limbs, only the head remains attached to the torso.

BOOM!

The windshield glass cracks into a brilliant pattern as thousands of shards are showered into the cab upon the faces of Katie and Bob. The majority of glass though, is somehow still held in place. The clarity of the windshield is now rendered obsolete as it appears thick and dark from inside the cab due to the amount of blood splattered on it.

Bob's screams fill the truck and the desperate whimpering of Katie is heard as the truck swirls in a desperate attempt to arrest its movement. The truck skids to a stop off the road with the front end slamming into a tree, which sends Katie's head against the passenger side window, shattering the glass completely.

"What the hell just happened?" she screams out in pure desperation, her eyes welling up with tears as she tries to piece together the events. As she cries, Bob manages to turn off the car engine and his face is frozen in shock.

"Miller," he says softly in a shaky voice. "Holy hell," Bob yells out loud. "That's Coach Miller!"

Katie turns to him while breathing heavily. She tries to speak but nothing comes out of her dry mouth. Finally she mutters as she desperately attempts to process what's happened right in front of her. "Yeah," she motions with her lips and a slight nod of her head. Her hands go up to her chest, holding her violently beating heart.

"Oh my God, Bobby, where did he come from?"

Bob tries to answer her, but is quickly cut off by her heavy breathing; she is hyperventilating. Between breaths, she lets out a loud scream, "How the hell did you hit Coach Miller?"

A short, piercing scream echoes loudly off in the distance.

"It wasn't him," Katie mutters to herself in fear. The prior happiness had instantly vanished, replaced by a completely different person. Her normally tan skin has

77

paled leaving her white as a ghost. "It couldn't have been him, Bob! No way!"

Seeing her in total hysterics, he touches her shoulder and sadness crawls across his face. "You okay, Baby?" he asks nervously. Her only reply is heavy breathing and whimpers. He sits there for a minute watching her cry and thinking how he might help her. At least they were still alive he thought to himself.

"Yeah," she breathed out the answer heavily as her frantic nerves started to calm down.

"Stay here, okay sweetie?" he requested. She barely nodded in agreement, no longer whimpering or talking, just staring ahead with her eyes wide open. Bob proceeds to get out of the truck and the only light visible is that of the headlights as everything else fades into the background. He figures the torso must be 20 feet behind them back along the road.

Dreading finding it, and with no light to go looking for what had been thrown at the front of his truck, he stood in front of the engine examining the damage all around him. He found the hood of the truck a mangled mess and splattered with bits of intestines and other body parts. He hears a small sound behind him while noticing the majority of the headlights being absorbed by a plant in front of the scene. He motions to Katie who is in the front seat. "Hit the brights!" he shouts to Katie, who appears to have regained some composure. He can't see much of her, as there's blood all over the cracked windshield. She cautiously reaches over to pull the switch on the driver's side of the truck. As soon as the switch is clicked, a large furry creature on its hind legs and forearms launches itself into the air and slams Bob down to the ground. Katie is watching the massacre of her husband and her face is so incredibly disturbed it is barely recognizable as hers anymore. "Oh, God . . . no!"

The creature moves swiftly and its movements are so precise, it almost seems mechanical. It stands up over Bob who is lying flat on the ground. Bob's legs barely moving and without a struggle the creature picks up his body and tosses him underhandedly onto the roof of the truck. A roaring sound is heard, the God damn beast laughing at them in a deep growl. Mostly standing on its hind legs, the creature approaches his new prey. Reaching up, it pulls the squirming body of Bob down onto the hood and using its front paws, bashes him against the windshield, directly in front of Katie's face.

The window glass breaks even more, yet maintains some of its original form. It's dented beyond belief, and is now being coated with a fresh layer of her husband's blood. The first smash, his nose flattens, and a combination of blood and snot leaves its mark on the windshield. She lets out a loud, hopelessly pathetic scream, and feels utterly useless as she watches the life snuffed out of her love. Again, the creature pulls back on Bob's head and slams it against the glass harder, the side of his face being rubbed against the cut glass is scratched and cut. He is still conscious, feeling every bit of this pain.

The third and final hit, his head smashes jaw first against the almost broken windshield, breaking through leaving his bottom teeth and jaw inside of the glass. The beast rips his head up, but the jaw stays locked, until his skin at the corners of his mouth start to rip open and his jaw stretches to incapable limits.

POP!

A dramatic sound followed by an almost comically large stream of blood squirts inside the truck, covering Katie's face and squirting in her eyes. The jaw is broken, and her husband, Bob, is dead.

The werewolf casually tosses his body to the side, seeking another kill, seeking more excitement and fun. The creature peers through the hole Bob's jaw made in the windshield, and makes a strange groaning noise at her, almost as if it felt sorry for her. The creature itself was in some sort of agony, yet it was fueled by its instincts to the point where it was no longer in control of its actions. A moment of sympathy appears in its eyes, but this quickly disappears and the fierceness returns.

The creature backs off the hood and kicks the headlights out one after the other. It is now pitch black. In a last ditch effort to survive, Katie fumbles around in the darkness until she finds the button to lock all the doors of the vehicle, while frantically screaming for help.

Silence is all around her. Her whimpering is the only audible sound. Not even a cricket chirps in the distance, and she is left alone. It is this newfound sense of solitude after such an extreme situation that gives her the courage to move a little bit back in the truck, to the rear cab. As soon as she situates herself into the foot space of the truck, the back window she is furthest from shatters without warning, and the creature rips its arm through, trying to reach her, yet is unsuccessful. In a last ditch effort to survive she picks up one of her pies in the backseat and throws it at his face. The werewolf smiles and pulls the door off of the truck.

CHAPTER 11

The beeping of the heart monitor is the only sound heard in the room. Jordan lies on the bed motionless. Sheriff Tom sips on a small cup of coffee extracted from one of the cheap vending machines in the hospital lobby. His face is disturbed, concerned; he just wants his son to be okay. With his next sip, the boy stirs.

"Jordan!" The sheriff, startled, spills the cup of hot coffee all over himself and the floor. He quickly stands up and moves over to Jordan's side. "Jordan," he says again, desperately. "Can you hear me, Bud?" he asks intensely, almost yelling into Jordan's face. "Oh God, I love you! Do you know that I'm here?"

Jordan, his eyes confused and worried and at the same time comforted by the familiar face of his father, attempts to speak, "Dad?" He utters the sound muffled by his swollen lips. His speech is slurred, but the sheriff doesn't care. His son is alive, conscious, and able to recognize him. A large smile crosses his face as he leans down and gives his son a kiss on the forehead between all of the bandages.

"Dad, I'm sorry." He makes a small gagging sound, "I think, I think I'm going to puke!"

"It's okay; I have a basin for you." He readies a small bedpan under his son's chin and uses the electronic controls to raise the top half of the bed up.

"It was so weird dad . . . something I've never seen before." He is obviously still shocked from the event of being torn apart, literally and physically. "It was like a big dog and it came out of nowhere. God, Dad, it hurts so badly!" He kicks his legs and cries out in pain.

In a worried voice and with hurried motions, the sheriff quickly presses a small button easily within Jordan's reach. "Shh . . . " the father just wishes for his son to calm down, wanting him to be out of this painful misery. He speaks to him in a hushed voice as he motions to the button. "Jordan, Jordan. Do you see this? It's a morphine drip, okay? You see, just push this button here every time it hurts that much, okay? It will make you feel better in just a second."

Jordan's restless movements calm down and then grind to a halt. "Okay . . . .thank you da . . . " his voice fades into a slur as he starts to drift back to sleep. The sheriff sighs and leans back into his chair for a moment, throwing a single napkin on the mess of spilled coffee, then he leaves the room. Finding Dr. Marcus leaning against a wall in the hospital corridor, the sheriff approaches him cautiously.

"He just woke up . . . my son, he's going to be okay, right doc?" he smiles at the doctor.

"He did? That's fantastic; it must be a relief for you, aye Sheriff?"

"Yeah, a hell of a one," he says quietly. His eyes become very serious and heavy for a moment, and tears start to form.

"Doc, I just don't know. With everything that's been going on, how can I be sure that it would be safe for all those kids to be up there? God, Doc, could you imagine what the hell could happen if there's something out there that we don't know about and it goes after all those kids. Jesus, Doc, I don't want to see any more kids dead."

Dr. Marcus looks at him with pity and only has a few words to say before sending him on his way. "I understand and I don't envy you one bit . . ."

The sheriff pauses for a moment, as though in personal reflection, wanting to say something else to the doctor.

"Sheriff, don't you have a meeting at one o'clock with a very angry school board and the City Council?"

The sheriff's face hardened. "As much as I don't want to, yes, yes I do. What time is it?

"Almost noon, sir," answered Dr. Marcus.

"Now look, Sheriff," says the mayor with a booming voice that is just as charming as it is deep and powerful, which no doubt helped him get elected. He stood over the townspeople, which fueled his ego tremendously. The meeting was very tense.

"We have all given this a lot of thought and I can't, for the life of me, see any reason why these kids cannot have their annual bonfire up there."

The sheriff's eyes appear to be bulging out of his head at the sound of this. "It's crazy," he wants to shout back, but his jaw remains firmly shut, knowing that the mayor could easily have him removed from his position as sheriff.

"Now, Sheriff Thompson, Mr. Fuller, the principal and I have discussed this and I'm going to override you. I have that power! I can do it."

The nerve of this guy, the sheriff's mind is filled with regret for helping elect the son of a bitch into office; now his decision may very well have killed the town's youth.

"Mayor!" he shot back with a stream of courage previously unseen from the sheriff toward the mayor. He continues, "You, sir, you may be able to override me, but I am telling you, if you do, and anything happens up there to those kids so help me God I will do everything in my power to get you out of office!"

His hands trembling, the mayor looks at him with disbelieving eyes, and for a moment, he lets the intimidation show. His face quickly changes back to the cocky politician-look reminiscent of JFK, although he isn't nearly as handsome.

"Sheriff, are you threatening me? Because I don't believe that's conduct very becoming of a sheriff," he shot back, in a confident tone, while batting an eye to his left and then his right, beckoning to the following of his supporters. Some meet him with a confident eye looking at him in an exceptionally proud manner; others simply avoid eye contact with the mayor

"No, Mayor," the sheriff paused for a moment. "Sir, I am not threatening you. I am merely stating a fact. If anything happens up there, it is all 100 percent on your shoulders."

An angry glance is exchanged between the two figures and the sheriff even starts to approach the mayor confrontationally, until a voice shouts out from the back of the crowd. It is Curt Bloom.

"Hey, I'm brand new here," he exclaims, standing up and coming to the front of the room so people can see him. The City Hall grows quiet and all eyes are on the newcomer.

"Uh, hi . . . I'm Curtis Bloom, and I'm replacing Mr. Miller as coach of the Hidden Valley football team." He looks around the room and not a damn thing is moving. The room is still and surprisingly quiet; all eyes looking intently back at him.

"Isn't there somewhere else we can allow these kids to have a party and do something for homecoming?" Bloom asks.

The sheriff shoots back with conviction. "Wait a minute, what the hell happened to Miller, Mr. Bloom?"

Mr. Fuller, a tall, slightly overweight man wearing a button up flannel tee interjects, "I got a phone call last week telling me that he had to leave town unexpectedly on personal business," his voice booms through the room as he stands up and adjusts his tie. "I don't think he'll be back for the rest of the school year. We had to get a substitute and Coach Bloom, here, came highly recommended."

In a fury of outrage, the sheriff stands up causing some ruckus in the crowd. "What the hell, Mr. Fuller, you got a phone call, and that's all?"

Not taking this outburst by the sheriff well, Mr. Fuller looks at him grimly. "Yes, Sheriff," he retorts with an angered voice and an almost menacing tone. "That's all we got - just a phone call."

The sheriff remains standing, his mouth slightly open as he is deep in thought and confused. He personally had a decent connection to Mr. Miller, or at least closer than anybody else in the town, besides the boys he coached, of course. Nobody asked a lot of questions about him, nor did those that were asked get answered. All that people were concerned with was that Coach Miller brought the boys to a championship game like he did at his last school. Everyone was hoping he would do it again here at Hidden Valley! He was a fantastic football coach, and the room was dampened with disappointment when the news was made public of his departure.

"Now that is the damndest thing; Coach Miller's been the coach here in Hidden Valley for what, 15 years?" the sheriff droned on, but the mayor interrupts him before he can answer his own question.

"No, actually, he coached here about 18 years, Sheriff," responds the mayor.

The mayor himself starts to ponder the matter of Miller's disappearance. "You know that is a little weird. I know Bob Miller really well and I would've at least thought he would have called me to talk about his leaving. Not just get up and leave like that - how strange."

His attention is directed toward Curt with newfound curiosity, ". . . and . . . Coach Bloom, right?"

Curtis Bloom nods his head yes toward the mayor, looking a bit of nervous.

"You have to understand that the party is a tradition that's been going on for 45 years. It has become the soul of this town. He smiles with pride as many people in the crowd shake their heads in agreement. "You know something? Every single homecoming dance we've ever had in the past, ever since we started holding them, ends with a big ol' bonfire behind the Hidden Valley Bed & Breakfast." He smiles to himself, remembering the fun he had up there as a student.

"All of the kids go, roast marshmallows and have a great time. It usually goes into the wee hours of the morning." The mayor's eyes are now twinkling with memories, pleasant memories. He seems to be almost selfish about this; he is so adamantly opposed to canceling this event, simply because he had such a good time when he was a kid. This ignorance is completely overwhelming, and when a dangerous mind-set is supported by a crowd . . . well . . . that's when things get scary.

"I'll be damned if the young kids don't get to enjoy themselves this year!" he yelled.

After the meeting ended and the crowd cleared, only a few of the mayor's little cult-like following remained, scattered amongst City Hall. In the hallway outside of the Mayor's Office, Donovan Gray and Tommy are being escorted to the Mayor's Office by an elderly secretary. Donovan has a large smile on his face.

At least the boy's smile is not nearly as reminiscent of the mayor's shit-eating grin, the sheriff thinks to himself.

As they reach the mayor's office door, the secretary knocks and opens it slightly, peeking her head through. "Mr. Mayor?" she asks in a voice that has been compromised by years of cigarette smoke. The people in the hall can hear rustling in the office as he comes to the front door in a bit of confusion.

"Yesssss, what is it?" the mayor asks with irritated curiosity, his 'yes' sternly dragged out to show that he is not happy with the interruption.

The secretary whispers something to the mayor that is indistinguishable and he responds in surprise. "He is? They are?"

He then proceeds to sound like a happy television star on a fifties television show. He seems in a wonderful mood, although he is clearly acting. "Oh! Well, not a problem," he tells her, as he steps out into the hallway and heads back to the meeting room greeting Donovan on the way.

"Donovan! I thought you were supposed to be here at one o'clock?"

Donovan stands up straight from leaning against the wall as the mayor addresses him. "Uh, yes, sir, I was," he says nervously. Gaining confidence or at least making himself appear as though he has some confidence, he answers, "I just got out of the meeting with the rally squad and the senior members of the football team. We kind of understand where the sheriff is coming from on his stance about the bonfire.

He nods his head to the sheriff as Sheriff Thompson gives a smile and a nod back to Donovan. Feeling he has total approval from the sheriff, Donovan goes on to explain the football team's solution to the dilemma.

The sheriff is skeptical that it will be worthwhile to listen to Donovan since a high school football team is not an ensemble of professionals put together to solve a democratic issue. *But then, look at many governments,* the sheriff thinks to himself.

"So, we have a compromise for the sheriff," Donovan states as he gestures a hand to the sheriff. "I know, Mayor, you said you were going to override him, but that sounds harsh, doesn't it?"

In not so hushed tones, there was unanimous approval throughout the citizens still left in the room, except for the mayor. "Here's our compromise - you condone the bonfire, Sheriff, and we agree that everybody, EVERYBODY, will be out of there by midnight and as long as your deputies turn their backs a little, we would not have a problem with having a couple deputies there overseeing the bonfire."

The entire room stares at the sheriff, waiting for him to give some type of acknowledgement to the deal Donovan has just suggested. The sheriff sighs heavily.

"Donovan, that is a good compromise and I'm proud of you guys for trying to work this all out, but I cannot condone something that I truly believe is dangerous. I realize my stance may be a little different because . . ."

He starts to tear up and falls silent, thinking for a minute and regaining his composure.

"Well, if the mayor still overrules me and agrees to that compromise - but I would want more than a couple deputies out there to keep an eye on everything."

Curt Bloom steps into the forefront once again. "Well, I, for one, think this is a fantastic compromise and I think it's something you and the people should all agree on because it is safe for everybody . . . I am just saying, Sheriff, Mayor!"

The mayor, feeling cocky and not comprehending the true power of the dice he is about to roll, makes his decision, making a furtive dominant glance toward the sheriff.

"I do, hereby, overrule you Sheriff Thompson and agree to this compromise brought forth by the young people of our town. I also authorize you to place at least two deputies up there behind the old Hidden Valley Bed & Breakfast for the safety of all those attending the homecoming bonfire."

Sheriff Tom Thompson sighs, shakes his head and looks down dejectedly at his feet in pure defeat, then mutters, "I will do as I'm ordered, Mr. Mayor."

The mayor's personal secretary comes back into the room, this time directly addressing the sheriff. "Sheriff, I just got a call for you. They said there's another bad situation and they need you to come over immediately."

His face becomes pale, and fearful. "Shit, now what?" he asks himself out loud in an attempt to convince himself that whatever has happened, it's something different than the previous few times they urgently requested his presence.

Losing his composure, he quickly leaves the room, yelling on the way out, "Okay, Mayor, you do whatever the hell you want!"

Donovan, in a moment of curiosity, quickly changes the topic back. "Does that mean we get to have our bonfire tonight, Mr. Mayor?"

Shaking his head, it is obvious the mayor has the same concern as the sheriff. For a split second, he thinks about following his better judgment and telling Donovan that, no, it's cancelled. However, he could think of no real reason to change his mind - another murder could not possibly have happened.

"Yes, Donovan, you go tell all your friends that the bonfire is on - and have a damn good time tonight, because we expect you all to win us a state championship this year!" Donovan and Tommy give each other a high five and then a fist bump saying, "Awesome," as they leave the mayor's office. Sounding once again like a young kid, Donovan thanks the mayor several times over, before leaving with a final statement.

"Thank you, Mr. Mayor, Mr. Fuller. Coach, we look forward to seeing you on the track."

"State championship, what? Nobody said anything to me about that!" Coach Bloom exclaims in total panic that is interrupted by Mr. Fuller.

"Yep, hell, we want to go to the state championship every year!"

Curt let out a big sigh of relief, "But . . ."

"We haven't had a championship in 25 years. We probably won't get one this year either, but we keep hoping," the mayor added.

A small smile comes across Curt's face.

Chapter 12

At the bed and breakfast Judy is quickly trying to get things put together so she can take Tristan in for his doctor's appointment. Tristan is, as usual, if not playing the piano he is outside tanning and swimming with the other guests at the bed and breakfast. Tristan is the only child Judy has ever had. He's extremely good looking, blonde hair, blue eyes small but has a very toned and defined tanned body. He has a great smile and an incredible personality. He is very protective of his mother and his mother is very protective of him.

Tristan, for a number of years, has been homeschooled by Judy. This next school year Tristan will be in eighth grade, middle school and it is the last year before he starts attending high school. Judy has decided even though she doesn't want to let him attend the middle school in Hidden Valley, she feels it is time that Tristan begin preparing for high school. Since Tristan is 13, Judy has decided that he needs to have a complete physical. She called Dr. Marcus's office and set an appointment. Tristan is not exactly sure about this, because Judy explained what Dr. Marcus is going to have to do, to perform a physical on Tristan. Judy opens the door to the back of the bed and breakfast and hollers out for Tristan to wrap up in his towel and come up and get ready to go to this doctor's appointment.

Tristan looks at his mother, "Do I really have to do this?"

Judy answers, "Yes, you do."

Tristan picks up his towel and wraps it around his waist and goes on in to the bed and breakfast. Tristan runs up to his room, dropping his towel on the way for his mother to pick up laughing as his mother says, "Get that naked butt of yours upstairs and put some clothes on now, we have to go."

In the car Tristan is asking Judy questions about Dr. Marcus. "Mom, Dr. Marcus is old isn't he?"

Judy just looks over at him and smiles, "He's not that old honey, but he has been a doctor for a long time."

Tristan shakes his head, "Yeah, that's what I mean he's been a doctor a long time. He's done lots of physicals, right?"

Judy shakes her head, yes.

"Then I suppose I shouldn't feel nervous or anything because he's seen many naked boys before and naked girls, right?"

Judy smiles and shakes her head, "Yes, there is nothing for you to be nervous about. Everything will be fine. Dr. Marcus sees many people from children all the way up to, well your Aunt Katie, for example."

Tristan looks at his mother with a smile on his face and says, "Aunt Katie, she's really old!" as Tristan laughs out loud.

"Your aunt is not that old, Tristan, she's only 15 years older than me."

"Yeah, mother, your 38 and you're old." They both start to laugh, which is definitely making Tristan feel more comfortable about his pending physical with Dr. Marcus.

They reach Dr. Marcus's office. Dr. Marcus has a very modern clinic at the Hidden Valley General Hospital complex. It is probably one of the most modern buildings in the entire town as most of the buildings have been here for many years, built in the 30s, 40s and 50s. Sitting in the waiting room Tristan has picks up a magazine called *Boys Life* and is very interested in the article pertaining to hitting puberty and how to deal with it. Judy has noticed that he is reading that particular article in the magazine and wonders to herself if he has hit puberty or not. She feels Dr. Marcus will tell her later, so she decides not to enter into a conversation with Tristan about his choice of reading material. Just then Dr. Marcus's nurse comes out and calls Tristan's name.

Tristan and Judy stand up and start toward the door. The nurse stops Judy and says, "You know this is a complete physical for your son." She looks at Tristan, "I think he would be more comfortable if you did not come into the room with him."

Tristan stops and thinks for a minute and looks at his mother and then looks away and then looks back at his mom and says, "Yeah, why don't you wait out here in the waiting room and when Dr. Marcus wants you to come in then you can come in, okay, mother?"

Judy gets an extremely surprised look on her face. Her baby has just told her that he really doesn't want her in the examining room with him while Dr. Marcus has him take off all of his clothes and examine him. She thinks to herself *oh my God, he really is growing up, isn't he?* She smiles, reaches down and pats his cheek, "All right, you go. When you're all done with your examination and Dr. Marcus wants to talk to both of us, I will come in at that time."

The nurse smiles and tells Judy that as soon as the doctor wants her in the room she will come out and get her.

Judy is a little stunned and taken back by the fact that she's not going to be in the examining room with her child for the very first time in his life. She's not sure if she's happy or sad about it because it means her little boy is not so little anymore and just may need his own private time with his doctor. *Oh my God,* she thinks to herself, *I don't know if I can deal with this, but I guess I'm just going to have to* as she goes over and sits down in the waiting room chair. She watches the door to the hallway leading to the examining rooms close leaving her behind. Her little boy goes in for his first complete physical exam since he was a toddler.

The nurse takes Tristan to the examining room and tells him to take everything off except for his underwear. Tristan looks at her with a look of confusion in his eyes and says, "My underwear?"

She smiles, "Yes."

Tristan thinks for a second, "Mmm, I don't wear underwear."

The nurse turns back around, looks at him and smiles, "Oh, that's okay, I will get you a gown." Tristan looks very embarrassed at the nurse who turns back around and smiles at him, "It's okay, honey, a lot of boys up here in Hidden Valley evidently don't wear underwear. Especially where you live, I'm sure as with most of the other boys, you mostly run around with nothing on swimming and sunbathing, so you're not alone. That's why we keep this special type of gown for you boys," as she hands him one to put on.

Tristan has a big smile on his face, "Thank you."

The nurse tells him to tap on the door as soon as he is undressed and she'll come in and take his vital signs for the doctor. Tristan looks at her, smiles and nods.

She leaves the room and Tristan exhales with a sigh of relief still a bit embarrassed as he wasn't expecting to have to get completely undressed to see the doctor. Even though Judy had told him that the doctor was going to want to look at his entire body, he didn't quite realize that he was going to have to be naked in the doctor's office.

Tristan gets undressed and puts on the little paper gown and to his surprise he realizes that even if he ties it behind his back his butt is probably going to show. He quickly hops up onto the examining room table and then realizes he did not knock on the door to let the nurse know he was ready. He jumps back down off the table, knocks on the door and quickly runs and hops back up on the examining table so the nurse cannot see that his bottom is exposed. The nurse comes back in and takes all of his vital signs - blood pressure, heart rate, temperature and then goes out to let Dr. Marcus know he is ready to be seen.

Tristan is sitting on the examining table looking around the room at all of the different things when the door opens and in comes Dr. Marcus. "Good morning, Tristan, how are you? My goodness you have certainly grown up since the last time I've seen you." Dr. Marcus looks at Tristan's chart, "You're 13 now, right?"

Tristan smiles and shakes his head, "Yes."

"That's just great. Let's see, you're here for a complete physical examination - your very first as you should be entering puberty, right?

Tristan looks at Dr. Marcus and says, "I think so, I'm not sure Dr. Marcus."

"Well, Tristan, I'll tell you in a minute if you are, okay?" Tristan smiles and shakes his head.

Dr. Marcus reaches his hand out to give Tristan a handshake. Tristan looks at it and catches Dr. Marcus offguard when he comes back with a fist bump. Dr. Marcus looks at him and then clenches his fist and bumps Tristan's with his.

"So Tristan, how are you feeling these days?"

Tristan looks at Dr. Marcus skeptically, "I'm okay, I guess. I feel pretty normal, the same as I always have Dr. Marcus.

"Very good," Dr. Marcus starts to examine Tristan looking in his ears, up his nose, listening to his heart, his lungs, checking his reflexes, all of the standard medical procedures involved in a physical examination. "Have you noticed any change in your voice, Tristan?"

Tristan looks at him and shakes his head, "No, it's the same."

"It hasn't started to crack or anything?" asked the doctor.

"What do you mean by cracking?" asked Tristan.

"While you're talking does your voice suddenly get higher and sound different?"

"No, not ever - why?"

"Usually that happens when you start into puberty, Tristan." Dr. Marcus asks Tristan to stand up and take off the robe so he can examine him.

Tristan's eyes open wide, "Dr. Marcus, you want me to take off this robe so you can look at me?" asked Tristan.

"Yes, Tristan," said Dr. Marcus, "I need to look at your legs and everything to make sure that you are developing properly and growing correctly.

Tristan nervously takes off the robe and stands there naked for Dr. Marcus to examine him. Dr. Marcus asks Tristan to stand up straight putting his legs together as tightly as he can so he can see if his legs are growing straight. Dr. Marcus tells Tristan to turn around and he spins him around looking at his back and down his butt cheeks at the back of his legs.

"Tristan, do you stand with a bend in your knee most of the time?" questions Dr. Marcus.

96

"Maybe," said Tristan, "I don't know. I've never really thought about it."

"I want you to stand up straighter, Tristan, so you don't get a bend to your knees, okay?" Dr. Marcus has Tristan turn around and he looks at Tristan's private area, which makes Tristan embarrassed and uncomfortable. "It is okay, Tristan, you don't need to be nervous, I'm not gonna hurt you, I promise," said Dr. Marcus. "Are you sure your voice is not starting to change at all, Tristan?" questioned Dr. Marcus.

Tristan shakes his head no, "I don't think so. Why?"

"Well, if it's not, I would say it's probably going to start pretty soon. I'm pretty sure you have started into puberty, Tristan." Dr. Marcus was expecting to see a smile on Tristan's face as he normally does when he tells a young boy he is starting puberty. Instead, Tristan looks fearful.

Tristan's looks at Dr. Marcus seriously, "Are you sure? You really think I have started entering into puberty?"

Dr. Marcus is surprised by Tristan's questions and takes a step back and looks at him, "Yes, Tristan, I'm sure you have started into puberty."

Tristan turns around and looks at himself in the mirror in the doctor's office, he turn and looks back at Dr. Marcus, "How long does it usually take for puberty to be done?"

"It could take up to a year, but with most boys it usually takes about six months for puberty to completely transform. Why do you ask, Tristan?"

Tristan has a very concerned look on his face and thinks for a second then turns back to look in the mirror. "Does that mean I'll start growing hair on my face, Dr. Marcus, that I'll have to shave?"

Dr. Marcus smiles and laughs a little, "No, Tristan, just because you've entered into puberty doesn't mean that you will get facial hair. You might not have to shave until you hit your late teens or maybe even your twenties. It just depends on how your body works."

"Oh, okay. Thank you, Dr. Marcus," said Tristan. He tries to get the look of fear off his face, but he really doesn't do a very good job of changing facial expressions.

Dr. Marcus can see that Tristan is very concerned about something, which concerns Dr. Marcus because he can't read Tristan quite as well as he can usually read the other boys that he sees in his office on a regular basis. Dr. Marcus steps back and takes a really good look at Tristan who is still standing there naked looking at himself in the mirror. Dr. Marcus thinks to himself, *there is something about this boy - I can't quite figure it out. I will have to keep it in the back of my mind for later, for the next time I see him.*

Dr. Marcus looks at Tristan, "You can go ahead and get dressed, Tristan, and I'll tell the nurse to have your mother come in and we'll talk for a few minutes. "Oh, is there any other questions you have for me or anything you want to tell me before your mother joins us?"

Tristan looks at Dr. Marcus and shakes his head, "No, I think you answered most of my questions, Dr. Marcus."

"Okay, you get dressed and we'll bring your mother into the room." Dr. Marcus walks out the door.

Tristan looks at himself one more time in the mirror, very closely examining his entire body. He appears scared and very worried and his eyes start to swell up with tears. He shakes his head and reaches over grabs his clothes and gets dressed.

A few minutes later the door to the examining room reopens with Dr. Marcus and Judy entering.

Dr. Marcus has a big smile on his face while explaining to Judy that Tristan looks absolutely fantastic and everything seems to be great except for the fact that he wants him to stand up straighter. "I'm concerned that Tristan stands with his knees bent and he needs to get in the habit of standing taller and straighter because he's not a very tall boy. Reminding him to straighten those knees will be beneficial later on," said Dr. Marcus.

Judy agrees and smiles, "Thank you very much, Dr. Marcus." She looks over at Tristan, "Now that wasn't so bad, was it?"

Tristan shakes his head no. Judy looks back at Dr. Marcus and tells him about the conversation they had in the car on their way to the appointment.

Dr. Marcus laughs and looks at Tristan, "I certainly hope it wasn't as bad as you may have thought it was going to be."

Tristan smiles back, "No, it was okay."

Dr. Marcus looks at Judy, "Say by the way, how is that crazy old brother-in-law of yours?" as he smiles at Judy.

Judy laughs, "Bob? He is Bob, just as crazy as ever, always up to something that drives my poor sister Katie insane, but they love each other. They've been together for 30 years now, you know. He built Katie that new high case, the one that had all the shelves in it for her pies - it looked so lovely and beautiful, the only problem was when she filled it full pies it all fell apart and smashed the pies all over the floor. She was so mad, I would have loved to have been there it must've been so funny."

Tristan chimes in, "Uncle Bob is crazy, but he's funny. He always has a good story to tell, he makes me laugh all the time."

"Please tell them the next time you see them that I said hi and for Bob to stop causing Katie high blood pressure," as he laughs out loud.

"I sure will Dr. Marcus and thank you for taking such good care of Tristan for me today."

"You are welcome. Judy, you take care of that boy and take care yourself and I'll see you in about a year. Tristan, if you have any questions about your body or any of the changes that it's going through, let me know okay?"

"Okay, Dr. Marcus, but I think I know what's gonna happen to my body – at least I'm pretty sure I do, but thank you and I'll keep you in mind if I have any questions."

Judy and Tristan leave Dr. Marcus's office, get in the car and head back to the bed and breakfast.

"That wasn't so bad now was it Tristan?"

"No, I guess not, but somebody really needs to tell Dr. Marcus his hands are really cold. Especially when he touches you down there, his hands should be warmer, mother."

Judy smiles and laughs, "Tristan, you are so funny. I love you so much."

CHAPTER 13

The sheriff walks into the station and everyone is working frantically on the phones, conversing with each other, and documenting notes on paper. The sheriff wears a fearful expression and he is still denying his initial thoughts about what may have happened. His mouth is wide open and his voice booms through the station, everyone becomes significantly quieter.

"Where the hell is Cooper? What the hell is going on?"

Many people stop what they are doing and just stare at him until Deputy Bodie Cooper stands up from a chair and walks toward the sheriff ready to share the bad news with him.

"Sheriff, we have a problem. We have had some more killings!"

It was official, somebody else had died. This situation is spiraling out of control. The sheriff becomes frantic and become short of breath.

"What are you talking about and who is it?" he barks out harshly in a fashion similar to a dictator during his speeches.

"Well, they think it's the Parkers, both Katie and Bob, but they can't really tell due to the mess that was made of 'em."

"What the hell - Katie and Bob?" Shaking his head, the sheriff is at a total loss for words.

Deputy Bodie hates telling the already worried and depressed sheriff the situation, but it is his job. "Yeah and there's one more, Coach Miller," he revealed quietly avoiding eye contact.

"Coach Miller?" the sheriff repeated, with a lack of emotion. He was obviously overwrought with the news. His career mode kicked in once again, and using his best effort, he tries to turn off his emotions.

"We were just talking about him over at the meeting with the mayor. Let's go, Cooper, we better get out there."

The road to the Hidden Valley Bed & Breakfast is relatively calm as they drive up to the crime scene. The sun is shining through the leaves on the trees, puddles reflect the foliage on the ground. It is very beautiful. Around the next bend, however, is when things start to become nightmarish. The first thing the sheriff sees is the bloody trail left behind on the dirt road by the mangled torso of Coach Miller. The blood trail is coagulated and covered with flies. Around the trail a few analysts are stooping over the evidence. Stopping at a line of caution tape, they look ahead and see the pickup truck off the edge of the road and marks in the dirt from the struggle that had ensued.

"Jesus Christ, what the hell happened, Bodie?" the sheriff cries out as he turns to Deputy Cooper.

"Holy shit, Sheriff, I have no idea. This appears to be a triple homicide."

They walk up to the scene as a variety of deputies and police officers are still securing the area, picking up the markers as they finish taking photographs of the area.

The Parker's truck is beat to hell and is a bloody mess. Walking up in disbelief, he tries to keep his professionalism, but his emotions are overwhelming. The sheriff becomes short of breath again, and starts to gasp as he sees Bob Parker's distorted body, his jaw severed from his body, lying next to the wreckage. The jaw had dug itself slightly into the ground from the force of impact.

The sheriff stands over him, completely frozen in a combination of fear and sympathy.

"Sheriff . . . Sheriff . . . Sheriff!" A deputy said for the third time. The sheriff snaps out of his deep train of thought and turns his attention toward the deputy.

"Sheriff, come over this way," as he walks up to the driver's side of the jumbled mess of twisted metal, blood and broken glass. Sheriff Thompson walks over to the other side of the truck following the deputy with a sense of caution. The deputy points toward the truck's backseat from the driver's seat window.

That's Katie Parker in there . . . " He points to a jumbled pile of blood and guts, topped in a sadistic fashion with sugary frosting from the pies. Her face is torn open and the only thing that is recognizable as human are bits of the yellow dress she was wearing, and a few unbroken rib bones sticking through the mangled mess.

"Are you sure?" the sheriff asks, hoping for another answer, but the first deputy responds exactly how the sheriff expects him to.

"Yes, Sheriff, we are. And, over there on the ground is Bob." Glancing over, he sees a team poking and inspecting the bloody mess.

"Where's Coach Miller, Deputy?"

"I'm sure he's the first thing you saw as you drove up here. That blood trail over there?" he said, motioning off into the distance.

"He's over there, Sheriff - Jesus Christ - or what's left of him . . . "

Concerned about the sheriff's heavy breathing, he

looks at him with concern. "Jesus, Sheriff, are you okay?"

Realizing just how much he is struggling at the scene, he attempts to wipe his face clean of all emotion and quickly shifts the topic. Looking away and pretending to scratch his head, the sheriff wipes a tear away from his cheek. "Is the medical examiner here?" he shouts out to anybody that might be listening and just like that, an answer is heard.

"Yes, Sheriff, I'm over here," Dr. Hyde replies as he motions to the sheriff to come see the remains of Coach Miller.

"You need to come over here, sheriff!" he encourages frantically. "You need to take a look at this!"

Walking over to Dr. Hyde he takes long, energized steps, anxious for his tour of the crime scene to be complete. He comes across the nude torso of Bob Miller without arms or legs face down in the ditch.

"Holy shit, what happened, Doc?"

The doctor looks at him with a hard to read expression, pauses, and then takes a deep breath. "Well . . . it looks like we have some bad, nasty type of animals out here. I think there's more than one because they ripped the hell out of these guys. I also find it odd that they ate all of Katie's pasta and some of the pies that didn't get ruined."

The sheriff's heart stops in its tracks, "What?"

The doctor looks at him and with firm confirmation, "That's right. I said they ate all the pasta, and from the look of the inside of the truck, she had a bunch of food with her. They were probably making a delivery to her sister Judy's place at the Hidden Valley Bed & Breakfast."

The sheriff's thoughts directed themselves toward Judy, Katie's sister. "Has anybody gone and talked to Judy yet?"

"Eh . . . No, Sheriff, we were waiting to talk with you before we did that."

He nods his head somberly. "That's good, I will go inform her in person."

The thought of her expression and response cross his mind as he imagines relaying the death of her sister to Judy. "She is going to be devastated." The sheriff glances down at his feet, which have bits of grass sticking to the bottoms attached by dried blood of one of the three victims. Sighing heavily, Sheriff Thompson walks to his car to head up to the Hidden Valley Bed & Breakfast. He stops momentarily and turns back around, pointing a finger at Deputy Bodie.

"Bodie!" he instructs firmly as the deputy perks his head up. "You stay here and help get this place cleaned up. See if you can find out who the hell would be the next of kin for Bob Miller. I will get back to you after I go up and talk to Judy."

"Yes, sir, Sheriff, this is a hell of a mess," Bodie replies as Sheriff Thompson drives off to the Hidden Valley Bed & Breakfast.

CHAPTER 14

The rest of the road up to the B & B was as peaceful as before, but thoughts of the mangled corpses still ruminated through his mind. After a fifteen minute drive Sheriff Thompson walks up the steps to the front door. As he approaches the bed and breakfast, Judy is already at the doorway standing behind the old screen door, patching a hole. Seeing the sheriff, Judy opens the door with a welcoming smile and yells for Tristan to come outside.

"Hello there, Sheriff! What are you doing up here? Been some time since I've seen you, you're looking pretty fit, Tom!"

Her face changes from a smile to a look of extreme disappointment as she realizes the frown upon his face. He is breathing heavily, his mouth is clenched and his eyes are wide and moist.

"Sheriff, what's wrong?" she asks in a panicky manner.

Exhaling heavily, the sheriff shuffles his feet and looks up at her with very sad eyes. "Judy, I really wish I was just up here to visit . . . but I'm afraid that I do indeed have some very bad news for you to hear." His voice cracks at the end of his sentence. Doing his best to remain composed the sheriff looks down, avoiding direct eye contact with her, in fear that he will breakdown and cry.

"What's wrong, Sheriff? Oh my, God! It's Katie. What happened, Sheriff?" She senses what the sheriff has come to tell her.

"Sheriff . . . tell me it's not Katie!" she exclaims with pure sadness and without a glimmer of hope that it would be anyone else but her.

With a frown, and being barely able to speak as he is choking back tears, he looks at her, and confirms the fact. "I'm so . . . sorry, Judy," he apologizes as he looks back down at the ground. "I'm afraid it is both Katie and Bob."

She openly starts to weep. Her eyes look like they have given up all hope of ever seeing anything pleasurable again.

"They were both killed by wild animals last night on their way up here, Judy."

In denial, she shoots back at the sheriff in an outrage, and Tristan runs back inside the bed and breakfast, hiding from the confrontation.

"That can't be. I just talked to her yesterday evening!" She is slightly hyperventilating. "She said she was going to come up today - she wasn't supposed to come up last night. It can't be her, Sheriff. It can't be her!" Judy starts to cry hysterically and runs down the steps to the sheriff. Falling into the sheriff's arms, she wails over and over again that it couldn't be her sister.

Curt rushes out of the door of the B & B in confusion and concern. He observes the sheriff holding Judy tightly in his arms out of necessity. The sheriff has regained his composure and has his emotions under control.

"Judy, what's wrong?" Curt asks, hearing her desperate pleas to God for her sister to still be alive. Sheriff Thompson jumps in response to Curt's presence.

"Where the hell did you come from? I just left you at a meeting, Curt!"

"I rent a room here, Sheriff, I didn't exactly move into the town," he reports readily, and then gets to his real concern.

"What's wrong with, Judy?"

With a sniff, she turns around and addresses him, "My sister . . . my sister, Katie, she's dead," she whimpered before she began crying again.

"What? Katie? Did something happen at the bakery?" Curt is confused.

Reaffirming his authority, the sheriff gently stops hugging Judy and places one arm around her shoulders and the other on her arm next to him to keep her propped up.

"Nothing happened at the bakery, but Katie and her husband, Bob, were both killed last night by what looks to be wild animals."

Curt is caught off guard and stumbles backward not believing what he has just heard. "Oh my, God, she was so nice to me," he says in disbelief.

"Yes, they were both really great people. I'm glad that you're here, Curt, because Judy certainly needs someone to be with her right now."

Curt steps off the porch and reaches out and takes Judy into his arms, consoling her. He looks up and addresses the sheriff, "It's okay, Sheriff, I will be here for her. I'm so, so sorry. Let me know if you find those animals, okay?"

Sheriff Thompson gets in his car and leaves without a goodbye and doesn't look at Curt or Judy.

"We'll try," he mutters to himself as he shuts the car door and starts the engine. Judy and Curt watch him drive away. Tristan watches from the attic of the bed and breakfast, peeking from behind ruffled blinds.

Not ready to go back to the crime scene yet, the sheriff starts thinking of every excuse possible not to go back to the bloody massacre. Making a long sigh, the troubled man glances at his gas gauge and realizes it is on a quarter of a tank. Morris's Gas Station is the only stop between his destination and the Hidden Valley Bed & Breakfast.

He picks up his radio and calls out to the station, "Hidden Valley Sheriff's Station - come in."

"Hello, Sheriff, this is Sandy," the voice on the radio crackles back.

"Sandy, let Cooper know that I have to stop and get some gas at Morris's place. Tell him I want a report when I get back on everything that he's found at the scene so far. Also, ask him if he found Bob Miller's next of kin." Through a stream of static, his words are barely distinguishable back at the station.

"Okay, Sheriff, sure thing. Oh, and Sheriff, be careful at Morris's place. For God's sake, don't use the bathroom; we may never find you again, Sheriff."

"Sandy, I'll just piss in the woods. I'd never use that shithole."

"I hear that, Sheriff. See you soon."

A few miles down the road, he turns into what appears to be a junkyard. Barely distinguishable behind the piles of trash is a single, very old and rusted gas pump. Resisting the urge to drive past, the sheriff pulls up to the pump and parks his car. The brief respite this stop affords him is preferable to seeing any more of his friends butchered.

Overgrown weeds are everywhere and a couple of rusty screen doors rest against the front of the building. It looks to be abandoned, but the sheriff knows that the lowlife, Morris, is floating around somewhere.

The sheriff puts the car in reverse and backs up. He turns the wheel to pull horizontally to the front of the building next to the gas pump. Through the rear window, he sees the silhouette of a man. It is the owner, a disheveled hillbilly, standing there and his sudden appearance makes Sheriff Thompson jump with an audible word.

"Jesus!"

Morris tilts his head and walks forward peering into the back window in a very creepy manner. His mouth is open, his skin is pale and he looks undernourished. There is a sore on his cheek similar to what you may see on drug user. Morris has let himself go; he looked much healthier some years ago when the sheriff last saw the man. He usually keeps to himself up here, mostly because nobody gets along with him.

"HOLY SHIT!" the sheriff whispers heavily under his breath, his heart pumping at an incredibly fast rate. Morris lifts his hand up and motions for the sheriff to roll down his window. With slow motion, almost as though he is in a trance, the sheriff complies.

"Hi, Morris, sorry . . . "

The man initially replies by coughing up phlegm and spitting it down toward the ground, instead it lands on his pants leg. With a decayed, near toothless mouth, he smiles at the sheriff, "Hey, there, Sheriff. Can I help you with somethin'?"

Looking at him in disgust, yet wanting to be polite, he responds, "Yeah, Morris. I need some gas. You scared the fucking shit out of me."

"A y'up. A lot of people say that about me," he snickers as he coughs sickly, then hawks up another loogie.

Sheriff Thompson's tongue is frozen for a second. "Uh, I was also hoping maybe you could tell me if you've seen some weird, wild animals around here lately? Maybe a wild herd of dogs or something of that nature."

Morris looks at him with hollow, empty, but brilliantly blue eyes and skin with the veins bulging out. He speaks slowly to the sheriff in a hushed voice. "Well now, Sheriff, there's always some kind of weird, wild animals running around here. Wild dogs, and I see a lot of coyotes, Sheriff," he smiles slightly. "Why you wanna know about 'em for anyways?

"Well, Morris, I'm trying to find out what the hell's going on up here. Some wild animal or animals killed Katie and Bob Parker and it looks like it also killed Coach Miller."

"Oh, well now . . . that's a damn shame for sure, Sheriff. That Ms. Katie, she made a damn good pie. I . . . I liked her hair . . . too," he grunted with a very creepy smile, lost in the thought of Ms. Katie.

Sheriff Thompson looked at him in disgust, and shook his head in dismay. Feeling the need to get away from the strange man, if Morris could be described as a man, he opened the car door and got out of the car.

"Yes, she did, Morris. You got any soda pop in that store?"

Morris laughed slightly in a drawled out manner while glaring at him with those hollow eyes. "Yes I do, Sheriff. . ." he paused for a few moments and then continued, ". . . And it's cold, too." Morris lets out a perverted laugh. "It's good . . . really good."

Not sure how to reply, the sheriff simply walks toward the store with a disturbed look on his face. He opens the rusted screen door and walks inside looking around at the darkly lit store. The only light comes from the sunlight shining through the dirty windows; the light bulb must have burned out ages ago. The place is dusty and filthy dirty. Antlers and stuffed animals adorn the walls and shelves, the highlight of which is a stuffed ferret hanging down from the ceiling by a fishing hook tied to a ceiling beam.

"How quaint," he says to himself as he walks past the front counter looking at the various items. There is a rack full of porno magazines. Most are crumpled and soiled. He continues on into the store. There is a metal cooler that is humming. He slides it open and inside there are cups of worms squirming around, very lively. "They must be the only fresh things in this place," he says under his breath. He grabs one of only two cans of pop and slams the cooler shut.

"Fucking gross," he says out loud to nobody.

Seeing a door next to him that is slightly ajar, he walks to it quickly and pushes it open further, no longer wanting to be inside. The sheriff stands in the doorway looking in. The bathroom is trashed. The walls are dirty and there is broken glass on the floor. He walks over to the toilet and lifts the lid expecting the worst; however, the basin is clean, too clean. It's very surprising. The toilet is immaculate. He looks surprised. He pulls his pants open and relieves himself while looking around the bathroom. He hears a noise to his right and upon further investigation finds a small hole in the wall. He looks over to the source of the noise, and at first sees nothing, but continues to hear scratching sounds that cause him to look further.

Finally, he sees an inch-wide hole in the wall amongst the papers stapled to it. He squints, trying to look at it closely. He zips his pants up, walks a few steps toward the hole and leans forward, trying to look through it from a distance of a few feet.

"Is this son of a bitch watching me?" he mutters. He is startled and walks closer to the hole kicking papers, porno mags and a beer bottle out of the way. As he is looking closely at the hole, suddenly a hairy leg sticks out of it . . . followed by another and a large, furry tarantula crawls out of the hole stretching out one of its legs in an attempt to touch his face. Grabbing the knob, he swings the door open and finishes buttoning up his pants. Stepping out into the disarray of the store, the sheriff bumps right into Morris, who laughs at the sheriff's fear.

Sheriff, you all right?" he asks in a slow monotone voice with a perverted smile on his face.

"Morris, you need to clean this fucking place up. You have a tarantula in that bathroom. If it bites someone, it could kill them."

"Oh now, come on, Sheriff." His grin is very unsettling. "It's just a friendly little spider -and you're not afraid of friendly little spiders, are ya, Sheriff?" Morris just smiles as the sheriff shakes his head and turns to walk away toward his car.

"Your bill, Sheriff."

"Yeah, let me just get ya my credit card, Morris."

The frail, lanky man shakes his head in disapproval. "I don't take no cards, Sheriff. Cash only."

"Well shit, just a minute, let me go see what I have. How much do I owe you Morris?"

"That is $75.80 with the pop."

"Shit, $75.80, really?" the sheriff reluctantly searches through his wallet and pulls out a $100 bill as a large smile crosses Morris's face. "This is all I got; I'm sure you won't have an issue with it."

"Oh, wow . . . well, I'm sure it's not counterfeit coming from you, Sheriff." Morris grins ear to ear and lets out a sickly giggle, interrupted by the sounds of phlegm in his throat.

"No, I mean, do you have change?" the sheriff asked.

Morris cocked his head at him in confusion. "Nope, you're my first customer in a long while, Sheriff. I'm surprised the pump still works!" he exclaimed, showing off his unsightly tongue, which appeared brown with fungal growth making the sheriff turn his face away in disgust.

"Oh shit, just keep the change and use it to clean this fucking place up and get some God damn mouthwash, Morris!"

The sheriff hurries outside and is anxious to get away from the stale area inside the store, not that the smell of the place outside was any better. The sheriff gets back into his car and starts it up as Morris stands there smiling and shaking his head.

Sheriff Thompson nods a relieved goodbye and, like a jackrabbit being chased by a dog, exits out of the gas station, highlighting how anxious he is to leave the place far behind.

CHAPTER 15

Inside the small diner, a few people sit at assorted tables. An elderly man, Dave, sits at the counter sipping a cup of coffee that appears as white as a milkshake, while reading a newspaper. A very attractive waitress, whose apron hugs her curves, stands wiping off the countertop.

Mr. Fuller, who is the owner of the diner, stands at the register checking tickets of the day's sales. The cook, Denny, sets a plate up in the window to the kitchen and hits the bell.

"DING! DING!" the little bell rings and echoes throughout the diner.

"Order up, Jane."

The waitress puts down her towel, walks over to the window, lifts her apron up and uses it to grab the hot plate. "Thanks, Denny!" she says with an adorably sexy voice, and a batting of her eyelashes - Denny blushes in return. She turns and walks over to the man at the counter, and his eyes light up in surprise at how good the food looks.

"Here you go, Dave. Plate's hot, so you'll want to be careful, okay?"

Dave looks up and smiles, trembling as he does from age, he picks up his fork and stabs a French fry. "Thanks, sweetie," he says as he puts it in his mouth.

"Not a problem, Dave. Would you like me to top off your coffee?"

Dave reaches up, makes a fist and covers his mouth as he quickly chews the rest of the food in his mouth. "Sure thing. That would be fantastic."

In a split second she leaves and returns with a commercial grade coffee pot to fill up Dave's cup for about the fifth time.

"So, is there anything in the paper today I should know about?" Jane asks with a slight giggle.

"Nah, it's the same old stuff. The gas price is still going up, the economy is in the shitter and the end of the world is coming . . . yada, yada, yada," he says shaking his head, now in a grumpy mood.

Jane simply smiles and returns the pot back to the coffee maker while looking at the elderly man. "Well, you be sure to give me a heads up if they pick the date that the world will end. I'll probably take the day off, okay?" Jane smiles at him.

He forces a smirk and remains silent, in unison with the rest of the diner's guests.

The door opens and a group of about ten kids come streaming in. Among them is Donovan Gray. Jane's cheeks grow bright red, as even the presence of the boy makes her blush and feel wonderful. Completely oblivious to the rest of the diner, she stares at him, and finally, his eyes meet hers. She can't help but smile, showing off her perfect teeth. She waves at Donovan who is staring at her with admiration as he waves back to her.

Her face, still beet red and forcing back a giggle, she runs up to him and gives him a hug, followed by a kiss on the cheek.

"Hey, honey! What are you guys all doing here?" she asks the group, maintaining eye contact with Donovan and expecting an answer from nobody else.

With that, he replies to her, ignoring her affection. "We're all here to talk about the bonfire tonight. The mayor told us we can have it so we are going to par - tay!" he announces proudly, even puffing his chest out a bit as he tells her, saying it loudly enough so the entire diner can hear without any effort to listen.

Billy, who is Donovan's friend, chimes in from the back of the crowd with a somewhat high-pitched voice. "Yeah, the mayor said we can have the bonfire and Donovan told him that we'd be done by midnight, so it made everybody happy."

Another voice resonates through the diner, as the boys are all very excited about the night's events. "Yeah, but I don't know how much partying we are going to do with two deputies hanging around," mulled Elliot.

In a somewhat concerned voice, another boy starts to speak, but this is quickly muted by Donovan's bad-boy style, which it seems many people turn a blind eye toward. Donovan's face goes from pride to sheer annoyance as he looks back at Billy, the boy who had just spoken out. With a degrading tone, he speaks to both Billy and Elliot.

"Yeah, well, I got that all taken care of - shut the fuck up!"

Unfazed by Donovan's yelling, Billy dons a very confused look and lashes back at him. "What do you mean you got it all taken care of man? You gonna sock 'em?"

"No you douche! Listen up!" Donovan says in a hushed voice. "After midnight the guys and I and a few girls are going to sneak back up to the bonfire and keep on partying!"

He looks around for a moment. Jane had walked off, tending to another customer in the old rustic diner, as he was ignoring her. Seeing the coast was clear, he proceeded on. "We will drink a little beer, listen to some music, and fuck ourselves a few girls!"

A serious look comes over Elliot's face, along with mixed reactions from the other kids. Elliot, angered at Donovan's reckless behavior, grows red in the face and confronts him. "What the hell are you talking about, Donovan?" he screams out, making all heads in the diner turn around towards them.

The boys glare back, and a few seconds of silence are exchanged in the diner before normal conversation and the sound of food being made starts up once more.

"You know what the coach taught us." Elliot continued, in a more controlled voice. "It's hard enough for me to control that shit without having sex, Donovan!"

"Listen, Elliot," Donovan says in a convincing tone, "And this goes for all of you guys."

Their heads perk up with interest and listen intently to what their 'leader' has to say. "I personally want to have sex with a girl again. I mean, shit!"

He looks over at his girlfriend, Jane, who is bent over the bar pouring hot coffee into Dave's cup. "See Jane over there?"

The boys nod unanimously.

"She thinks I'm this Mr. Goody Two Shoes proper little boy. Well, I'm tired of that shit and tonight I plan on showing Jane how proper a little boy I am! I need to!"

Many of the boys smile and speak in hushed whispers amongst themselves, but Elliot holds his stance. "What are you talking about, man?"

He looks frustrated, as though he is about to hit Donovan. "You know what happens. Just the smell of sex and I can't control myself and I know Donnie and Tommy can't either! You're always talking about sex, more so than everybody else!"

Donovan's eyebrows quickly turn to an angry frown. "Listen, I want to have sex with a girl again. I haven't been able to since the coach turned us. I think I can control myself! Just let me do it!"

Billy shot back with anger, "Donovan!" His eyes grew wild, "Are you fucking crazy? It's been six months since I went there behind the bed and breakfast and all I wanted to do was watch them. As soon as the smell hit me, I couldn't control myself. Do I need to say more?"

Elliot, angered with Donovan's ruthless decision, raises his voice even louder. "Yeah, Donovan," his voice echoes throughout the diner, "At least you had Jeremy. I'm getting ready to turn bi just like the coach wanted us to."

Donovan looks down at the ground with a look of sadness, despite how loudly it was said. His mind was preoccupied with thoughts of what his relationship with Jeremy used to be like. He smirks, but this is unseen, as he quickly covers it up. With mustered courage, after making sure people weren't listening, he spoke out to the boys, "Hey, we all knew what we were getting into," he said as he gazed at the small crowd.

"The coach told all of us this. We wanted this power, and we want this championship!"

Some of the boys nod their heads in agreement; others simply meet his gaze with a stare.

Donovan continues, "You can't tell me that we all didn't know what was going to happen. Coach Miller said because of how young we are if we were turned we wouldn't be able to control ourselves if we had sex. You've all heard the spiel. It takes years and years . . ."

Others in the group start to mutter the sentence along with Donovan, ". . . to be able to control not turning into that monster when you are having sex. It's bad enough on the full moon when we have to feed. You chase after

119

those wild animals, rip them apart and eat them. We all made the choice."

"Yeah," said Billy in agreement in a softly spoken voice, looking up at him with his eyes while his head pointed toward the ground. "The coach didn't twist any of our arms. That's why he told us if we couldn't handle not having sex, hook up with each other; if we turned into the wolf, we can defend ourselves. If my memory is right, none of us have ever gotten hurt, although something happened when he started taking on new football players."

There was a pause and Donnie's face paled, "Yeah, what about the new kid?" Everybody's head turned to him, in anticipation. "I know that he was doing more with Danny than coaching football. After he turned us three years ago, things happened and he started taking on new football players. I don't know how many more of us there are - he was fucking going crazy and now he is gone. Whatever you do tonight, Donovan and the rest of you guys, you better be fucking careful."

CHAPTER 16

The sun shone brilliantly through the Hidden Valley Bed & Breakfast's windows casting rays of light in the shapes of the windows down onto the floor bathing it in an orange light, which was interrupted by the occasional scattered shadow of a falling leaf from the trees above. The interior of the bed and breakfast is comprised of a very nice wooden theme. The orange rays only compliment the color of the wood, and the reflection of the sun blooms into the rest of the room, creating a heavenly glow. Curt admires this from inside the big glass doors and accompanying windows that cover almost an entire wall of the room. Looking outside through the windows, there is a small pond.

Tristan and Judy are sitting on the corner edge of Judy's bed in her room of the beautiful old rustic mansion that was built at the turn-of-the-century about 1901 or 1902. Many of the original aspects of the old mansion remain even though it has been beautifully updated and is very well maintained.

After admiring the view, Curt turns and walks down the hallway on the way to his room. He sees Tristan and Judy talking in her room and he does not want to disturb them, so he turns around and heads into the kitchen to grab a bottle of water. After he finishes the water, he tosses the bottle into the recycle bin and heads back down the hallway. Judy is in the hallway leaning against the wall adjacent to his room. Her arms are crossed and he doesn't need to be closer to her to see she is distraught. She is dressed in a fuzzy, white robe that looks exceptionally soft to the touch and looks as pleasing to the eye as Judy does.

Even though her hair is a total mess and she has no without makeup on, her skin glows in a natural fashion that could not be improved with makeup. Her robe is short, falling about five inches above her knees. The front is slightly apart, exposing a fair portion of her large breasts. For an older woman, she looks fantastic.

He debates simply walking into his room and leaving her to her solitude, fearing her attractive nature may arouse him, which would not be wise after she has just learned of the deaths of her sister and brother-in-law. Instead, he steps over to her and wraps his arms around her in a warm, embracing hug. For a moment she is shocked and her body stiffens, then her eyes close and he feels her body relax. For a few seconds they simply enjoy each other's touch and company. He breaks the hug and steps back and Judy sees the sympathy in his eyes.

Her hands grab his arms and she pulls him closer to her, pressing his body tightly against hers. She hugs him once again, sobbing slightly, and then heavily. The tears falling from her eyes wet his shoulder and as she weeps, he hugs her tighter and whispers into her ear, "I'm so sorry, Judy."

Between sobs and inhales, she cries out to him, "I just don't know what I'm going to do. She was always there for me. I could always count on her if I needed her."

Curt speaks to her compassionately and through his voice she feels that he absolutely understands her raw pain. The one person she had left in her family, the sister she knew from birth, was just ripped away from her.

Even though she has her son, and she is eternally grateful for him, she feels so alone. She is still mourning the recent death of her mother and now her sister's gone too.

"I didn't know her for more than one day, but when I met her, she seemed like an awesome person. She must have been, to have such a great sister." he said sincerely.

Like a spark ignited, Judy looks up and smiles at Curt, who takes her face in his hands and with his thumbs wipes tears away from her eyes as they run down her cheeks. "I'll try my hardest to be here for you, Judy."

Her feeble smile becomes a grin. She starts to sob a little more, but takes a deep breath as Curt slides his finger across her soft cheek, rubbing away the tears and with it, some of the pain from her loss.

"Oh, Curt," she chokes out her words. "From the first moment I saw you . . ." She pauses for a moment as if in a deep internal debate as to whether or not she should continue on and finish her thoughts, or maybe even share her desires. Her face subtly changes, though not enough for Curt to recognize. She speaks out, looking up at him just a bit as her body trembles, "I . . . knew . . . there was something special about you."

Judy changed the words she wanted to say, but her body continues to say what her voice had hidden from him. Her hips press against his subconsciously and she expresses the natural emotion of sexual desire by tightening her grip, but in her state of distress she believes it is just a tight hug. As he looks at her Judy's eyes grow passionate and full of fear, but she is equally overcome with a sense of seduction. It is truly amazing how much truth one's eyes can share. Without any hesitation, she kisses him softly on the cheek then presses her lips against the gruff on his chin and pauses for a few moments with her eyes closed.

"There is something," she pauses once more, for a slightly shorter time than before and with troubled eyes reflecting the stress of her situation, she looks at him. The bags below her beautiful eyes sag ever so slightly, creating quite a contrast. Her age is not that of a young adult her face appears youthful, as does the rest of her body, which peaks out of the slit of her soft, white robe. The robe feels as though it is made of rabbit fur, creating a soft thrill of pleasantries for both of them to enjoy. Underneath her robe, her body is bare. Curt cannot help but look down at her exposed cleavage, her breasts being pushed upward from the pressure of their bodies intertwined in the hug. Her beautiful but sad eyes shine in the reflected sunlight as she removes her hands from his body and puts her forearms against his chest, holding Curt's shoulders tenderly while she examines his face in delight.

He has such strong features, a jaw line that is sharp and defined, coated with stubble that compliments the rest of his face. Pleasantly contrasting with his tanned skin and dark complexion are a set of perfect hazel eyes. Not to mention is long, thick eyelashes any female would be jealous to have - one of the many reasons she is so charmed by him, for sure.

"I don't know Curt . . ." she exhales, momentarily breaking eye contact. She takes a deep breath and looks directly into his eyes. Still unsettled by the tumultuous feelings running through her, she takes the time to judge the moment, if only for a second, before saying, "There is something I really want to experience with you . . ."

She doesn't finish her sentence before aggressively pushing her head forward and kissing him on his lips. Curt realizes on some level that he should end this gently as Judy is grieving and not thinking clearly, but before he can even begin to think about stopping this action he is overwhelmed by the amount of pleasurable shock her soft lips have cast over him. It's most certain he wouldn't have been able to resist even if she had moved in at the slowest pace possible. This kiss was much more than a kiss for both of them. It was an instinctual release of the sexual tension they have both felt vibrating between they since they met. Also feeding into this sexual frenzy, are the situations they each find themselves, which make them more vulnerable to reaching out to gain comfort from another person. Curt has literally walked into this strange town of Hidden Valley with these mysterious deaths and, of course, Judy's bereavement on the death of her relatives.

"It has been so long," whispers Judy in his ear and she kisses him once more.

The words echo in Curt's mind, nearly causing him to panic, though he doesn't consider retracting his lips from hers, and for a second or two they embrace passionately. Judy's bottom lip quivers a bit as she pulls away from him. Curt, however, leans in ever so slightly as she pulls back, wanting to embrace her even more.

"This is crazy . . . knowing you for only a few days . . ." she stops and looks down at Curt's chest. She feels ashamed and unsure about what just happened, however, she thoroughly enjoyed every bit of it. Her words are softly spoken, yet powerful to hear, " . . . I feel like I've known you all of my life."

Curt freezes, feeling as though she had somehow read his every thought, for at that exact moment in time, those very words were churning through his head, "Me too," Curt softly murmurs back to her as his closed eyelids seal off his vision and he embraces her further. His arms hold her tightly, protecting her fragile shell from unwanted feelings of loss and sadness, if only for this brief moment. Even though it is highly inappropriate for the current situation, the way he was holding her close, even though she was in a state of complete dismay, started to arouse him sexually.

No! Not now, the voice inside his head chanted over and over again, but with each passing moment his body starts to throb and pulsate with even more impact than the last. He can tell by her body language that she may be receptive to it, but at the same time Curt does not wish to take advantage of her desperation and loneliness. Suddenly, it's too late, his member is already pressing tightly against his jeans and into her thigh. Out of embarrassment, he falls into a silent, expression-free panic. The only indication of something wrong is his chest thumping wildly as his heart beats furiously in out-of-control nervousness. His face stays like stone.

Judy's eyes widen as she feels him pressing solidly against her thigh and as she looks down, her face does not mask her surprise. Now the emotions wind through his body up to his face, he looks away and down to the ground in embarrassment. A tiny smile crosses his face at the same time. Judy's chilled fingers touch his jaw softly guiding his mouth toward her gorgeous lips where a long, slow, passionate kiss is exchanged between the two of them. Her fingers run along his cheek and jaw, moving to the back of his head, which she presses lightly upon, locking him into the kiss.

Slowly she moves her lips away from his and places her hand back on his shoulder as a puzzling look comes across her face. Her lips are open as if she is ready to speak, but all she manages is a stutter. She looks away, shaking her head in disappointment, or perhaps even guilt, for allowing herself to think whatever was going to come out of her mouth. Against her better judgment, she looks at him with determination to speak her mind.

"I know it may seem wrong . . ." she pauses for a moment and nervously swallows. "It doesn't seem wrong . . . I know it is, Curt. I just met you . . . and . . . well . . . Curt . . ." His eyes stare back at hers as she pauses yet again, his eyes displaying nothing but curiosity and concern.

Judy continues, "Okay, in light of everything going on . . . this whole fucked up situation . . . right now . . . I just really need to feel you inside of me."

Before he even has time to react to what she is saying, her mouth meets his with passion. She chaotically kisses his mouth, not even taking time to make sure her lips meet his. Her lips are all over his face, and he pulsates perhaps even more than he ever has, his jeans becoming very tight amongst the rest of his body as his member pounds against his leg.

"Wai . . ." he starts to speak, but she meets his verbal outburst with even more desire.

"Are you sure you want to do this right now?" he questions when she takes a breath.

Curt's mind is racing at the speed of light. His body conversely detaches from his contemplation and he starts to return her romantic gestures until she gives him a look of indecision. This only appears for a moment, however, as she pecks him on the cheek and reluctantly smiles at him without exposing the inside of her mouth, turning it into a cute smirk.

"God, I need you so bad right now, I've never been so sure of anything in my life," she said. Her eyes turn from a passionately seductive appearance to calm, loving look. Curt's feelings of guilt ease, yet he is still holding back, for reasons perhaps unknown even to him.

"Okay," he exhales, knowing that both of their urges were going to break soon. Timidly, he looks deeply into her eyes; he wants to say so much to her.

"There are so many things that I wish I could tell you, Judy. I feel it's not the appropriate time to do so, but . . " he lets out a very long sigh and with it, he expresses worrisome feelings. Cocking her head in slight confusion, she leans forward, closer to him, as if ready to console him.

"Just know that it's been a while, you need to be patient with me, okay?" he said for reassurance.

Before he even finishes his sentence, she lets out a pent up wave of relief, followed by a small giggle. A smile appears, once again, upon his face, but it doesn't mask the amount of tension he is feeling, as it is painfully obvious at a simple glance that he is nervous.

Judy replies, "Well," trying to hold back a smirk, "I guess we're both in the same boat then, Curt."

Her exceptional eyes stare at him, not breaking contact, as they shine. "Curt," Judy whispers with an incredible amount of passion as she leans her body into him, her breasts once again pressing upward, exposing themselves as her robe unravels with no hands available to tighten it. She starts massaging Curt's back. Her bare breasts are pressing against his shirt, he can no longer resist her. Quickly, and with little restraint, she reaches over and starts to kiss him with unrelenting energy. His hands on her shoulders, he pulls at the soft robe and slides it over her shoulders until it hangs at her elbows. Her upper body is completely exposed, revealing a sexy toned, flat stomach and curvy hips.

He releases a deep exhale as her hands move down along his fit stomach. Her fingers slide between his front side and his belt, tugging lightly. Every caress from his fingers makes her shudder in enjoyment and he shudders from her caresses as well. She kisses his cheek, his neck, eventually trailing her tongue along his smooth body and down across his abs, her face lighting up in enjoyment.

Curt's breathing gets heavier and heavier stifling his oxygen intake in an irregular fashion. Her teeth pull at his belt, loosening it from the fitting, and pulling it loose while her fingers, still on his skin, scratch him lightly with her perfect nails.

His pants bulge open; she doesn't even need to unzip him. She looks up at him teasingly, but Curt pays no attention; he is looking up, breathing heavily in a very seductive but slightly nervous manner. His expression is puzzling to her, as it looks like that of extreme concentration, like he is not enjoying her touch. His breathing tells her otherwise, though. Looking back down at him, she sees more than exposed skin, and she realizes he is not wearing anything underneath his jeans. Smiling, she stands back up, cupping him with her hand and moving her fingers along his bulge through the lower part of his jeans.

She slowly leans into his ear, "It's okay, I'm not wearing anything either . . ." she whispers, and nips the side of his ear, lightly tugging on his earlobe and breathing softly into it as her grip tightens, vibrating her hand slightly as it pulsates. Although Judy is smiling brightly at this moment, her eyes tell a slightly different story. She is still deeply mourning the loss of her sister and though the moment now is pleasant, it isn't seamless. As her eyes well up and moisture puddles at the bottom of her eyelashes, she brushes her tears away covertly along his hairline, taking a deep breath and offering him an impeccable smile.

He takes Judy's hand and turns away from her, leading her into his bedroom and giving her a light tap toward the bed as he closes and locks the door. He pulls his pants down a little bit more, revealing himself to her and gives her a light push on the shoulders. Her body falls backwards onto the soft bed, her breasts slide and bounce across her chest in a very stimulating manner. Anxiously, he stands over her. Her robe lies on the bed top beneath her as her perfect, full body shines in the light of the setting sun.

Looking deeply into Judy's eyes, he smiles at her and presses himself in between her soft lips. The warmth is the most intense feeling; her cavity is slippery and embracing. Almost immediately he gently pushes himself in a bit further; he feels orgasmic! He feels as though just from that bit of stimulation, he could finish in a matter of seconds. It clearly has been a long while for him and he is more than ready to let his load loose. Maybe it's embarrassment from this issue, but Curt's face becomes overwhelmed with fear and a puzzled look. Quickly, he slides his erect penis out of her and turns away before she can question him, and he quickly rushes off into the bathroom.

"Oh shit, I'm sorry, Judy, but I need to take a piss. I will be right back!" he yells on his way to the bathroom.

Judy shakes her head with a questioning smile as the door to the bathroom slams shut with Curt inside, the force of which shakes the paintings on the walls and leaving Judy in a very confused and slightly turned off state. From just inside the bathroom door, comes very heavy, raspy, deep breathing, as though Curt is in excruciating pain. Curt stands naked over the sink, his body sweating profusely, and every one of his muscles is tensed up as tightly as they can be, appearing as if he had just finished a very intense work out. A look of extreme desperation is upon his face, which soon rolls into anger as he stares into his own reflection in the delicate mirror, forearms propping up his body, but slipping from all of the sweat.

"I can control this, do you understand me!" he harshly barks in a very deep growl toward his reflection in the mirror. Curt Bloom's skin appears to become darker and his irises literally shift color to an intense brown.

"You will not . . ." Curt starts to grit his teeth and strain every single muscle in his body as he makes a strenuous effort to control himself.

"You will not come out right now! I am in control, you are not."

The white in his eyes, now bloodshot, with spots of yellow poking through blurs his vision as he tries to maintain eye contact with his own reflection. In an exhausted voice, he grunts out the words, "I will control you, you understand me you son-of-a bitch!"

His skin starts to roughen up and he can feel his skull shifting around, morphing a bit, as well as the rest of his body, and then, in an instant, all appears normal. His body is back to its natural state, though his eyes are a bit irritated, the brilliant hazel is now dull and almost lifeless in comparison, yet still captivating to the unassuming eye.

"Okay then . . .I see that we have an understanding."

Standing up straight, slipping momentarily on his own sweat lying between his feet on the floor, he bends over sorely to flush the toilet, peels off his sweat soaked jeans and grabs a soft red towel from the rack next to the shower to dry off. His body is as wet as though it has just emerged from the shower only two feet away from him. There is a puddle of sweat upon the floor and he uses the towel with his feet as a mop, splashing water upon his face. A shiver overcomes his body, shaking him from his head to his toes, and when it reaches its destination, a sense of clarity comes over him once again, and a newfound strength erupts. Energy is now pulsating through his body like a rushing freight train late for its destination.

He takes a deep breath as a relaxed smile slowly fans

across his face. Curt opens the door to the bedroom
where Judy lies naked with the robe placed over her for
warmth. In the few minutes Curt was in the bathroom,
the sun's rays are no longer shining brilliantly through the
windows as before. Small specks of light reflect off of
the leaves outdoors. The leaf shadows dance along on the
ground, up the side of the bed and breakfast, and arrive
lightly through the windows onto Judy's, once again,
naked body. As the winds that shake the branches whip
through the forest they hit the house, creating a rather
eerie howl. None of this plays any importance to Curt
and Judy, as they are both preoccupied with thoughts of
each other.

Curt throws his body onto the floor and crawls like an
animal back up onto the bed, making playful roaring
sounds, which soon mingle with her girlish giggles. He
begins kissing her soft lower legs, moving up to her inner
thighs still growling at her and gnawing lightly with his
teeth into her thighs and hips. In a fury, he forcefully
pushes her shoulders down onto the bed and her body
bounces back up from the momentum of his ambitious
energy.

Judy soon becomes overwhelmed by his playful
charm and giggles in uncertainty as he holds her down on
the bed, putting most of his weight on her shoulders. He
is fully erect and instead of being slow and gentle as
before, he thrusts himself inside of her, but her body is
not ready for the roughness and she whimpers and moans
in a mixture of pain and satisfaction. Forcefully he
thrusts again and she is totally submissive, completely at
his mercy. Her face shows pleasure and some fear for
what his next actions may be. Her look tells Curt his
aggressiveness is not only welcome, but perhaps even
yearned for.

Realizing how extremely rough he has approached

her, thoughts of guilt rush through his mind, yet the animalistic urges to have his way with her are so strong! He debates for a split second as to whether or not he should stop and be gentle, or maybe he should just lay down with her and keep her close to him as they peacefully embrace with no more sex. She is in need of a friend right now, not just a sex partner. Suddenly, he gets a slap on the face and his thoughts vanish from his mind as Judy yells, "What the hell are you doing, Curt! Fuck me already!"

CHAPTER 17

Donovan's eyes survey the diner as several older folks clear out and the sun starts to set. It is getting too late for them, as most go to sleep early and wake at the crack of dawn. Donovan is trying to focus on other things, as his friends are talking back and forth over some bullshit. His eyes are trying to stay off of Jane's beautiful figure. He can't help but think of how he is finally going to see underneath all of those clothes and, for the first time, taste her body and fully celebrate their relationship. His eyes fixate upon her slender yet curvy frame. When Jane walks, her hips sway from side to side making a more than seductive movement with her behind; unintentionally, of course, but still a delightful treat for all those who look as intently at her body as Donovan does.

Jane walks over to a lingering customer, an elderly man with gray hair, whom she has been serving since that afternoon. Now, at six o'clock p.m., it appears he has made the diner his new home. Dave looks up at her beautiful face, and the old man can't help but crack a smile, one induced by dirty thoughts. "You know, about what you said earlier darling, if the world ended, you better be here serving me in the diner, 'cause I want nobody other than you to serve me like you've been doing all week!"

Wanting him to leave the diner, she smiles at him and giggles slightly, turning on her charm in hopes of a bigger tip. He is old, but rather wealthy and although he is a pain to take care of at times, Dave always tips well.

In her sweetest voice she replies, "I don't know, sweetie, if I only have one day left, I'm sure not going to spend it here . . . no offense to you, of course."

The old man looks up as his head slowly shakes uncontrollably due to his age, or possibly because of the number of pills he's been taking. "Oh, Jane, no offense taken by this old geezer, I would be expectin' you to want to be with your boy, Donovan, and your family of course."

He stops for a little self-reflection, as if he is pondering who he has left in his life to spend his last day on earth with. A look of discomfort spreads across his face, and he quickly shifts topics. "Say, how's that boyfriend of yours doing? Are we going to win that state championship this year?"

Jane's glowing face and bright smile falter slightly, in hesitation at his question, "Uh, yeah, he's doing great, Dave!"

She looks around the diner, specifically back at Donovan's crew. They are still moseying around the diner looking more than ready for the big party. Finally, her eyes meet Donovan's and he greets her with a smile. Turning back to Dave, with a slightly uncomfortable smile upon her face, she looks at him and boosts up her confidence using the same energy she learned in drama class years ago.

"Yes, if he has it his way we will definitely win that state championship!" As soon as the words spill out of her mouth she turns quickly around with a smirk on her face. Trying to look busy, she picks up her towel and goes back to wiping the counter down. Concerned, Dave looks at her and frowns for a moment, shakes his head, and goes back to eating his food.

"ROAR!" Donovan shouts as he comes from behind her and wraps her petite waist in his arms holding her tightly with a smile upon his face. She looks uncomfortable and shy, and glances around for her boss before letting loose a smile and returning his affection.

She escapes from his grasp so that she can give him a

warm hug and a small kiss on the cheek.

"Hey, baby, are you ready to party tonight?" he asks in a seductive manner as he presses his hips into hers and looks lustfully into her eyes.

"Yeah, I've heard that before Donovan," she answers in a very irritated mood, as she breaks away from his grip. Donovan's demeanor changes from sensual to sad as he sees her looking so dejected. Without looking up from the counter she addresses him resentfully, "What are you really doing here anyway?"

Donovan smiles half-heartedly and looks puzzled for a moment. His feelings are hurt by the way she is asking, but he can't let the prying eyes and ears of his friends see any weakness on his part, "Like I told you, we're talking about the party after the bonfire!"

She isn't fazed and keeps her head turned away from him as she continues to scrub the same spot on the counter over and over again. There is not a single thing on the counter besides the polish she is rubbing away as she furiously scrubs.

"And, that isn't the reaction I was hoping for, Jane," he adds.

Realizing her frustration is very high, Jane sighs and forces herself to lighten up, relaxing the tension in her body. Exhausted, she turns around to look at Donovan; she has had a long day at the diner, and customers like Dave, although pleasant to talk to, can sometimes be a bother, especially when they specifically request service from her on a daily basis.

"I will show you tonight after the party. I promise," Donovan says in a somewhat defeated, yet still confident voice, as Jane tries to relax. Despite her best efforts, she still remains tense and defensive.

"Oh, yeah, like the night before the big game?" she inquires.

It becomes obvious to Donovan that he has been a disappointment to her on a few levels, which only fuels his urge to prove to her that he can satisfy her.

"We've never done it before, why is tonight going to be different?"

Donovan's face swings from looking prideful to complete defeat. He looks down at the ground, his shoulders slumping and his eyes refusing to make contact with hers, as beautiful as they are.

"Look, I'm sorry. I didn't mean it like that," she apologizes.

Ignoring her apology and building himself back up again, Donovan's eyes light up as his head bobs slightly in excitement. "I do have a surprise for you!"

Somewhat intrigued by his sudden emotional change, Jane looks at him, her eyebrows accentuating her sudden interest. "Oh, yeah?" she queries, as she cocks her head toward him. "What's that Donovan?"

"Here's what I'm talking about babe . . . after the bonfire, we are going to sneak back up and drink some beer, have some real fun, and I am going to show you just how much of a 'goody-two-shoes' boy I really am."

Now cocky once again, his hands grab her hips, pulling her closer to him trying to be seductive. The old man simply smiles as he watches the two out of the corner of his eye, no doubt reflecting on memories of when he was younger. Not wanting to be construed as a perverted old man watching teenagers be intimate, he turns his attention to his newspaper and continues to sit there, drinking his coffee and enjoying the evening.

CHAPTER 18

Jordan's tired and sore body rises from the uncomfortable hospital bed. The sheets are stained with dried blood that has leaked through his bandages and they need to be changed, but he hates the pain he experiences whenever the orderly does so. The smell of his exposed flesh, coupled with the antibiotic cream they soak it in, is dangerously powerful. It becomes especially excruciating whenever a bandage is freshly removed. At least now Jordan is a bit more conscious and understanding of the world around him than he was in his prior state. However, he is nowhere near ready to step foot into the outside world. His wounds are deep, and he has several all over his body.

His muscle fibers have been torn in half, cut by his attacker's sharp claws. He knows that he may never regain full movement of his arm again, even though he never heard a doctor state that possibility. Because of the wounds that were inflicted upon him, the damage is painfully obvious to him.

All in all though, he is lucky to be alive after what he has been through. He sits up in the dimly lit room and looks around at all of the tiny green and red lights from the machines around him, the ones helping him stay alive and well. The hospital is quiet. He doesn't hear another patient coughing or any nurses in the hall. It is rather strange and eerie at the same time. If he muttered a word, he feels as though it would echo throughout the hospital. Looking around the hospital room, a sense of despair comes over him. He's so lonely here, and hospitals are very depressing to begin with. The neon lights flooding through the room keep him awake with their unnaturally unpleasant light and low humming as electricity runs through the bulbs. The undecorated walls covered with dim green and tan colors are difficult to look at, and after this emergency visit, Jordan is certain that he would rather die than spend another stay here.

Suddenly, almost as an answer to his wishes, he hears the distant sound of footsteps out in the hall. As much as he hates to see his father so concerned for his wellbeing, as that is all he remembers from his father's prior visit, he really could use a visit from him.

"Maybe it's him!" he speaks aloud to himself, hoping that someone was in the room accompanying him. But no, his small voice echoes through the empty room until the sound meets the distant footsteps. Not one other person had been in his room the entire evening, as the nurses had left him to rest. The footsteps draw nearer to him, growing louder and louder. With every sound, Jordan's anticipation grows higher and higher. How pleased his father would be to see him alive and sitting up! How proud dad would be to see his son was tough enough to stick around through all of this pain and trouble, surviving against all odds! He begins to feel prideful and almost heroic. He could picture his father bursting through the doors, gasping in excitement! The footsteps are right beside his room. Here he comes; it must be his father who has come into the room with him! A large smile spreads over Jordan's face as he debates about looking over to see the familiar figure, or simply waiting for his voice to sound out first.

"Hey, Jordan, I'm Coach Bloom."

Shattered, Jordan's hopes and cares were completely shattered; he slumps down as the unfamiliar man looks at him, reading how upset he is. Jordan really wants to fade back into a coma, away from this miserable hospital and the reality of his situation.

"I'm . . . a . . . I'm" he stuttered for a moment, very intrigued as to what exactly caused him to get so sad and emotional upon hearing Curt Bloom's voice instead of his father's.

"Jordan, I'm Coach Miller's replacement," shared Bloom.

Now, combined with his look of disappointment was an overpowering wave of fear that sent Jordan's entire body into a cold shiver, as though somebody had just dumped his naked and frail body into a cold ocean. A large frown appears on his face, coupled with raised eyebrows, and a tear starts streaming down his cheek, onto the hospital gown.

Realizing he is expressing weakness in front of this new coach, the person who expects him to be tough, he looks to the opposite side of the room away from Coach Bloom and tries to conceal his tears. In the coldest, most detached, yet strongest voice he could muster, he speaks back to him, "Yeah, nice to meet you."

It was obvious from the state he is in, Jordan has a right to be feeble, but crying was not acceptable to the coach, or at least this is what Jordan had led himself to believe. Noticing Jordan's hostility, Coach Bloom speaks to him in a very understanding voice. "It's very nice to finally meet you, Jordan."

A few moments of silence go by, and only a loud sigh was exhibited by the wounded boy.

"I want us to be friends, Jordan."

Friends,he wants to be friends with me? That's not what a coach is; being a coach is a job. You can't be friends with your work. Angered and very skeptical, yet keeping his composure, Jordan addresses his thoughts on the matter. "What do you mean, friends?" he said with distrust. "Aren't you going to be my coach?"

Even though Jordan's first impression didn't seem to be very high, Coach Bloom's compassionate and strong-willed nature allowed him to easily see the pain and frustration the boy was going through. "Yes, Jordan. I will be your coach and more. I'm sure you understand, I'm sorry I didn't get here sooner, but there's nothing I could do about it."

In resentment and confusion, he snapped back at the coach. "I don't even know what the hell you're talking about!"

Coach Bloom reached out and closed the door to the hospital room slowly, without saying a word, and quietly walked over to him, speaking in a very soft, creepy voice to Jordan. "Yes, you do," he whispered to him softly as he slowly leaned over his bed-ridden body. "I'm sure you are feeling it by now, Jordan. Let me help you. I'm not like Coach Miller, Jordan," he added.

Breathing rapidly and unsure of this unfamiliar man's intentions, Jordan shied away from his strange approach toward him. Alone in the hospital bed with nobody around to oversee him and the nurse's button out of sight, Jordan starts to panic and his heart beats rapidly, a cold sweat overcoming his entire body.

"What do you want to help me with?" Jordan screamed out in frustration, but his yelling was quickly met by the coach putting his finger to his lips, hushing him with a sick smirk on his face as he reached down and softly touched his fingers to Jordan's arm.

"I'm sure you know what I want to help you with . . ."

In an instantaneous burst of fear, pain shot through Jordan's body as he squirmed as much as he could to get away from Coach Bloom's touch. His face and body were completely overwhelmed with absolute terror and disbelief. "Oh my God! No!" Jordan tried to scream out, but he spoke nothing audibly, as no air would come out of his mouth.

"It'll be okay, Jordan, if you let me help you through this." Coach Bloom's hand now has a firm grip on his forearm, holding it down to the hospital bed as Jordan tries to inch away, struggling like a worm getting sucked into a bird's beak. The further Jordan falls into horrible feelings of hopelessness and desperation, the more the coach appears to enjoy himself and the more his grip tightens on Jordan's arm. His arm is now so tightly squished that his hand is starting to turn purple from lack of proper blood flow.

Click.

The door to the hospital room opens slowly and the figure Jordan had so yearned for just moments ago now stands tall in the open doorway.

"DAD!" He wanted to yell out, but was still completely unable to force words out of his mouth, or even place a single thought in the right order in his head. Shaking with fear, perhaps even embarrassed to tell his father of Coach Bloom's actions, he sighs. The sheriff has a look of suspicion and surprise on his face when he sees Coach Bloom is in the room standing over his son, who looks pale and downright scared. Bloom quickly and clandestinely hits the button labeled "Pain Management" and intravenously, a dose of morphine is administered into Jordan's bloodstream causing him to become very relaxed and drowsy, momentarily letting all of his troubles simply float away.

"Coach?" the sheriff looks and sounds puzzled. A moment of silence and a strong look is shared between the two adults. The sheriff lets down his guard quickly after seeing Jordan's face relax.

"You came to meet my boy I see! He's actually doing much better than anybody anticipated him to be at this point in his recovery."

Confidently facing the sheriff and slipping on a smile, he gives the sheriff a nod of acknowledgement. "Yes, Sheriff, and I was just getting ready to leave. He's been having a lot of pain this morning." The coach pauses and forces a concerned look upon his face as he lowers his voice and draws his face in closer to the sheriff. "Just between you and me though, Sheriff, it's dangerous to let him have instant pain relief like that; maybe you should mention it to an orderly . . . that stuff is nothing to mess around with, but you don't have to listen to me."

The sheriff looks at Jordan's relaxed face and with nary a word, turns back toward Coach Bloom and gives him a silent nod of appreciation.

"Your son and I have had a wonderful talk, Sheriff. I told him that his place on the baseball team is secure and waiting for him as soon as he gets well! Everybody always says how great he is when he's up to bat. I can't just let buzz like that go unrecognized; he looks like a talented kid."

A smile cracks the sheriff's tired face, and he turns red as the compliments about the child he is lucky enough to still have alive flood out of Coach Bloom's mouth.

"That's very nice of you, Bloom," the sheriff smiles as he shakes his head in appreciation. If the sheriff has a single weakness, it would be his children and the pride he feels for them. He's incredibly flattered and dons a grin ear-to-ear.

"Well, you know, Sheriff, I've heard a lot more wonderful things about your son," Coach Bloom said, looking directly into the sheriff's weary eyes. He can see the sheriff has not been getting much sleep with everything that's been going on in this town and his personal life.

" . . . And, I just want to say, Sheriff, that I am very lucky to have him on our team. Maybe we can get that state championship everybody's been wanting if he makes a full recovery soon."

The sheriff, however, breaks out of his elated state of ego and starts to question in his mind why, if they had such a phenomenal conversation together, did Coach Bloom look so worried when he entered the room. The sheriff gains a look of suspicion on his face and extends his hand for a handshake. Coach Bloom immediately reciprocates, yet the sheriff does not stop looking into his eyes during the extended shake. There is a heavy sense of doubt in the sheriff's eyes, until Bloom breaks the tension with a smile. Feeling slightly intimidated Bloom rushes off toward the doorway.

Jordan is still conscious, but barely. He sees his dad as a blurred figure standing out in front of him, the general shape of his body a double vision mess, still Jordan recognizes his father's voice from when he was speaking with Coach Bloom. The initial wave of the morphine dose has vanished quickly, perhaps due to his high tolerance of the drug, which he has used often for frequent pain the past few days.

"Okay, guys, I will you see you later after we have the bonfire tonight!" Coach Bloom says as he exits the room.

CHAPTER 19

Jordan is disoriented and still slightly fearful. At this particular moment he cannot remember why and looks slowly over at his father. "Dad?" he says in a very calm, flat voice. "Why are you are letting 'em have the bonfire?" he slurs out as his head turns to look over at his father. He is unable to hold his head in place and it simply falls limp onto the pillow.

"Jordan, after what happened to your sister . . . and now you . . . there isn't much I can do about it, the . . ."

Speaking as though he was dreaming in a nightmare, the boy slurs out in an almost incomprehensible fashion. "Dadddd, it's toooooooooo dangerous out there . . ." His eyelids grow heavy and drool starts to come out of the right corner of his mouth, but he forces himself back into a more alert state. "Something is going to happen again, I just know it!"

Jordan's eyes light up fearfully, as his father's eyes dim in pain, not wanting to admit it even to himself. "Relax son . . . I have a couple of deputies heading up there and it's going to be all over by midnight, so we will do the best we can to keep everybody as safe as possible."

A series of knocks come at the mostly open door, and through its opening a very familiar face appears. It is Mark, Zach's father.

"Sheriff, Jordan, how are you two doing?" he asks in a

forcefully happy voice. It is obvious he is distraught seeing Jordan in such a state; it is such a contrast to his usually strong condition.

Jordan, responding only to a new voice, not necessarily his presence, mumbles, "I'm doing better, thank you, Mr. . . ."

As if in an attempt to detract attention from his son's delirious state, the sheriff stands up and immediately extends a hand to Mark Gooden.

"Mark, it's great to see you," he replies as he strongly shakes his hand and then sits down in a small chair. "There's another chair right here, Mark, if you want to take a seat for a while."

Mark considers the offer for a moment; however he decides he doesn't wish to place himself for a long period of time in the same room as a drugged out, half-alive boy. It is simply too disheartening for him to see. There is a certain amount of jealousy he feels toward the sheriff. The sheriff still has a kid left, barely, but he can still talk to him. Parts of Jeremy and Zach are in an evidence bag now, or frozen somewhere in a laboratory. Though his jealousy is not a serious contending issue on the surface, on a subconscious level, it is immensely deep.

"Thank you for coming to check in on Jordan; that means a great deal to me," the sheriff sighs.

Mark is occupied thinking about Jordan's state, and the reality of the situation sinks in once again. Shaking his head and hesitating slightly, Mark quickly rushes the words out of his mouth, "Well, Sheriff, we were almost family."

With a warm smile, the sheriff looks at him and speaks softly, "We will always be family, Mark."

His face heavy with a sense of purpose, Mark gets straight to the point, "So, Sheriff, I talked to Dr. Hyde today . . . and, well, uh, I learned a lot."

"ARRGH!!" Jordan suddenly screams out in utter pain and frantically searches his bedside for the button to administer more of the intoxicating pain reliever into his bloodstream. The sheriff debates whether or not to stop him, but at the same time, cannot bear to see his son in such misery. Within seconds of the panic, and with thoughts of telling Jordan to stop relying on the drug on the edge of the sheriff's tongue, the monotone beeping noise is heard once again. The crying dies down as the drug flows through his bloodstream and Jordan falls into a deep sleep.

His blood curdling screams still resonate through the sheriff's mind. Obviously shaken up from the amount of pain his son is experiencing, he looks at Jordan with concerned and tired eyes. "It's okay, son . . . please try to relax."

Jordan's body instantaneously obeys the sheriff's words, almost as though it was looking for a reason to put his conscious mind to rest. Jordan's head slumps to the right side on his pillow, his lips part slightly, until he remains outright motionless. His body lying there in the hospital bed, he looks almost as though he is dead. Both the sheriff and Mark are still for a moment watching him intently, with worry filling their eyes. He sleeps and the machine's alarm doesn't sound so with a final realization that he has just succumbed to the pain-relieving power of the drug, they both take a sigh of relief and a spark of a smile comes across his father's face. Mark, however, still looks troubled.

"So . . . Mark . . . I read Brittany's diary after Dr. Hyde gave me the toxicology reports," the sheriff said as Mark let out a heavy sigh, looked down at the ceramic tiles of the hospital floor and shook his head in disbelief.

"You know, I am really not surprised!" Mark admits, his voice resounding with emotional distress. He thinks about how he could have been more accepting of the gay community in general and then perhaps Zach would have been honest with him and felt more accepted. Now, however, it's just too late for him to make amends. Zach was gone and so was his other son.

"Now that I look back, they were definitely more than friends. They were inseparable. It's kind of crazy, because at the same time, I knew Zach loved Brittany," Mark shared.

Without skipping a beat, the sheriff took a deep breath, and with confidence, looked directly at the worried man. Mark's eyes appeared to be sunken in and his skin was dry, exaggerating his wrinkles. He was taking this loss very, very hard.

The sheriff spoke to him, "I can tell you, without any doubt, Brittany wrote in her diary that Zach was the one she loved; she loved him desperately."

A small grin appeared on Mark's face as he was instantly whisked away into a memory of overseeing Brittany and Zach wrapped in each other's arms on the living room couch. They would spend an hour or two in silence just gazing into each other's eyes, with occasional light kisses creating a wholesome experience.

" . . . and Jeremy . . . "

The sheriff's eyes widened in nervousness for what he was about to say. "Well," his voice turned soft and slightly raspy, as his smile faltered. "Well, let's just say that my daughter had a definite appetite for sex!"

Finally, the tension in the room broke, and they exchanged smiles with each other. "You know, Bud," the sheriff shared, leaning in a little with a twinkle in his eye, "she also knew about Zach and Jeremy."

His face returned to a serious look, the air heavy with despair. "She loved them both, Mark, but she did love Zach the most, and he received most of her affection."

Chuckling a little, and looking away to the small paintings on the hospital walls, the ones meant to help the patient feel a little more at home, he added, "She wrote 'Brittany Goodman' a number of times in her diary."

The sheriff's eyes welled up with tears and Mark leaned over, patting him on the leg. "Sheriff, there was no other girl that I could imagine Zach with. You have to get whoever killed them. We've got to get those bastards even if it is an animal, because if it's human, it's still an animal for what it did to our kids."

CHAPTER 20

"The sheriff gave into them all!" Billy's crackling voice yelled out, echoing through the green woods near Morris' Beer & Gas. The woods were fairly calm tonight.

"He's going to let them have the bonfire, they say it's supposed to be over at midnight, but after that time a group of the guys and some girls are all sneaking back out there! They're all going to get wasted and start fucking each other - you know what's going to happen, Morris!" exclaimed Billy.

Billy's voice is now filled with extreme anxiety, his eyes wide with fear, and with good reason. Several of his friends, no, more like his family, were going to be completely reckless and endanger not only their lives, but everybody's in the town. Morris stood there, his pale skin looking almost translucent as purple veins were exposed all over his skin, his eyes wide, staring blankly at Billy.

With a slow stir, he spoke methodically, yet surprisingly articulately, "Well then, Billy boy, I guess we'll just have to visit them tonight, won't we?" A smile cracked upon his old face, and he let out a chuckle that in its nature was sinister.

"What do you want me to do, Morris? Should I be there? You know what will happen to me. I can't control it!" Billy said escalating in volume and trembling with anxiety. Billy's face is flushed from a tremendous mixture of fear and judgment.

"I will kill them Morris! I will kill my friends! I don't want to; that scares me so much! I hate this curse; I hate this stupid state that I have to control constantly! I'm not me when I'm like that, Morris!" yelled Billy.

"I have no power to resist any of it!" He is in a total outrage, his voice yelling as loud as he can, his throat becoming hoarse from the shouting. Despite this burst of emotion, Morris stands before the boy, not frightened, untouched by anything other than his own devious thoughts. Smiling like a pervert, he licks his lips while continually making eye contact with Billy.

"Well then . . . " Morris's voice trembles as he speaks, his poor posture becoming even worse as he leans in closer to Billy's face. "Those little boys will be having sex with those girls now, will they?"

He leans back, but steps closer to Billy, making him very, very uncomfortable.

"Coach Miller told them what to do if they wanted to have sex. They needed to buddy up with each other, you know, be team players, take one for the team, you know what I'm saying right, Billy? Well, not every player on the team must be a team player if they don't take one for the team, Billy boy.

He looked Billy dead in the eyes in a menacing way, and the smirk upon his face grew into a smile, displaying the few out-of- shape, yellow teeth he had left in his mouth. "I don't blame them either, Billy. It was bound to happen, kid . . . and . . ." His smile grew wider and his eyes appeared to bulge out of their sockets. Looking directly at him, he revealed, ". . . and, I'm hungry, Billy boy! I'm hungry for some real meat!"

Morris looks at him, parting his mouth a bit, sliding his tongue out of the corner of his mouth, licking his lips while Billy backs away cautiously, unsure of Morris's intentions.

"Morris . . . what happened to Coach Miller? What's going on?" he started yelling, his fists clenched by his side, brows angled in an angry fashion toward the old, seemingly feeble man.

"Everything is fucked up and out of control!" he exclaimed, his face red with outrage, his voice bouncing off the sides of the tall trees surrounding them, creating a powerful echo and sending a flock of birds upright into the air in fright.

"Oh, Billy," Morris says with a cautious, excited tone. "You, my dear boy, have a lot to learn. I'll watch over you tonight . . . I won't let anything happen. Now get out of here. Everything is going to be just fine, Billy."

He gives him a stare not saying another word for a very awkward thirty seconds. Billy takes a few more steps backward, and then starts to jog back down the path onto the road between town and the bed and breakfast.

"Oh yes, Billy boy . . . everything is going to be just fine . . ." Morris mumbles with a slight grin.

CHAPTER 21

Curt Bloom and Judy stand in the brightly lit kitchen in the bed and breakfast. The sun has completely set and the skies are filled with a dark blue tint. The kitchen is elaborately furnished in a very well-decorated rustic manner. Though the inn has had many guests throughout the years, Judy has made sure to keep it in near perfect condition. The marble countertops are so well designed they look like a mirror, with a slightly darker reflection.

"I have to get ready for homecoming tonight," says Curt in a rather disgruntled tone.

"So, when will you be back, Curt?" she sighs as she opens up the cupboard to place a stack of fresh plates upon the shelf.

"Probably around one a.m., Judy." Curt walks up behind her and puts his hands on her tummy.

"I will miss you," expresses Judy, and as she speaks, Curt's eyes widen with joy.

After a few seconds he smiles and says, "I can't believe how special you are to me."

Judy turns in his arms and after a moment of staring into Curt's eyes, she grins, forewarning, "You have not seen anything yet. Just wait. I'll never let you go." Curt's smile widens as he hears this. Judy stops and thinks for a second, realizing what Curt has shared, she turns to him in concern.

"Oh my, did I hear you say they are having a

153

bonfire?"

He sighs deeply and gives a look of forced acceptance to the fact. "Yep, that's what I said Judy!"

She is stunned, "How can they allow that? It's much too dangerous, Curt! I don't want you to be anywhere near there!"

Curt, with a lot of confidence behind his words, firmly states that she doesn't need to worry about him. "There will be deputies keeping an eye on things. I'm sure everything will be fine, Judy! Besides I'm not going to let anything happen to me, Judy."

With a very caring expression on his face, he tightens his grip on her soft body. As silence fills the room, worry fills their faces.

Curt, however, shakes off the gloom and doom, "Especially now that I've found you, Judy."

Looking up, she meets his gaze with confidence and holds him tighter, not letting go. "Well, I don't like it one bit, Curt," she said in a whiney and sad voice, knowing she couldn't do a damn thing about him leaving.

"I am shocked that this whole party is going on. For God sakes," she begins to grow angry, looking Curt directly in his eyes, not accusing him, not even angry at him, but at the situation as a whole. "We don't even know what's happening up there. The sheriff's boy just got attacked in the campsite behind the inn, probably by the same thing that killed my sister, her husband, Coach Miller and those kids!"

She begins to weep in his arms as Curt pats her on the back. He then begins rubbing it softly and in a reassuring manner he shares, "I know how you feel, honey, and that's why I'm going up there tonight . . . I don't want any more losses, and the more people they have there, the safer we will be if anything does happen."

CHAPTER 22

"Okay, Cooper!" the sheriff instructs in a serious, energetic tone, reminiscent of that of a general planning a war strategy. No doubt he was in the same mindset as one at war. As a general would strive to protect his country, he strives to protect the people of his town. Unfortunately, unlike a general, he has very limited power and resources at his disposal.

"I want you and your two men up there. And, for Christ's sake, keep an eye out for anything that looks suspicious, would you? When midnight comes, I want that whole thing closed down." The sheriff's intimidating voice rises as Cooper tentatively listens.

"I want that fire put out and I need every one of those kids home. Do you understand me, Cooper?"

Standing with his full attention toward the sheriff, he looks at him nervously, "Yes sir, Sheriff. I sure do!"

As much as Cooper knows the sheriff on a personal level, when he gets into his control mode and wants a job done right, he is a very intimidating man.

"We will definitely keep our eyes open for anything out of the ordinary, Sheriff," he said as though he was standing at attention, and nodded to the sheriff.

"And, Cooper, don't let those kids make an ass of you just because they said that they are going to go home at midnight. Don't believe them! Keep your eyes open!" the sheriff spoke in a discerning tone. Cooper stares at him intently, listening to every word he says and burning it into his memory to the best of his ability.

This is the first time the town has had a serious issue such as this, and luckily albeit curiously, the press hasn't been a bother in any of the cases. Sure, rumors have spread to neighboring towns, but things have been mostly kept under wraps. It is all rather strange. It seems that the people of Hidden Valley are a very tightly interwoven community and are treating these losses as their very own. A brutal massacre, brushed off as though it is a simple ghost tale. Very few are taking heed to the obvious dangers surrounding the area.

"Sheriff, I am not going to let you down on this one. If anything happens to those kids, I don't think there will be any way to keep the press off of our backs. If that happens, then we are all in trouble."

"Correction, Cooper. You will be in trouble," the sheriff says firmly, pointing an accusatory finger in his direction, followed by a step back by the nervous deputy.

"Because, I am turning it all over to you, do you have a plan?" the sheriff inquires.

Shocked, yet honored to be carrying such a responsibility, much like the sheriff usually does, the deputy takes over kicking into a purely work-based mentality.

"Yes sir, I do," he chanted loudly and confidently, puffing out his chest as he speaks to his boss. Cooper then thinks of the future, one day he will take the sheriff's place. *And, when I do, hopefully this whole shenanigan will be over*, he thinks to himself.

"I have two deputies and I'm going to have them walking the perimeter the whole time everyone's there. I am going to be in amongst the kids having the bonfire, so I can see what's going on," outlined the deputy.

"Okay, having the two deputies surrounding the

perimeter is a good plan, but having you down in the middle with all the kids who are partying and supposed to be having a good time for their homecoming? Really, Cooper?" the sheriff questions, cocking his head with a smile on his face.

"We want the kids to stay at the bonfire, we don't want them wandering away into the woods. We want them to have a good time, Cooper. While we want them to be safe, the town will be in an outrage if, God forbid, their treasured tradition is under arrest. The officers will turn a blind eye to whatever happens there for one night so those kids can have a good time. Bodie, we are there to protect them, we don't want them to feel as though we are going to arrest them."

Cooper is frozen in thought, puzzled and slightly embarrassed by his plan. He loses his previously confident grin and bows his head, "Oh, so I suppose I should probably walk around the perimeter too?"

Still shaking his head, and once again looking very serious, the sheriff addresses Bodie's proposal. "I think that is a good plan. Get your men together and get out there and start setting up for tonight."

There is a loud knock on the sheriff's closed office door and he looks over in confusion. The door opens without his approval. It is obvious that Curt Bloom is getting too comfortable around him and a little cocky, as well. Remaining professional, yet giving him a subtle glare as he enters the room, the sheriff addresses him with curiosity and some resentment, "What can I do for you, Mr. Bloom?"

Bloom looks eager to speak with the sheriff, but is not as welcomed as he had hoped. "Sorry if I'm interrupting, Sheriff, but I was wondering if you were going to go up and see your son tonight?"

The Sheriff's brows, which were previously showing

signs of frustration, are now raised in an emotional outburst.

Bloom rambles on, "I mean, from what I understand all these kids look forward to this night all year long and he's stuck up there in the hospital. I don't know sir." He shuffles his feet against the dark cherry-stained wooden floor of the office. "I just feel kind of bad for him, up there all alone."

"Yes, Bloom, that's a good thought." The Sheriff sighs deeply and places his chin in the palms of his hands, his elbows resting on his rich wooden desk that is littered with papers and various office supplies. His eyelids close, no doubt heavy with concern.

"I do want to go up there, I know he's all alone, but with everything that is going on tonight I feel as if I shouldn't, or rather, can't . . ."

"Well, I just thought I would stop in and see how you're doing. Hey, uh, Sheriff?" The sheriff's eyebrows raise, but not a single word the does he speak.

"You know, on my way home, I would be more than happy to stop by and remind Jordan that he's got three more of these events coming up before he graduates. I'm sure it must seem like the end of the world for the little guy right now."

With a sense of distrust, the sheriff looks at Bloom. He is having an internal conflict over the matter; he shakes his head as if clearing any doubt from his mind, and gives the coach a very, long heartfelt stare before speaking his answer.

"Yeah," the sheriff nods his head slightly in compliance with the seemingly kind offer the coach has just presented to him. The only thing bothering him about this is why Bloom is so interested in his son, and why there seemed to be tension in the hospital room when he walked in and saw Bloom with his son the day before. "I appreciate that. It would be very nice of you, if it's not an inconvenience."

The sheriff is a very kind man and does not wish to make any accusations toward other people unless he has conclusive evidence. In this case, he only has his intuition and an awkward conversation between them, and that alone is not enough to start putting restrictions upon his visitation rights. Against his better judgment, the sheriff gives his full approval to Bloom.

"Alright, Sheriff!" he says in an arrogant manner. "I'm going to check out the dance and then I'll be heading home. After some thought I don't think I'm interested in attending the bonfire any longer, so I'll stop by and see your boy."

Detecting the hesitation in the sheriff's face (even Deputy Bodie standing in the corner, gives the sheriff a puzzled look over the manner in which he delivered his response) he figures he should at least ask the sheriff's permission once again.

"Yeah, yeah, that's great, Bloom. I really appreciate it. Just watch yourself out there; things have been kind of crazy around here at night."

CHAPTER 23

The bass from the sound system shakes most of the area around the school; melodic thumps shred off into the distance as music shakes the windows on cars parked just outside. The small town is very lucky to have such an amazing sound system donated for the event, even if it is a bit overkill. If one were to walk into the school's parking lot, past the occasional rocking car with lustful teenagers inside, the sound waves resonating on the ground would vibrate their feet with an absolutely tremendous force.

Inside the gymnasium, there are a few hundred kids having an exceptional time laughing and dancing. Even the teachers have an excuse to party. They are mingling amongst the crowd, dancing and taking advantage of the punchbowl being spiked by some of the high school students.

Many of the kids were dressed up in tuxedos and prom dresses, but there were a select few just wearing dress pants with their accompanying button down shirts tucked tightly into their slacks in a cheesy manner. Some of the boys manage to pull off the look without a cocked eyebrow, but most looked slightly ridiculous. It is obvious that formal events don't happen often in the small town. The students' behavior was wild, exotic and energetic.

Donovan danced awkwardly in the middle of the dance floor with his date, Jane. Donovan's status in the school has skyrocketed amongst the boys because he is lucky enough to be courting the beautiful Jane. They are not engaged in formal dancing. The beat of the music is very fast and hot, so it is only natural that at the volume it is being played, the teens are reacting in the same fashion.

Donovan stands, swaying his hips and his torso to the wild and eccentric techno beat, his face a bright red, as he is already slightly intoxicated. Jane acts very differently than the proper lady Donovan encountered earlier that evening. Holding him true to his word, her hips slipped in comfortably along his pelvic area, grinding with him, pressing her ass against his thigh, and his erection, as they continually dance to the hot beat.

Her hands are flailing in the air awkwardly and over his body as best she can in this position. Suddenly she bends over, shaking and massaging Donovan with her behind as her hands grasp his ankle. Clawing upwards, she moves her torso back up with sexy twists and thrusts until her hand meets with his manhood and she starts to move her hand up and down, pressing through his pants with her palm. The pleasure almost forces him to stop moving to the beat as ecstasy overcomes his body.

Donovan returns this action by placing one hand on her swaying hips, moving toward her inner thigh and using his other hand to perfectly cup one of her perky breasts. She slaps his hand away and spins around toward him, pressing her breasts tightly against his chest and kissing him on the neck. She is making sure he keeps his promise to her tonight.

"Tonight is your night, Baby. I am going to do so many nasty things to you," he yells over the music as he smiles at her, clasping her firm butt-cheek with his right

161

hand.

"Ok, but it better not be all talk," she yells back in a drunken daze staring at him with seductive eyes. Not too far from the two, Billy and Elliot are dancing in much the same manner with their dates. Donnie is dancing very loosely with his date, Sally. Sally, a very attractive slender girl, is a very mature teenage girl who is extremely sexually aroused and interested in Donnie. The lights flashing, her sexy movements and flowing hair presented like a series of photographs.

"You are going to come up to the party after, right, babe?" Donnie shouts into her ear. The answer is barely audible or distinguishable from the blaring music. Her leg wraps around his as she rubs herself along Donnie's leg in a sensual manner as she dances, teasingly exposing her chest to him.

"You couldn't keep me away. I have a surprise for you in the car on our way up there," she said as she cups his manhood, and a look of surprise lights up his face.

"Ahhh," his next words burst out of his mouth as his body is overwhelmed with pleasure. "You know I can't . . ." he takes a few deep breaths as her grip tightens; his face is the picture of full blown ecstasy.

". . . Have sex the night . . ." he grabs her arm and forces her hand away and regains his composure.

"Okay!" she surrenders.

He lets out a laugh between deep breaths, now heavily debating whether or not to indulge in her pleasurable offer, and then suddenly, his senses rush back to him. "I have a game tomorrow night babe, and I can't have sex before; you know the rules."

She looks at him in disgust, in obvious annoyance, then puts on her seduction mode once again and rubs herself against his erection, her panties warm and soaked, getting her not-so-formal skirt moist as well.

"A blow job isn't sex, baby; just ask Bill Clinton!" She stares at him with a devious little sexual twinkle; she is obviously on a mission tonight. She is rather frustrated with him. It isn't supposed to be the girls who chase after sex so obviously and intensely, and it's most certainly not the guy's place to refuse a petite hot and ready body.

"Well, yeah, but . . ." he said back in hesitation.

"There's no ifs, ands or buts about it, baby," she says as her lips meet his, her hands continuing to move up and down his body, and she playfully pulls down his fly a little bit, making him breathe heavily in anticipation.

While this is going on, a really good looking young guy by the name of Danny comes into the room. He is one of the boys associated with Donovan's circle of friends. Somewhat of an outsider to them, he is still respected and acknowledged. He is smaller than the other boys and has a very unique look and an attractive face. He confidently strides across the dance floor, looking at all of the boys and girls surrounding him and feels the open sexuality in the air. There is no question in his mind that he is the best looking guy there, and if moral obligations were not taken into consideration, all of the boys, as well as the girls, would be all over him.

Danny has gained a sort of messianic reputation as far as the students among the high school are concerned. He's supposed to be the next best quarterback for the football team and the girls are irresistibly attracted to this, especially as the two previous hotshots, Zach and Jeremy, are now out of the picture. Coach Miller has had a very close relationship with Danny that started about six months ago. Some even questioned its level of intimacy.

Danny struts self-assuredly past a few of the other boys in a darker corner of the room, looking up and down every last body and winking at an attractive blonde male. Their body language and their movements give enough indication as to what has been going on between them in the past.

Tonight Danny has his mind set in a completely opposite direction. On the floor, standing apart from the rest of the girls, she has on thick eyeliner, wears her hair in pig-tails and a bright red, almost gothic-oriented lipstick with the rest of the accompanying makeup. Her eyes are piercing and dark, seductive and almost malicious. She is wearing her very tightly-fitted cheerleader outfit, doing different twists and cheering patterns, with a very seductive twist. Her energy is purely wild. Odd that she would have a gothic twist tonight; something was most certainly different about her.

She was usually very preppy and would never be caught acting in such a way, but tonight she simply didn't care. Everybody in the entire room appeared to be under an incantation; sexuality was airborne at the dance, and none of the respective authorities seemed to care that the teens were going absolutely wild. Her hips and ass are very curvy and full, however her chest is somewhat lacking, which somehow fit her very well. Without skipping a beat, almost as if he was in a trance, his eyes lock with hers and she seductively gestures him over. He walks right to her as if he has been hypnotized.

"Hey, Sammy, I must say you are just fucking amazing-looking and I cannot wait to see you out of that outfit," he smiles slyly, gripping her tightly in his arms. She bends backwards very smoothly in his arms and her feet lift off of the ground, pivoting her hips on his. Unlike Donnie, he is fazed by this, but it does not overwhelm him. He remains calm, cool and collected, holding her up and thrusting his hips into hers. As she spins back up using her stomach muscles, she kisses him on the lips and looks him in the eye with deadly passion.

"Danny, tonight I'm going to show you what being a

boy is all about." Strangely, and in an animalistic nature, she licks his lips and cheek in a very hot, arduous way. "Trust me. I am going to take you someplace you've never been before in your life."

He looks up slightly, his eyes still locked with hers, and licks his own lips in a very seductive and spine-chilling manner. He grabs her arms tightly and roughly, their energy feeding off of each other, and building even more passion. His nails dig into her skin, almost to the point of cutting her, and with the music beat as an excuse he shakes and jerks her back and forth to the pulse of the bass.

"I hope you like it rough baby . . ." he says as he harshly bites her lip, but not enough to pierce the skin, as her eyes light up with fire. She is very turned on.

"Whips and kisses. Baby, I'm yours. Oh, God! I'm burning right now." A grin comes across her face and she looks at him, her nails scraping along his back. "Just fuck me, baby!"

She smiles at him, having absolutely no thought of anything but rough sex, but Danny's eyes are filled with much more than just passion.

Danny reaches over and gives her a very aggressive kiss on the lips, holding her throat as he does. She uses her long nails to squeeze his rear end and starts to claw at it. Danny, now incredibly hot, suddenly widens his eyes in fear as he screams out in pure energetic pain! He quickly pushes himself away; something is trying to come out. His head is tingly as the sensation of the stretching of his skull overcomes him, his fingers trying to elongate and every muscle tensing in his body! Somewhat frightened, yet completely turned on by this freaky behavior, Sammy looks at him curiously, and breathes heavily. Danny erupts into madness and lets out a bloodthirsty roar!

"Stop," his voice is unusually deep, his face red and angry, and he appears as though he is ready to beat somebody to a bloody pulp!

"This has to wait until tonight!" His voice is increasing in pitch with every word that comes out of his mouth. She takes a step back, but her hips still lean towards him and she lets out a captivated sigh. "Mmm, you really do get freaky, don't you, you nasty boy!"

Sammy is somewhat frightened, yet she is incredibly turned on by his odd behavior. Danny simply looks at her and shakes his head, the veins in his neck notably pulsating. Using all his might to compose himself, he walks away to serve himself some spiked punch.

CHAPTER 24

"Baby, I want you so much," Donovan speaks to Jane as his hands ignore her silky dark blue dress, feeling every one of her curves perfectly with his fingertips. About to return his affection with a passionate kiss, suddenly a high-pitched voice interrupts them.

"Hey, Donovan, have you seen Billy? He was supposed to pick me up an hour ago," Beth nearly screams over the music, hitting his girlfriend on the arm lightly to get the pair's attention.

"No, Beth!" he shouts back to her in a blur. The alcohol is starting to take over his body, He is slurring his words and he feels it is making the night even sexier in a strange way.

"Hey, Beth, Billy told me he was picking you up earlier today. I don't know; he has been acting like a weird little fuck lately!" His words unrestrained as the alcohol flows through his bloodstream, making her face seem so much prettier than usual. The room seems to shake with every flicker of the light and for a moment, they lights synchronize with each other perfectly, even though it is just a random strobe pattern.

It took Donovan a minute to realize that Jane was talking to Beth even more passionately than he had just hollered out to her on the dance floor. "I'm sure he'll show up, Beth!" Jane yelled to Beth, still rubbing her tight body all over Donovan.

"He's probably just busy," she pauses for a moment. The alcohol seduces her with its inebriating ways, "You know, doing some stupid 'Billy' thing!" Jane erupted in laughter. Beth, however, was clearly sober, unlike everybody else in the group.

"Wow!" she exclaims in a painfully disappointed manner, frustration searing inside of her. She pauses for a moment and looks around for her date. "This is supposed to be our last night to see each other before I go to Europe next week for the exchange program!"

Donovan, who is usually contained, belligerently yells out to her in an accusatory manner. "Did you try to call him on his cell?"

She releases a heavy sigh, and barks back at him harshly, "Yeah, Donovan, I did, like six fucking times!"

"I don't know, Beth! He's a God damn douche!" Feeling horrible about the words that spewed out of his mouth without any form of restraint, he gains a look of sympathy and guilt, and tries to make an apology.

"He told me he was excited about the two of you sneaking back up there tonight with us after the bonfire! Don't worry girl, he's excited to see you!"

"Yeah, I was too . . ."

With extreme disappointment and feeling foolish for expecting him to keep their date, she produces a little smile as she watches the couple in front of her embrace. Sighing deeply, she forces herself to move with the beat, trying to dance the pain away.

Suddenly the room erupts into wild, drunken cheers as the door to the gym opens up and the lights illuminate Elliot, who has just arrived from the diner, and his date Rhonda, as they stumble into the gymnasium, obviously already intoxicated. Elliot's face reflects a regal expression as he walks in as pompous as ever. Through all of her makeup it's difficult to detect, but Rhonda seems embarrassed.

Elliot stands prideful as people continue to cheer, and much like a leader addressing his people, he holds up his hands and nods with an elegant smile upon his face. The students, acting like his subjects, quiet down and smile in anticipation.

"My loyal subjects, your King and Queen have arrived, let this not stop the festivities, my friends!" he proudly brags, as his date keels over with laughter.

"Everybody," his booming voice echoes throughout the gym, the music volume has been lowered to a murmur. "Now I command you all to party down!" He bellows out taking his queen into his arms and kissing her passionately. He then joins the rest of the crowd as the fast and loud music erupts on the dance floor.

Much like a rave, the party continues on. Amongst the crowd, nowhere near as energetic as the kids around him, Coach Bloom jostles his way through the slew of kids who are having the time of their lives. Having just entered the room a few minutes earlier, he looks around puzzled at how rowdy the crowd has gotten. Searching the students, he finally spots who he is looking for, Donovan Gray.

"Hey, Donovan!" he yells to him, waving his arms in the air trying to catch his attention, but to no avail. Donovan stands alone, his date apparently having left him. Coach Bloom finally arrives near Donovan, placing a firm hand on his shoulder from behind, and Donovan smiles, in surprise.

"Hey, Donovan, I know we haven't gotten to talk too much, but I'm looking forward to a really good game tomorrow!"

Watching Donovan the coach starts to realize that Donovan is heavily under the influence of alcohol.

Oh shit, the kid better not have a hangover tomorrow, he thinks to himself without revealing an ounce of doubt on his face. He forms an unusual smile on his face. He reaches out and grabs Donovan's hand, shakes it a little bit, but holds it for a little longer than usual. Donovan looks up into the coach's eyes and there is an immediate understanding.

"Yeah, thanks, Coach, I will do my best!"

Donovan falls, appearing to be mesmerized while studying the Coach for about a beat and a half of the song that is playing.

"I look forward to having a good rest of the year with you Donovan. I'm here to help you get through this, okay?" offers Coach Bloom. He looks at Donovan's slouched state and smiles at him.

The doors to the gym open once again, revealing a few kids out in the hall making out with each other against the walls. Billy stands in the open doorway, surveys the party, and starts to come in, bobbing his head to the music, but mostly looking disheveled, nervous, and very cautious. Looking around, he sees Beth making her way to Donovan with a few cups of the questionable punch, which is nearly gone. She abruptly halts when she sees Donovan, who is still talking to Coach Bloom. She panics and turns back around, nodding to Danny as she brushes by him.

Cautiously, Billy avoids Donovan as well and heads toward Danny. In a very nervous fashion he addresses him, his arms are crossed and he is shaking.

"Hey, man, you're going up tonight right?" asks Billy.

Danny is startled by this strangely fearful appearance of Billy. "Yeah, man, settle down. Jesus! I plan on going up there and having a good time, too."

"Danny, man, you have to be careful. Remember, it's really hard to control . . .I know you almost lost it back there a couple of minutes ago," Billy said in an intoxicated state, bitter and confident.

"I don't give a fuck, Billy!" he screams at him.

"Ask me if I want to control it," Danny challenged. Billy looks at him, seeing Danny's sinister smile, and breathes heavily. He takes a few steps backwards, at which time he is bumped into by a careless dancer.

"Danny, what the hell are you saying?" yells Billy.

Danny shakes his head in frustration, "I'm saying what happens happens Billy! I'm fucking sick and tired of restraining myself. I need it man, I can't stop it, and I don't want to anymore!"

A large evil smile erupts on his face, as he speaks. "It's like a drug, Billy, the harder you try not to give in and let it fill your body with that extreme feeling, the more you want it. The rush, the pure animalistic, natural mindless self-indulgence! You know how it is, Billy!"

Billy's face shows fear; he immediately turns around and rushes into the crowd, burying himself in it and vanishing from Danny's sight as Danny erupts with diabolical laughter.

As the music quiets down, Billy approaches Donovan. He had seen Donovan talking to the coach earlier. The coach is now absent, and Donovan and Donnie are talking. Billy joins the two of them as Donovan is talking.

"I don't know, man," he shares with them in a rushed and puzzled voice. "It was really weird! The coach just came up to me and said he was looking forward to a good game tomorrow night and then when he shook my hand..."

Donnie's brows rise in anticipation of Billy's thoughts.

"I think he's one of us," said Billy.

"What? No, man. There's no way! That would be

crazy," Donovan shouts out in a confused, drunken way as Billy shares this idea.

"Hey, guys . . . uh, Danny is acting really weird, too," said Billy.

They both give him a puzzled look. "What do you mean, dude?" Donnie asks, puzzled and very curious.

"Guys, he started swearing, saying that it was really difficult to control and he glared at me menacingly and started going on about how good it felt to give in to his animal side. He told me he didn't want to control it anymore."

"What the fuck?" Donovan blurts out, clearly outraged, feeling betrayed and shocked that he would say such a thing.

"God damn it!" Billy throws his arms down in frustration, and turns toward Donovan. "I told you that kid was trouble the first day coach turned him!"

With a serious look, Donovan throws his half-filled cup onto the floor, trying to sober up as much as possible.

"I knew something was going on between him and the coach! He's got this way about him. We need to keep a really close eye on him tonight," warns Billy.

He looks seriously at both Donovan and Donnie and said firmly, "You guys understand?"

Donovan shakes his head in agreement.

"Yeah, I understand! I've always thought that kid was dangerous. I don't know why Coach Miller trusted him like he did! Jane told me that he is extremely sexual toward everybody lately. She said he came into the café the other day and was acting very strange. He was talking to her, touching her face and hair, really sexual like and sort of violent - fucking bastard!

"I was told that if you are young - you know - when that happens . . ." Billy begins to look sheepish and somewhat ashamed for some reason. "That you start having sex young too, a lot of sex; the beast within you starts to desire sex and it kills more and more . . . it never ends and only gets worse!"

Donovan figures out why he is ashamed, and accusingly, speaks to him harshly. "Billy, who the hell told you that - Morris told you that, didn't he, Billy?"

Donnie erupts into frustration, along with Donovan who shakes his head harshly, and looks at him with murderous eyes. Taking a breath and speaking calmly but with authority Donovan said, "Billy, we've been told to stay away from Morris, you know better dude!"

Instantly, Billy puts himself in a defensive state, and takes a step closer to both of them aggressively. "He's not that bad!" He shouts in anger, before realizing how he is acting. Sheepishly, he takes a step back, with every intention of maintaining his prior distance.

"Besides, he is keeping an eye out for us tonight. He wants to be my friend and now that the coach is gone, I don't know who else I can talk to." Billy sighs, obviously hurt by the other's reactions toward him.

"Nobody else talks to him and barely any of you talk to me!" His frustrated face turns into a small, desolate smirk. The boys react with shock, neither knowing how to handle his feelings of loneliness or how to respond. Instead, both of them stay on topic, and avoid it all together.

Donovan shouts out in a desperate attempt to get the conversation back to the previous matter, "So! What else did he tell you, Billy?"

Billy looks around the area and motions the boys to follow him to a quieter section of the gym, further away from the speakers, which are lined up along one wall.

As they approach the corner, Billy starts to explain everything. "Prepare yourself guys . . ." he says with a sigh.

"He said that kids turned around the age of 10 or 12, you know, really young ones are the ones you have to really be careful of because they can become very strong, especially kids that get turned at 10 or 12, before puberty."

All three boys exchange fearful looks in fear that Danny may be too strong to handle.

"Yeah, I know," Billy said to them. The boys that stood in front of him had very worried faces, as he continues on with his explanation.

"By the time they are 14 or 15," he makes direct eye contact with Danny, who is glaring at him with a sadistic smile on his face from across the room, then takes a sigh, breaking it off.

"Yeah," he says, very disgruntled. "Once they become Danny's age they become very, very dangerous, and if they become sexually active, they don't know how to control it!" His words speed up in obvious fear over what might happen if Danny is allowed to party as he likes tonight, giving in to the nature of the beast.

"And, the sex gets out of control . . . then the beast . . . the beast takes control," he lets out a long sigh, his looks despaired, not wanting the words coming out of his mouth to be true, but he knows, as well as the other two do now, they are very true.

"Inside," Billy gestures over to Danny who is acting very erratically, shaking and running around the dance floor with a lot of sexual gestures. The kids around him are all watching, becoming a small audience. "He just wants more sex and then he wants to kill. It becomes an urge just like sex is, an instinct . . . a pure treacherous manifestation of dangerous desires and eventually the killing actually becomes the sex for him. The beast inside just wants more and more and he loses total control."

The boys listening to him shake their heads in disbelief, but they all know how true it is. Werewolves were no longer a legend to them, and they had not been ever since the coach had turned them.

"On a full moon you just go wild," Billy continued, his words speeding together as his eyes showed panic and excitement. "You don't have any control because you've killed humans and that's what you go after! Not the animals, like we do now! It feels so much better - you all know, the countless dreams we've had about just tearing somebody apart and it is almost orgasmic for us!"

His face saddens and his expression becomes a look of hurt. "After what happened six months ago, it's true; I have a hard time keeping it under control on the night of the full moon. I have to fight very hard to make the beast go after animals and not after humans . . . we all do! You can't tell me you don't! Everything is going to go to hell tonight!"

Billy is now very flustered, panicked, and hyperventilating as he leans back against the wall, sinking down to the floor. His skin is a pale gray, and he is perspiring profusely in dread.

Donovan feels frustrated as well, now realizing why he was warned so heavily about Morris. It is so obvious! Why couldn't he see it before?

"That's why Coach wanted us to stay away from Morris!" he shot out very loudly, grabbing the momentary attention of a few nearby students who were too intoxicated to really care. This conversation had now killed any buzz any of them might have had.

"He must go for the human kill."

Billy shakes his head in frustration, "No, I don't think so. Two months ago on the full moon, Morris and I completely tore apart a couple of deer; he seemed to enjoy it as much . . ."

"I don't care, Billy!" Donnie interrupted, grabbing his collar and pulling him up against the wall, pinning him tightly against it as he nervously shrieked in fear. Donnie snarled in frustration and spoke in a very angry, demonic voice, "I just want you to stay the fuck away from him, okay! He will hurt you!"

Suddenly, Donnie is pushed down to the ground as Billy falls right behind him, knocked down by a very angry Beth who had walked over toward them very drunk
.

"Bitch, you're on your period!" Somebody yells out from the crowd, but this doesn't phase her one bit as Beth proceeds to yell at Billy. Donnie stands up and steps back in shock getting a chuckle out of the situation.

"Can I ask what the hell happened to you?" she explodes in anger. "You were supposed to pick me up at six o'clock, babe! We are hardly going to be able to do any dancing now because of that stupid bonfire."

Propping himself back upon his feet and ignoring her attitude, he simply speaks to her with a glare, "Don't mess with me right now girl."

But he softens his prior words with, "I'll make it up to you after the bonfire is over tonight. We are going to sneak back up there after midnight. We will have some drinks and, babe; we'll have some fun then, okay?"

"Okay, sorry about knocking you over, I didn't mean to do that," she says in a shameful way as she hugs him tightly. He can't help but chuckle as he hugs her back. "But, you are going to dance at least one dance with me before we leave, right?" she asks, looking up at him with a very intoxicated face.

He smirks back, not wanting to dance, but agrees to anyway. "Okay, but I'm not very good at this dancing stuff."

She dons a smile so large you can hardly see the rest

of her face and she grabs his hand pulling him to the floor to start dancing. "You'll be just fine, let's go, baby!"

Beth and Billy head off to the dance floor and start dancing. Donovan and Donnie's moods are now lightened over the much needed comic relief. They can't help but laugh at her erratic behavior and how pussy-whipped the tough guy really is.

If it was a play, the cue would be exact, as Danny immediately interrupts Billy and Beth's fun, targeting Billy, whom he looks at with complete furiousness. Moving from one confrontation to another, Danny pulls his arm back and hits Billy square in the chest out of nowhere, knocking him backwards. He lands on the floor in a position resembling a crabwalk. Danny leans over and looms over him forebodingly.

"What's all this shit I hear you're telling these idiots, Billy! You asking me if I want to control it?"

Danny's demeanor is very controlled and confident as he gives a cocky and dominant look back and forth between Donovan and Billy, yelling, "Yeah, I'm not like you. You better watch out because I'm going to be the best quarterback this team has ever seen. The coach told me I was the best he's ever had!"

"We're not talking about sex, asshole!" Donovan sneered at Danny.

"God damn it!" he yells, getting very close to Donovan's face, but Donovan doesn't flinch. He returns his stare, challenging him; for a moment the two stare each other down.

"It wasn't like that with Coach. He taught me what my power really is good for and I don't know about you, Donovan, but I like the kill!"

The staring contest continues until Danny pushes him a little bit, forcing Donovan to break eye contact with him. Donovan quickly recovers, not standing down as

Danny had hoped.

"Listen to me you little shit. I'm the senior in this group, and you will do as you're told!"

Donovan grimaces and his body trembles as a very beastly look arrives upon his face. For a moment strands of hair begin to cover his arms, hands and face, quickly turning gray, his skin returns to normal, his clothes now covered with gray hairs that quickly tumble down to the floor beneath him.

"Do you understand me, douche?" he says harshly as Danny, who is taken back a bit, watches in fear. The rest of the crew and one of the school's freshmen look on in fear, motionless and not able to breathe for a few moments. His eyes as wide as his stoned little face can go, he turns with a series of sudden, out of place giggles. As he turns around to his friend, who is dancing amongst the crowd, unaware of the situation, he cries, "Oh my God!"

A stressed voice yells out in the direction of the crowd, "This stuff is great man! I'm trippin' balls now! Heh heh!"

The kid's laughter blends into the noise of the room as he disappears into the crowd, and Danny, who has now regained his composure during the interruption, yells back at Donovan.

"Donovan, don't threaten me, man. You can start numbering your days, fucker . . ."

A very foreboding look is quickly exchanged between the two, as Donovan walks away with a flaming sense of confidence, his middle finger held above his head as he assertively pushes his way through the crowd.

"I'll see you at the bonfire," Danny screams terrifyingly behind him as he pushes another student out of the way with complete and total vengeance. Donovan, himself, is not intimidated by his aggressor, yet turns around to Billy, who is concerned and starts to fall apart entirely. Perhaps a tear of horror would fall if he could muster it, but he is almost stationary as Donnie tries like hell to get Donovan to talk to him, but to no avail. Donovan sits down leaning his back against the wall in the corner of the gymnasium watching the kids make total fools out of themselves.

Amongst them, Donnie is dancing seductively with his date. Tommy, who has obviously had more than his share of the spiked punch, is dancing extremely seductively with everybody's date. It is definitely a comical moment that is needed by Donovan and all of the rest of the boys. Leave it to Tommy to get them laughing. Suddenly the music fades to a quick stop and an extremely familiar voice booms out over the speakers. "All right ladies and gentlemen, the last song of the night is about to play, and I plan to go out with a bang! So enjoy it everybody . . . especially Donovan Gray! Everybody give him a round of applause, he's over there, in the corner!"

It is Danny at the microphone, his voice booming across the gym, and, as the sound bounces off the walls and back into his ears, it also reverberates along his spine, causing a series of chills through his body. Danny had been cold and desolate and now he had the entire school cheering for him. The night had turned out to be a total disaster.

As the kids danced and the song "Revenge" lurched out of the speakers, Donovan couldn't muster the will to get up and join them. Instead he jumped up and ran out of the gymnasium in a fury, hopping over a series of drinks spilled across the dance floor, and slamming into the bathroom door, bursting it open and heading straight into the mirror.

Inside, the sound of a kid puking is heard in a stall,

and the cheers and laughter outside the bathroom are heavily muffled by the nearly soundproof door. Donovan looks at the amount of stress in his petrified face, yet surprisingly his hair is still combed to the side and his tuxedo looks rather nice. As much as he tries to cheer up, he just doesn't care.

He simply stares into his own dark eyes in the mirror. His eyes are getting lighter in color as he is still trying to fight back some of the change. For about five minutes he watches as his skin finishes returning to normal, the holes the hair follicles poked through shrinking, returning to their normal state, or at least close to it. Just as he is examining his skin, to his great fear, the holes quickly start to revert and grow larger. The beast within him trying to come out once again; his level of frustration is simply too high.

I will help you tonight, Donovan, a very deep, gurgled voice sounds in his head, but it feels as though it is his reflection itself speaking to him, looking deeply into his own eyes with a sinister expression. *It will be over soon.*

By this time, Donnie and Sally are already in the car. They are on their way up to the planned festivities, driving over the speed limit, of course, trailing behind a few other cars ahead of them. The car ahead of them, with two teens inside, swerves over to a little pit on the side of the road as someone tosses an empty beer can out the window. Simultaneously, out of the passenger's side someone pitches an empty glass bottle of liquor onto the narrow shoulder. Sally looks at him with wide eyes and a perky little smile, her breasts almost popping out of her dress as she leans in closer to Donnie. She places a hand on his thigh, and the other on his side, gripping him tightly.

"Hmm, I wonder what they're going to do, Donnie" she asks with a seductive twist, her eyes twinkling as she rubs her face on his, her nose pressing against his cheek. She slowly starts to unzip his pants. In a heavily breathy and frightened whisper he looks at her and says, "Wait," as he brushes her hand away from his crotch.

"Baby, Sally . . . I don't know if we should do this right now!"

Her face changes from one of complete seduction to a flash of concern, and then suddenly, she slides back into a confident demeanor. She looks at him as her hand is shoed away. She pulls the top of her dress down exposing her breasts. Trying not to look, he squares his head up with the windshield. From the corner of his eye, though, he can see her exposed body, teasing him, as he is teasing himself.

"I mean, this still might be considered sex, you know, and I can get in big trouble doing it the night before the game," he says to her, but her determination is very high and her body is very tempting to him, teasing him to indulge in the taboo.

"Donnie, no one is going to know, except you and me. Now enjoy every bit of it, baby," she says as she lifts up his shirt and starts to kiss his toned torso. Soon she is moving her mouth to all kinds of places and he is quickly becoming overwhelmed by extreme pleasure as she gets closer and closer to his private parts. It's been a long time since he has relieved himself, and he's really enjoying her kisses and caresses. His breathing is becoming heavier, and almost gurgled, struggling to keep control of the monster inside of him, which is fighting to come out.

CHAPTER 25

Coach Bloom walks into Jordan's room trying to keep up his spirits, yet he cannot help but show sorrow on his face. He knows just how much tonight means to Jordan, and how much he is missing out on. As he arrives at room number 401, where Jordan is making his recovery, Coach Bloom notices the door is slightly open. Somebody else must be paying him a visit. Assuming it is okay to make his entrance; Coach opens the door further to Jordan's hospital room and enters. He catches someone almost on top of Jordan, engaged in a very powerful kiss. It turns out to be Candace Walker, Jordan's older girlfriend.

Her lips are pressing against his, her tongue buried deep into his mouth. Coach is stunned at first and immediately turns away, a look of frustration covering his face. He immediately turns back at the couple and clears his throat, making his presence known. At the same time, he notices her hand down between Jordan's legs, on a notable bulge underneath a very thin, white hospital sheet.

Curt Bloom hurries over to the side of the bed where the button for the morphine pump is hanging on its designated hook as Candace steps away fearfully. He quickly presses the button in rapid succession; the machine however, only recognizes two of the presses and squirts a few pumps of morphine into Jordan, his erection quickly fading away.

"Hey, what are you doing?" Coach exclaims, his face flustered and becoming more and more frustrated as he looks at the girl.

"I was just simply taking care of him is all," she says, sounding very cynically innocent, and looking at him with eyes filled with complete malicious intention. It is obvious she is messing with him.

"Yes, I see that," he murmers softly in a disapproving tone. "Candace, that's your name, right?"

She shakes her head, affirming his assumption. "I think it's time for you to go home," suggests Coach Bloom.

She looks down at her feet in disappointment, knowing that her time with her injured boyfriend is over. She was simply trying to show Jordan some affection, and satisfy him as he wished, but the Coach assumed it was all her idea.

"Let Jordan get some sleep, okay?"

Ignoring his words, she heads over to the now irritated Jordan who lies on a fresh set of sheets and leans down by his side, softly kissing him on the lips for a moment longer. Her eyes become compassionate, realizing that she is leaving him alone on the night he is supposed to feel special.

"Baby, you want me to go home now?" she softly asks, her face saddened by the idea of leaving him alone.

"Yeah, it looks like he's just gonna fuck things up for us so I'll see you tomorrow . . . I love you . . ." the last of Jordan's words being slurred as the morphine starts to take effect. Candace looks at the coach with a glare, grabbing her stuff as she leaves the room with heavy footsteps.

As she takes her exit, Jordan interjects in as angry a fashion as his drugs will let him, "What are you doing here man? Why did you do that? I was feeling really good, and you just had to fuck it up! What - did you get jealous or something?"

Coach Bloom's face lights up with a surprised leer as he hears the jealousy statement. He shakes his head at it and smiles in laughter, "No, Jordan, not at all . . . and I know you were, but I also know that very shortly, you are going to start having a tremendous amount of pain."

Jordan, now very irritated with the coach, looks at him, disgust encompassing his face, as he shouts out to Coach Bloom, "I don't know what the fuck you're talking about, man!"

Trying to keep a calm face, he looks at Jordan, shakes his head and now, very seriously, starts talking to him. Coach Bloom's hand rests on the headboard.

"Listen to me, Jordan. I'm your friend; I'm not your enemy. You are starting to feel it already, aren't you?"

His voice is calm, slow, and somewhat comforting to Jordan; with the help of his morphine, he starts to listen, slightly panicked. His aggressiveness calms down immensely, yet tension is still present in his voice and upon his face, accentuating his already strong facial features. "What do you mean?" he shoots back in confusion.

"The pain," he repeats again, his voice soft yet stern as he replies to Jordan. "You know there's something different about you, don't you? You feel strange, unusual, and your recovery is unnaturally fast."

"Well, yeah, but that's just from these stupid drugs people keep putting in me! What the fuck is going on? You're so God damn creepy dude!"

"Jordan, you know how you got here, right? You know it was a werewolf," informs Bloom.

Jordan freezes in fear . . . his heart monitor starts to accelerate in its mono-tonic way as his breathing follows suit. He looks Coach Bloom straight in the eyes and stutters a bit. "N . . . no," he yells out, stunned and slightly surprised that the coach has suggested such a thing. After a long pause he looks at the coach and simply sighs. "No coach . . . there is no such thing . . ."

Slightly annoyed, as though he has had to do this many times before, he begins to rattle off what seems to be a prepared speech. "Jordan, let me tell you exactly how you're feeling at this very moment. You are feeling extremely aroused. You can actually smell the sex in the air because of all the stuff that's going on right now, and maybe you're even looking at me with a bit of excitement."

Jordan looks back at the coach with surprise and fear. "How, how do you know?" he stutters out.

Curt Bloom then continues to rattle off the symptoms. "These last few days you've been easily aggravated, people annoy you to almost no end, and you've had an immense hunger for next to raw meat. Thoughts of violence run through your mind and you can feel your body healing incredibly fast," Coach Bloom adds.

"What . . . what the fuck," he yells out in surprise his eyes wide, his head back toward the other side of the bed as far away from the coach as he can be while still remaining locked up in his hospital bed.

"Because, Jordan. I've been through it all; it's very hard!" He speaks now with a bit of pain buried under a tone of sympathy, as he reflects on his own transformation. "I understand that, Jordan. There's nothing that you can do to change back . . . I know about this town's secrets . . . I was sent here to help you and the others make it through this difficult time."

"Oh my God, this is crazy," Jordan takes several deep breaths, the morphine stopping him from inhaling fully. "Coach, I don't know if I am just sick or if the pain I'm feeling is from my injuries or what . . ." He rests his head against his pillow in a forced comfort by the drug inside him that courses through his veins as he speaks.

"But I do know one thing you are right about," he agrees, as his hips start to move forward slightly. "I'm so horny right now . . . and I don't know what to do because . . . because . . ."

His breathing escalates, becoming faster and deeper, his skin paling, and then gains a thickly saturated gray composure. Coach Bloom knows what is happening and quickly rushes over to the side of his bed depressing the button at an incredibly fast rate. A look of extreme worry comes over Curt and he audibly prays that his actions will help the poor boy, instead of killing him. His words indistinguishable from one another as he loudly prays, trying to stop the transformation.

"Jordan, Jordan! Can you hear me?" He shouts down at the shaking body on the bed, hoping that the drug and a familiar voice calling out his human name may retard or stop the transformation. "Jordan, I'm doing this for your own good kid!"

As though possessed, Jordan's hips throw themselves up in the air as his back arches and he flips around, standing on his feet and hands. His wounds rapidly healing over as they rip themselves open from his instantaneous movements. Peaks of newly grown hair start to shine through his skin. He tries to scream out in pain, but only air passes through his throat. Fearfully, Coach presses the button three more times, and the tiny hissing sounds of three more morphine shots are applied to him. Within seconds of this infusion of drugs Jordan's body falls back onto the bed, his sheets blood-soaked from his fresh wounds. His breathing quickly goes silent and his heart monitor as well.

Coach stays for a few minutes to reassure himself that

Jordan's vitals stay up, and then he softly pats him on the arm and begins to exit the room.

As Coach Bloom walks out of the room, Dr. Marcus comes in, giving Curt a very heavy look of concern. "Hey, Doc . . . he started to get a little crazy there so I gave him five squirts of morphine. He needs to sleep through this tonight."

The doctor grows concerned and sighs heavily. "You knew it would be very hard on him to deal with this tonight, in this condition. You forced his body to shut down, didn't you? I'll put some IV fluids in him and a catheter, also a low dose of Naloxone . . . shit, I was worried this would happen."

He pauses in a moment of self-reflection and begins to rub his hands together, very naturally stressed. "You will help him make it through this time?" the doctor inquires.

"Of course," the coach replies. "That's why you guys brought me here . . . to fix things. The only problem is, I'm not sure I can."

A heavy silence is exchanged between the two; void of noise filled with absolutely nothing but deep concern for their town and everybody in it. The doctor sighs and places his hand on Curt's shoulder.

"Well, we've sure gotten ourselves into one hell of a mess right now. How the hell did you guys let Coach Miller go this far?" Curt asks as the doctor removes his hand from Curt, and backs away cautiously, pointing a trembling finger at him.

"Did you . . . was it you that had him killed?"

With a slight grin and a reassuring look on his face he says, "No, Dr. Marcus, I didn't."

As if a spell had come over him, the doctor immediately relaxes. That was all he needed to hear on the matter, and strangely, he feels much more comfortable around Curt Bloom.

"No, Doc, I'm still trying to figure out who did it. Coach Bloom crossed his arms in discomfort, pondering the very difficult thought.

"As far as letting Miller go this far, I'm surprised they let him do it at all. It's crazy; somebody obviously owed him a very large favor."

With newly generated energy, Bloom spoke out excitedly, "And, nobody suspected a damn thing until about three weeks ago when that kid, Danny, started fucking things up. Coach had convinced him he is nothing but the next best, biggest quarterback of any football team ever in existence . . . it went to the damn kid's head."

Doctor Marcus shakes his head in agreement to the statement and gave out a very troubled sigh. "Well, Fuller called me a few weeks back and told me that he witnessed some very bizarre sexual behavior in that kid . . . even for a kid that had been turned. I went to talk to Miller and he got all defensive!" The doctor scowled at the memory of the confrontation.

"I knew he was up to no good! I asked how many other kids he had turned and the bastard just smiled at me and became very reserved."

Again, there was a pause in the room; both were very concerned and deeply worried at Miller's behavior. Doctor Marcus filled the void with the rustling of his pocket as he dug through it and pulled out a long blade. He handed it over to the coach who looked at it with a level of resentment, yet acceptance, before Dr. Marcus retracted his offering, and asking a question.

"Bloom, you're going up to that celebration tonight, right?"

"Yes sir," he responded with admiration for Dr. Marcus's position of staying far away from the potential danger erupting in the bonfire area.

"All right, Bloom, take this." Once again, he extends his hand to the coach who, with a sense of pride, takes the blade from his hand, and firmly holds the elegant silver dagger in his hand. The blade is incredibly sharp and polished. The handle is crafted of silver as well, and bound in thick, fine leather. The tip contains a skull and pointed ears, with sharp, finely pointed fangs extending outward.

"I always carry it with me now that we have him here . . . I would like to supply everybody here with one, too but you know as well as I, that it would raise too many questions."

He continues with a look of sadness, "You may need it tonight. If anyone gets out of control, put an end to it. It has to stop now. We cannot jeopardize everything over a few rogue boys."

Coach Bloom looks at Dr. Marcus with a look of honest concern on his face as he reassures, "I'll do my best to control the whole situation. I truly feel there is more to the circumstances than just what Coach Miller created."

Dr. Marcus turns and goes into Jordan's hospital room.

CHAPTER 26

The sheriff walks in and looks at Sandy. You can see a sincere look of concern on his face as he wonders how tonight is really going to go. He is scared that maybe, just maybe, he has given too much responsibility to Cooper, more responsibility than he and the other two deputies can really handle. So he looks over at Sandy and says, "Sandy, get Cooper on the radio; I want to know if they are all in position for tonight."

Sandy has been with the sheriff as his personal secretary and deputy for over 20 years. She knows him well and she knows that look on his face, that pensive look of concern, wondering if he's made the right decision, if what he's doing is right. She was with him when he lost his wife two years ago in the car accident and then six months ago when he lost Brittany. She knows he is starting to doubt himself, and doubt his decisions. She looks over at him and says, "You got it, Sheriff."

Sandy is sitting at the desk calling out to Deputy Cooper on the radio. "This is the Sheriff's Office to Cooper, are you there? Over."

"Yeah, this is Cooper," returns the voice over the radio. "What's up, Sandy?"

Sandy tells him what the sheriff asked her to find out. "The sheriff wants to know if you're all set up for tonight."

Cooper calls back on the radio and confirms, "Yeah, everything looks good."

Cooper asks Sandy, "Ask the sheriff if he plans on coming out here himself tonight?"

Sandy looks over at the sheriff with a smile on her face as she says to Cooper, "Will do, Cooper."

The sheriff is sitting at his desk and he looks back at Sandy, giving her a stern look with a little smile as Sandy says to him, "Did you hear that Sheriff?"

The sheriff looks at her, shakes his head and says, "Yes, I did. Let Cooper know that if I decide to head out there I don't know if I'll give him a warning or not, so he needs to be on his toes; we don't want the big bad werewolf to come bite him in the ass tonight."

The sheriff looks at Sandy with a look that says 'Go on; tell him.' Sandy radios back, "Cooper, the sheriff says that he may or may not show up, so stay on your toes tonight."

The sheriff looks over at Sandy and smiles. Sandy looks back and shrugs her shoulders and smiles back. "You didn't actually think I was going to say it the way you told me, did you?"

The sheriff looks at Sandy and shakes his head, frustrated as hell and says, "Heaven forbid anybody does anything exactly the way that I tell them to do it."

Up at the bonfire, Cooper is very frustrated and is shaking his head as he looks over at the other deputy and says," Jesus Christ, sometimes I just don't know if the sheriff really trusts me."

The other deputy, looks at Cooper and says to him, "Come on, Cooper, we all trust you." He smiles without Cooper seeing it.

Morris is inside his gas station getting himself ready to go out tonight and doing odds and ends when the screen door opens and in walks Robert with no shirt on.

Robert is very good-looking for a young boy. He's been in Morris's gas station many times; he walks with a swagger, and has blonde hair and blue eyes. At 16 years old, he thinks he's really tough. He walks around the store looking at the merchandise as Morris keeps a very close eye on him.

He walks up to one of the glass cases and sees the shiny silver dagger, similar to the one Dr. Marcus gave to Coach Bloom.

He continues to look around. As Robert catches Morris looking the other way out the screen door, he grabs a couple of candy bars and stuffs them into the pocket of his shorts. He then realizes that by sticking the candy in his pocket it makes him have a bulge in front of his shorts that looks much larger than his manhood. He really is afraid Morris might notice it, so he takes one of the candy bars out of his pocket and actually puts it down inside of his shorts. Then he smiles because he's happy with the way it makes him appear to have a much bigger penis.

Morris turns and walks back to the counter. Morris can't help but notice the large bulge in Robert's shorts that makes it look like he has a much bigger penis than he really has. Morris smiles and knows exactly what he has done.

Robert walks around looking at things until he's near the door. He goes to open it and Morris turns, looks at him and yells, "Hey!"

Robert turns with a scared look on his face, afraid that Morris has figured out that he's taken some candy bars. Morris looks back at him and smiles with a broken-toothed smile and says, "Be sure to stop back again."

At the same time, a car that has just finished fueling up outside drives away from the gas station. Robert walks out of the building, heading over toward the back of the gas station. He looks behind him to make sure Morris isn't following him. He walks back a ways into the woods.

Robert ponders about what a stupid fuck Morris is and starts to laugh out loud as he pulls one of the candy bars out of his pocket, looks at it and opens it with a smile. He takes a huge bite and starts chewing as he simultaneously hears something in the woods. He turns and looks around asking, "Who's there?" He waits a minute, hears nothing more, and decides that no one must be there so he continues to chew on his candy bar.

At the same time, he starts playing with the other candy bar in his shorts pocket, stroking it as though it's his cock. He starts grinding his hips in the air. All of a sudden he hears a snarl and a growl. He spins around again and looks into the woods still not seeing anything, and after a few more seconds of chewing his candy bar he gets a very weird look on his face. He looks down at the candy bar and sees that there are little white maggots crawling all over the candy bar and onto his hands. The maggots are squirming and crawling around on his hands, oozing from the candy bar and wrapper. He throws the candy bar down in disgust and shakes the maggots off of his hand, spitting out the candy bar bite in his mouth. As he spits it out he says, "Oh, my God," and continues to spit out pieces of the candy bar. The maggots are crawling all over the chocolate bar on the ground and he spits more out as he says, "That is fucking sick."

Robert hears the snap of a branch that cracks somewhere in the distance. He spins around again and searches quickly for the source worried he might be caught for stealing. He yells out once again, "Who's there?" When no one answers, Robert tries to become macho but fear takes over his face as he yells out, "That's what I thought! You're just a pussy." He then pulls the other candy bar out of his pants, opens it up and examines it closely. When he realizes it looks fresher than the other bar, he takes a nice big bite.

He smiles and pops another bite into his mouth, chewing quickly and swallowing hard. At that moment, a werewolf jumps out of the woods and slashes at him. In one quick motion, the werewolf slashes Robert's neck open. Robert stands there briefly immobilized and then his head tilts back, revealing a wide open neck cavity. Blood and the partially chewed candy bar squirt from his esophagus and the open wound.

He slumps to the ground, motionless, next to the maggoty candy bar mess.

Back at the store, Morris is getting himself ready to go out for the night. Smiling with memories of the day, he's whistling a tune that's quite upbeat. He walks over to the glass case, opening it and taking out the silver dagger. He smiles mischievously as he slides it into his back pocket and mumbles to himself, "Oh, we are going to party tonight."

CHAPTER 27

Back in the hills above the bed & breakfast the high school kids are showing up for the much anticipated bonfire. As the bonfire festivities begin, everybody is whooping and hollering and having a good time.

The music is playing loudly and the kids start to roast marshmallows over a hot fire pit. Some kids are dancing. A case of beer gets popped up and the cans start getting passed around.

Donovan is dancing with Jane. They're laughing and having a great time.

Billy shows up with Beth. Beth is all over him. Billy is kissing her very sensually; she is being very sexually aggressive with him, not only kissing him passionately but smoothly sliding her hand down the inside of his pants and playing with his penis. It is obvious that Billy is becoming a wreck. Beth has a smile on her face, forecasting a great time for both of them. Billy is struggling to maintain himself, determined not to lose the battle with the monster already so early in the evening.

Donnie and Sally show up. Donnie has a look of excitement and pleasure on his face.

Donnie runs over to Donovan, grabs him and pulls him aside for a chat. Donnie is as excited as a young child being granted a toy that he has wanted for many years. He reaches out and grabs Donovan, speaking with delight into Donovan's ear he says, "Dude, oh my God.

Sally gave me the best blow job in the car on the way up here and, dude, I controlled it." He reaches up to receive a high five from Donovan.

Donovan looks at him with an expression of surprise, excitement and happiness. He cannot believe what he is hearing and says, "What, are you serious? You controlled it?"

Donnie looks at him with a touch of embarrassment, but embarrassment in a good way. He's accomplished what they wanted to accomplish for so long. Does this mean the end of not being able to have sex with a girl?

"Yeah, man," Donnie laughs slightly. "It was . . . it was hard. I thought I was losing it at one point, but then I had this unbelievable orgasm without any warning, and I shot all of it in her mouth."

Donovan's eyes light up with glee and excitement. "You're shitting me," he laughs.

Donnie grins with pride and happiness like they have just accomplished the state championship alone between the two of them. "No, I am NOT kidding. Sally got so pissed off. But then she kissed me and told me it was really good. She also told me I owed her one."

Donovan thought for a moment, looked back over at Donnie and grabbed him tightly on the arm. He looked into his eyes with love and admiration, and thought of all that they had both been through together saying, "Dude, if you can control it, I know I can. I was actually thinking of not doing anything tonight, but now, yeah, it's going to be a good night, Donnie boy."

Donnie, in his excitement over hearing this latest development, reaches over and gives Donovan a big bear hug and then pushes him back and looks him in the eyes, "Just remember, Donovan, you cannot lose the thought, you are in control."

Donovan looks at Donnie and shakes his head in

acknowledgement and smiles that reassuring smile only Donovan has and says, "Don't worry, I am in control."

Back at the bonfire, the music is playing loudly. The kids are dancing, drinking beer, eating marshmallows and having a great time. Most of the kids, by this time, have smoked a lot of weed, drunk a lot of beer, and removed a lot of clothing. Most of the boys have stripped down to their underwear wanting to show off what they have in their boxers.

With all the drinking, partying and dancing going on between the boys and girls the smell of sex begins to permeate the air. Oh how the smell of sex can just drive a poor little werewolf insane. Morris can smell it; he knows this will be a night for a great party and he can hardly wait for it to start.

The kids are kissing and a lot of heavy petting is going on amongst them. The kids, wrapped up in their own revelry, vaguely remember Deputy Cooper and the other deputies are there chaperoning. As Cooper is surveying the area out of nowhere, it seems, Coach Bloom walks up to him.

Deputy Cooper looks shocked because he hadn't see Bloom anywhere around, and all of a sudden he turns and Bloom is there standing in front of him.

"What are you doing here?" he inquires.

The coach looks over at Deputy Cooper and smiles and nods his head sharing, "I just came by to check on the kids and make sure things are going okay because this is a school condoned event. We have some responsibility here and since I'm the new kid on the block - here I am."

Deputy Cooper looks at him with a tinge of jealousy and says, "Yeah, well I'm supposed to be up here keeping an eye on things, but I have to turn a blind eye to all the things that I'm seeing down there."

Coach Bloom responds, "Deputy, there's been a lot of

stuff happening here lately. I think the sheriff wants to give the kids a bit of latitude to enjoy themselves . . . to cut loose a little."

The deputy shakes his head, disagreeing with him. "Damn it, Coach, I am a deputy sheriff and I should be stopping some of the things that I'm watching go on down there! I don't understand the sheriff's mindset right now!"

Coach Bloom smiles, "Well, I think I do. I think he's made the right choice. You have to remember that he was forced into allowing this bonfire to happen in the first place. Just keep your eyes open and make sure that nobody does anything to hurt anybody else, and make sure you prevent anybody from drinking so much that they shouldn't get behind the wheel of a car, okay?"

With a sarcastic look on his face Cooper says, "That's what I've been told."

Meanwhile back down at the bonfire, a couple of girls are starting to get pretty rowdy. One of the girls takes her shirt off and then her bra and a few of the other girls follow suit. The boys start whooping and hollering and the party gets even crazier.

The sheriff walks up and stands there with his arms folded and looks down at the bonfire where all the kids wearing very little to no clothing are in close proximity. Many of the boys are fully naked and some of the girls are pretty close to being fully undressed. The sheriff observes one group of kids who have shifted over to the side of the bonfire, engaging in a sex orgy of sorts, boys with boys, girls with girls, boys with girls. And in the dark nearby, Morris smells it all and just can't wait for the party to begin.

The sheriff has an angry look on his face as he yells, "Where's Cooper?" The second deputy looks around for him, doesn't see him, and says to the sheriff, "He was walking right around there sir," pointing over to an area nearby. All of a sudden Deputy Cooper comes into view from that same direction. Cooper is looking around the corner as he's walking toward the sheriff with a look of surprise on his face and exclaims, "Well, Sheriff, you came up!"

The sheriff has a very sullen and sad look on his face, "Cooper, what the hell is going on down there?"

Deputy Cooper looks at the sheriff in surprise and retorts, "They are partying, Sheriff."

The sheriff shakes his head with a look of disgust, "I can see that, Cooper! I told you to let them have a good time. I didn't tell you to condone a freaking orgy!"

Deputy Cooper looks very frustrated, almost angry, when he meekly replies, "You said to let them party, Sheriff, and to turn a blind eye."

Now the sheriff is just more frustrated; he smiles and shakes his head, "Jesus Christ, Cooper. Yes on the little things like a little weed or a little beer, not a fucking kegger and an orgy. Now get down there with the other two deputies and tell the kids to put their clothes back on. It's time for them to go home."

Deputy Cooper puts his hands up in the air wondering what the hell he has done wrong, "Shit, Sheriff, I'm just trying to do what you told me to do."

The sheriff looks sternly at Cooper and says in a demanding voice, "Cooper!"

Deputy Cooper throws his hands up in the air again in frustration, "Okay, Sheriff. Let's go down there and break up this party."

Sheriff looks at Cooper with a smile on his face and says, "Cooper be nice; nobody needs to get hurt. Nobody needs to be arrested. Do you understand me, Cooper?"

With a look of disappointment on his face Cooper agrees, "Yes, Sheriff, I understand you. I will just send them home."

Coach Bloom walks up to the sheriff with a smile on his face almost laughing as he leans over and whispers to the sheriff, "He is one funny guy, Sheriff."

"No Bloom," the Sheriff sneers back at Bloom, "He is a moron!" Coach Bloom looks at the sheriff, pats him on the back, and announces, "Well, I think the night was pretty uneventful. And you're a pretty good guy to let these kids party like this tonight. I think they really needed it."

The sheriff looks at Bloom, gives him a smile, nodding his head as he grimaces, "Yeah, that's what they say. I'm just a fucking, sweetheart." Just then, Tommy who is completely naked and obviously extremely drunk sees the sheriff and with his hands stretched out all the way from his sides screams, "Hey, Sheriff, this was the best fucking night of my life and you are the most awesome guy ever, love you man," in that little Kentucky slang of his. The Sheriff looks at Bloom and they both start to laugh.

Down at the bonfire Deputy Cooper is walking around with the other two deputies telling everybody to put their clothes back on and encouraging them to go home. He offers rides home to anyone who has had too much to drink, wanting them to arrive home safely.

In unison, the kids all start talking back to Deputy Cooper yelling that they don't want to go home and some choice words are heard in the bargain.

Looking down from atop the hill, Morris is sitting on an old stump, surveying the area and thinking to himself, *Oh, tonight is going to be a wonderful night. How many of you are going to sneak back up here? I'll be here waiting. We'll have our own little party.*

Back down at the bonfire most of the kids are starting to do what the deputies have asked them to do and put their clothes on. It's a hot 84 degree night with the bonfire making it even hotter in the area. Donovan is trying to encourage the other guys to listen to the deputies as he is getting dressed. He selectively tells some kids it is time to pack up and go home, while secretly reminding others that they are planning on sneaking back up later that night to continue where they left off.

He reminds the guys who are starting to put the fire out to just bring it down to a small fire so that when they come back up later, they can light the fire up again.

The kids start piling into their cars, driving off one by one. Donovan pulls Elliot, Billy, Donnie and Danny together. "Okay, you guys, remember, an hour from now, we come back up. And, Danny, are you bringing Sammy back up with you?"

Danny looks at Donovan with a questioning look in his eye and confirms, "That's my plan."

Donovan looks back over at Danny with a stern look on his face, "Danny, don't fuck with us. The only reason you've been brought into this group is because the coach turned you without talking to us, all because he liked you. Now we have to look out for you."

Danny gets really angry, "Look, dude, whatever was between me and the coach, that was between me and Coach. Now that he's dead, it's just me, and you've got to deal with it."

Donovan gets pissed, anger raging in his eyes, "All I'm saying, Danny, is we don't want any trouble tonight. We just want to have fun and party. Do you understand?"

Danny smiles with a smartass look on his face. "Hey, party is my middle name. And, that's what I plan on doing tonight."

Elliot becomes really angry, his eyes starting to turn a little bit yellow, which happens just before the werewolf starts to take over. "Danny, do not ruin anything tonight;

there's enough shit going on around here and people are going to find out and then it's all going to go to hell," snarls Elliot, with a little bit of werewolf appearing in his persona. Danny stumbles back with a look of fear in his eyes as Donovan begins to leave the bonfire area.

"Okay, let's go! We will all meet up at the diner in one hour. If anybody's watching, they will think we are just going to go to the diner to hang out and get something to eat. Then, when we know its okay to come back up here, we will really party boys."

Donovan looks over at Danny. "Danny, you've got to be very careful. Are you sure you can control it?"

Danny smiles and says, "Remember what I said; ask me if I want to control it." Donovan just shakes his head and snarls, glaring his canine teeth back at Danny as he backs off. They get in their cars and leave for the diner.

The sheriff is standing with Deputy Cooper on the top of the hill. He looks over at Cooper, "Looks like they're all starting to leave and doing what they are supposed to do. It looks like it was a good night. So, I guess I gotta say it; 'Good job, Cooper.'"

Deputy Cooper, with a look of shock and pride on his face smiles slyly at the sheriff, "Well, thank you, Sheriff."

Sheriff smiles back, "Now, I want you and one of the deputies to hang around here for about an hour. Make sure no one decides to come back and pull the double cross on us. You understand that, Cooper?"

"Yes sir, Sheriff, I do. If any of those kids come back, do I get to arrest them then?"

The sheriff stops, turning to look back at Cooper, "Yes, yes, Cooper, yes, you do and, you call me if that happens."

Cooper gets a big smile on his face and shakes his head at the sheriff. The sheriff turns and walks toward his car. He stops and looks around and glancing back down at the bonfire, remarks, "I don't know what it is, Cooper, but something is telling me that this night is not over."

"Sheriff, I think it's all going to be just fine and I'll stay up here for an hour and make sure that it stays that way. Good night, Sheriff."

"Good night, Cooper." The sheriff gets into his car, starts the ignition and takes off. Cooper is watching him as he drives away. He shakes his head and whispers aloud. "There ain't nothing going to happen except me not getting enough sleep."

CHAPTER 28

Back at the diner all the kids are pulling into the parking lot and running into the diner. They squish into a booth, some ordering food and others just a drink. Mr. Fuller is there and thinking of calling in a few more workers because of how busy it is.

Donovan, Jane, Donnie and Sally are sitting at one booth while Billy and Beth enter the swivel door and go to another booth. Sally comes over to where Jane is sitting. "Hey, Jane, I'm going to go to the bathroom. You wanna come with me?"

Jane looks up and smiles, "Sure, let's go."

Donnie looks at the two girls and with a fatherly tone says, "Don't be telling wild stories to each other while you are gone." Donnie smiles at Sally. She laughs and smiles back at him as they get up and walk away.

Once in the bathroom Sally can't wait to tell Jane exactly what's going on. "So are you excited about going back up and spending the night with the boys?"

"Yes, I am. Donovan and I haven't had sex yet, even though I've given him every opportunity. So, tonight it's supposed to happen. I was starting to think he might be gay."

Sally smiles and shakes her head, "Yeah, I know. It's been really weird. Nothing has happened with Donnie and me until tonight."

Jane looks at Sally and corrects her, "Well, you mean until later tonight . . .right?"

"Something has already happened," says Sally, "one hell of a blow job. The little shit didn't tell me he was getting ready to orgasm and he blew all of it in my mouth. I thought I was going to choke to death, there was so much."

Jane looks at Sally as she is washing her hands, with a smile on her face, "Are you kidding me? He didn't even warn you?"

Sally shakes her head, "No, he said he had no warning; he didn't realize he was going to orgasm at that moment."

Jane starts to laugh almost uncontrollably, then pulls it together, "Oh, I would be so mad. Donovan better not do that to me tonight."

"Yeah, well I gotta tell you, I don't know how many blow jobs you've done, but it tasted so sweet, it was actually good."

Jane looked really surprised, "Are you kidding me? It's always so salty. Yuck."

"I know, it normally is, but not Donnie's. I actually hope he does it again tonight," she smiles and laughs. Jane smiles and laughs back, "You, oh, you are sooooo bad!"

Back at the booth Donovan and Donnie are talking to Elliot. Donnie questions Elliot, "So, are you guys ready to head up?"

"Yeah, we are, but I don't think we should all go at the same time. If someone sees us they will know something's going on and we will get caught."

"Yeah, I think you're right. Let's do this. Jane and I will leave in just a few minutes when the girls get back from the bathroom and then about every 15 to 20 minutes one couple leaves. And while Jane and I are waiting for you guys to show up, we will set things up."

Donnie shakes his head agreeing, "That's a great idea.

Let's not start the bonfire until after all of us are there. That way it'll be at least another hour and no one will be around thinking something is going on."

Just then the girls return to the table.

Donovan smiles at them and announces, "Jane and I will leave now. Donnie, you and Sally leave in about 20 minutes and you tell all the rest of them to leave in that same timeframe about every 20 minutes."

Donovan and Jane leave the diner, climb into his car and take off for the woods. When they arrive, they set up a camp and tent.

A werewolf is slowly and quietly moving through the woods. He comes up to a thicket of branches that he slowly spreads apart, eyeing Donovan and Jane at the camp. Jane sits next to the fire eating a roasted marshmallow.

Donovan sits down next to her, "Did you save any for me?" Jane reaches into a plastic bag and throws him a marshmallow. He catches it, picks up a stick and spears the marshmallow on it.

He holds it over the fire. He leans back and looks up, "See, it's beautiful out here at night, so peaceful."

Jane looks around. "It's alright, but I'm interested in more than just looking at the stars." Donovan looks at her and smiles. Jane reaches over and snuggles up to him. She slowly and seductively moves her hand down to his crotch and starts to unbutton his jeans. She looks up and gives him a kiss, opening his pants and sliding her hand inside of his underwear.

Donovan looks surprised and excited at the same time, "What are you doing?"

Jane smiles at him, "We are alone. I think it's time for me to give you a little bit of pleasure before you give me a lot of pleasure."

Donovan looks at Jane with a mixture of excitement

and fear, not sure if this is what he should or should not do, but in the moment he can't say 'no.' "Okay. I think that sounds like a fantastic plan," he agrees.

Jane runs her hands underneath Donovan's shirt lightly touching his chest. With both hands she lifts his shirt right up over the top of his head. She then slowly kisses his chest from the top of his neck all the way down through his belly button right to the top of his crotch.

She stops momentarily and looks up at him and smiles. She puts her head down between his legs and starts performing oral sex on him. Donovan has a look of excitement on his face. He all of a sudden realizes that he is struggling with the beast inside of him. He shakes his head a couple of times as if to say 'no, I am in control.'

He puts his hands on top of Jane's head, experiencing pleasure like he's never experienced before, while trying to control the monster, trying to make him understand that he is the one that is in control. His eyes start to turn yellow. He is starting to lose control. He tries to push Jane's head away so he can try to regain control and all of a sudden he reaches climax with no warning, just like it happened to Donnie. He releases a large amount of semen on his pants and all over her face and her dress.

Donovan has such an extreme look of joy and total satisfaction on his face when he smiles and says, "Oh my God, baby. I am so sorry. I had absolutely no warning at all, but it was so incredibly awesome!"

Jane looks at him with cum all over her mouth, her eyebrows and in her hair, trying to wipe it out and accusing, "I cannot believe you did that! Sally said that Donnie did exactly the same thing to her tonight and now you did it to me. Is this some little game that you and Donnie are playing?"

Donovan looks at her with a pleased look on his face, trying to make her understand. "No, not at all. It's just, I guess it's been a long time. I mean, you know how Donnie and I are really into our sports and what it means. I'm sorry, baby. Really, I am."

Jane smiles at him with love in her eyes. "I don't care. But I do have to say one thing, Sally was right. Maybe because you haven't done anything in so long, your cum tastes good, really good!"

Donovan caresses Jane and gives her a big kiss getting some of his own semen in his mouth as he smiles and looks at her and shares, "Wow, that is kind of sweet isn't it? I have to agree it's pretty good." Jane just looks at him as Donovan predicts, "Come on, baby, I promise I will make you feel really good tonight."

At that moment Donnie and Sally show up at the campground. Donnie looks around and has a big smile on his face when he realizes that he's just walked in on Donovan and Jane messing around. "Well, now, what have you two been up to? Did we start to party a little bit already?"

Donnie looks at both Donovan and Jane and can see that something has just happened sexually between them because Donovan's pants are off and he has that 'I just had sex' look on his face. As he smirks and looks away, Donnie spies little white stains on Donovan's boxers and all over Jane's dress.

Sally looks over at Jane and smiles, "Oh, no, I would say that maybe someone has learned for herself now." As she laughs, Jane looks up at her with a glare and then breaks out laughing.

Donnie and Donovan look at each other and smile and Donovan questions, "Jesus, you girls tell each other everything, don't you?"

CHAPTER 29

Back at the bed and breakfast, Curt and Judy are in bed together chatting. They have been there for a while, getting ready to go to sleep.

Judy affirms to Curt, "I'm really glad everything went well tonight, honey. I was pretty worried."

Curt smiles at her, "I told you everything was going to be okay. I just needed to go up there and make sure everything was fine." Curt reaches over and starts to give Judy a very passionate kiss, wanting to start making love again, when all of a sudden he stops and sits up straight.

Judy is stumped and looks at Curt with concern, "Curt, what's wrong?"

"I'm not sure, but I think something's going on out there," he replies.

"What? What are you talking about?"

Curt looks concerned and sits up even straighter in bed, "I've got to go. Oh my God, those kids are back."

"What are you talking about? What the hell are you talking about, Curt?"

Curt hops out of bed and starts to pull his boxer shorts on. He's in such a hurry he reaches over and grabs his pants and shirt and runs out of the room.

Curt looks back at Judy with a very stern look, "If I'm not back in two hours, you call the sheriff."

"Call the sheriff? Curt, what is wrong?"

Curt shakes his head, "Nothing. I hope, but if I'm

wrong, it could be very bad."

Curt exits the house, running down the porch with his clothes in his hands. He stops, looks briefly at his clothes, and throws them over on the side of the porch. He then looks up toward where the bonfire was earlier and he starts to run.

As he is running, he transforms into a werewolf.

Back at the bonfire all of the kids have arrived. Donovan and Jane, Donnie and Sally, Billy and Beth, Elliot and Rhonda and Danny and Sammy are all sitting around the campfire laughing and talking about how they managed to pull this one off. The boys are all in their boxers. Beth has her blouse off with just her bra on. Rhonda has her blouse and bra off exposing her breasts. See I told you everything was going to be fine said Donovan. He looks around at the other guys and especially Billy and says, "Billy, look at this night its perfect with the stars, what more could you ask for? Being here with these gorgeous ladies, right girls?" The girls all get a smile on their face and giggle.

Beth looks at Billy, "It's a perfect night for my last night here, tomorrow by this time I will be on my way to Paris for six months." She sensuously looks at Billy and starts to tickle his belly; he laughs, reaches over and gives her a big kiss. She pushes a marshmallow into Billy's mouth. Billy grabs her and becomes much more affectionate telling her how much he loves her in front of everyone. All the boys look at each other and smile.

Jane is becoming very passionate with Donovan when she tells him, "Donovan, I think maybe it's time that you keep that promise to me."

"Okay, right after I finish my marshmallow."

Jane looks at him sideways thinking, *are you kidding me?* "Fine, whatever," Jane turns and walks away. She stops after a few steps, "Yeah, good luck with that marshmallow."

Donovan looks at his stick, "Shit." He sits up and lifts his stick out of the bonfire. The marshmallow is completely black.

Back up on the hilltop, Morris is spying on the scene. He stands up from the stump on which he was sitting. He looks down where the bonfire is and the kids are sitting around laughing and talking.

Morris has a mean leer on his face, thinking, *I think it's show time.* Morris transforms into a werewolf and starts down toward the bonfire.

Back at the bonfire, Donovan looks at the burnt marshmallow on his stick, smiles, looks back up again at Jane walking away and tosses the stick and the marshmallow into the fire. He immediately hops up and goes toward her as they enter the tent together.

Elliot and Rhonda have already snuck over to the other side of the tent. Elliott starts kissing Rhonda passionately. He stops and he looks deep into her eyes, he wants this night so very much, he wants to experience the ultimate of sexual pleasure. But Elliot is questioning himself, can he control the beast inside and what happens if he can't? He could hurt Rhonda if not kill her, and that fear becomes very strong for Elliott. "I just don't think this is right, as much as I want you and want to have sex tonight, what if we lose that game tomorrow. We will all be questioning ourselves - was that moment of sexual gratification worth taking away what everybody has wanted all year - to win the state championship." Rhonda, being one of the cheerleaders and very supportive of the football team, looks at Elliott with a loving, passionate look on her face, "There will always be another night and I will love you even more." Elliott says, "Let's sneak out of here, no one will ever know." Rhonda smiles and shakes her head yes.

Donnie and Sally follow Donovan and Jane into the same tent.

Billy and Beth have a sleeping bag right next to the fire. They're kissing and enjoying each other's company, both mostly naked.

Danny and Sammy are on the opposite side of the bonfire, inside of Danny's sleeping bag. Sammy is underneath Danny with her breasts exposed. Danny is kissing her passionately and grinding her, with a little up-and-down motion, very aggressively. Danny has a look of total sexual pleasure on his face. He starts sweating profusely while trying to struggle with his beast inside. The sexual pleasure and the anticipation of a sexual kill are more and more powerful as Danny is fully engaged sexually with Sammy. Sammy is totally enjoying the aggressive sexual experience of having Danny on top of her, grunting and grinding and getting more and more excited. He is rocking back and forth, becoming more rough and forceful with Sammy. Sammy starts to beg him to settle down a bit, "Don't be so rough."

Danny just looks at her and smiles. The yellow in his eyes starts to glow. Sammy sees it, asking, "What's going on with you? You're being too rough, and you're hurting me."

Danny continues becoming rougher with greater sexual pleasure as the monster starts to transform. As his teeth become sharp, the hair starts to grow on the backs of his hands, as does all of the hair on his body and head. The hair starts to completely manifest itself around his head as his ears start to stretch out and become pointed like that of a dog. His hands start to transform from fingers to long claws. His upper chest starts to expand as his hips pop out and adjust into the back legs of a wolf. His strength and power is 300 times that of a human being as he continues to thrust with the power of the wolf. He lets out a shrill howl as the wolf would do, at the moment of climax. The sexual gratification becomes incredible as he rips Sammy's head off and starts to feed.

Billy and Beth have become very sexually involved. Beth is on top of Billy riding him and giving him the sexual pleasure that he had hoped for all night. Beth is kissing him passionately taking her nails and digging them into his chest as she rides him. All of a sudden the beast starts to materialize as Billy tells Beth that he is going to orgasm and just as he does, he transforms into the werewolf and grabs Beth and flips her over and starts to thrust with all the power that he has after transforming into the werewolf. Beth cannot believe what is happening. She becomes scared and screams when she can't get away from Billy. Billy is unable to control his urges, just like the night he killed Jeremy, Zach and Brittany.

Beth has a look of sheer terror on her face, frightened of what is happening, with Billy totally out of control. Sitting atop her, his penis still inside of her, he reaches down and rips her chest wide open, pulling her beating heart out and eats it in one huge swallow.

Moments later, Billy lays there on the ground, transformed back to a human, naked next to Beth's body. He looks over and sees her on the ground next to him all mangled, and he realizes he did it again. Her chest and belly are ripped open and her guts are hanging out.

Billy looks up and sees Morris over his shoulder as the werewolf is hulking over him. Billy is devastated, tears rolling down his cheeks not believing what he has just done to Beth. He yells at Morris, "Look! Look, what I did. You told me you would not let this happen. You told me everyone would be safe, you told me . . . oh my God, what have I done, Beth? You let me kill her, and you watched me, you watched me feed. You are nothing more than a monster, just like Coach told me."

Billy opens his mouth to scream and warn the other kids, and the werewolf quickly moves toward him grabs his tongue, and yanks it out of his mouth, quelling Billy's intended scream for help.

Blood spurts from Billy's mouth as Morris picks him up and throws him. Billy flies through the air and slams against a huge tree trunk with a thud, gurgling out a bunch of blood.

He quickly transforms back into a werewolf. He stands up and lunges at Morris who obviously did not expect Billy to transform once again to a werewolf. Billy lands a forceful punch square in Morris' chest. He flies backwards; the werewolf stands up and shakes his head and looks at Billy, as Billy is trying to snarl or howl, but he has no tongue to make noise for the others to hear.

He runs forward lunging at Morris. Morris quickly pulls the silver dagger from behind him and shoves it right into Billy's chest as he rushes toward him. Billy stops dead in his tracks. With a look of surprise at Morris, his eyes bulging, he drops down to his knees and then falls dead on the ground as he transfers back to a human Billy.

Danny is still sitting on top of Sammy with a fully erect penis still inserted in her, he looks below at her back covered with blood. He jumps up standing there naked and looks at her, realizing what he has done. He realizes that he has just killed a human again, and then fed on her. This makes his second human kill; he knows how close he is to going over to the other side.

A look of fear crosses his face. All of a sudden he looks up and sees that Morris, as the werewolf, is coming toward him. He is naked and covered with blood in human form realizing that Morris is coming after him for the kill. He takes off in human form, running through the woods. He knows he's not powerful enough to take on Morris. He knows that Morris could kill him with one swipe of his hand so he runs, and as he runs he transforms back into a werewolf, trying to escape from Morris.

Morris chases him through the woods and, at one point, gets very close, almost close enough to grab him. However, because Danny is smaller and more agile, he is able to slip away, accelerating with lightning speed. As he slips further away, Morris discontinues his chase, deciding to return to the campsite for more fun. The other kids there will be plenty for him.

Donnie and Donovan are both making so much noise having sex with their girls, Jane and Sally; they don't hear what has just happened outside the tent. Donnie is starting to get close to climax when he yells at Donovan, "Remember, you're in charge!" At that moment, both of the boys' eyes turn to yellow and the features of the wolves start to break through on their faces.

Donovan realizes that he's losing control. He tries to push away from Jane who has her eyes closed. She is enjoying every minute of the lovemaking session with Donovan. She reaches up and grabs his ass pulling him back closer to her once again as the monster starts to take more form and is taking more control. At that moment, his climax is reached. He is about 65 percent transformed into a werewolf and Jane opens her eyes.

When she sees what is happening, she becomes scared and screams piercingly. Donovan does not want to hurt her, but he reaches down and slaps her face to shut her up, contacting her with the arm that is already transformed into a werewolf limb and scratches her face with his claws. She starts crying hysterically trying to push Donovan away from her with all her might.

At the same time, Donnie and Sally have listened to the screams and witnessed what has happened right next to them. Donnie starts to orgasm and transform uncontrollably into a werewolf as well. He cannot control himself. He climaxes at the same time he completes his transformation.

Sally screams hysterically in fear and can't believe what she is seeing. She fights to try to get away. Both Donovan and Donnie are now werewolves and have never killed a human before, but the extreme sexual pleasure from the orgasm enhances their desire for the kill even though their immediate instinct is to try to back away from both of the girls. But the sexual pleasure has taken control with the beast as they continue to thrust to complete their full orgasm. At this very second with their penis fully erect and in each one of the girls, the tent rips apart with one mighty tear on the entire side, and Morris, the werewolf, is standing there salivating.

He sees Jane lying on the ground and he lunges for her. As he does, Donovan realizes that Morris is going for the kill and manages to spring himself at him and then Donnie jumps on him too, but Morris is older and much more powerful than both of them.

With one mighty swish of his arm he throws Donnie out of the tent clear across the campsite and into the bushes. He hits Donovan in the head. But Donovan immediately attacks him back and bites him on the neck. He pushes Donovan back with a forceful motion.

From behind his back, Morris grabs the silver dagger. At that minute, seemingly from nowhere, appears another werewolf, Coach Bloom? He grabs Morris and throws him down; the silver dagger goes flying through the air as Morris hits the ground and Coach Bloom attacks him.

They growl and snarl, ripping at each other. They bite each other back and forth ripping and biting. Snarling, scratching and knocking each other around with great strength. They beat each other back and forth.

While this battle rages, Donovan glances sideways and notices Donnie on the ground by the bushes. He has transformed back into human Donnie and is lying there naked and bloody.

Donovan becomes angry and lets out a piercing howling sound that only a wolf can make. He turns back and jumps into the middle of the fight with Coach Bloom and Morris.

Morris is on top of Bloom. Donovan jumps on Morris's back and starts to growl and rip in to Morris. Morris smacks Donovan so hard that something cracks in his body as he flies through the air and lands in a heap between Jane and Sally, who are both crying hysterically.

Donovan transforms back into human Donovan, bloody and naked, looking dead. Morris overtakes The coach and goes for his throat.

At that moment another werewolf appears; it's Jason from the junkyard. He grabs Morris and starts to rip into him hard, limbs flailing everywhere.

Morris is very powerful; he is able to take on both Jason and Bloom. They are snarling, growling, gnashing teeth, hitting, swiping and throwing. Morris hits Jason square in the head, knocking him to the ground. Bleeding and hurt, the coach comes at Morris. With one hard swift punch, Morris knocks him clear across the campsite.

Morris turns and sees Jason on the ground. Morris walks toward him and picks up the silver dagger. Jason is lying there hurt. He tries to get up and away, but Morris has come back for the kill.

At that moment, coach manages to bring out his own silver dagger as Morris lunges with all of his force for the final kill. The coach shoves the dagger into Morris's shoulder. Morris staggers back and looks at the dagger.

He reaches up and pulls it out of his shoulder, but it's too late. He knows it is. He looks at the coach, and then he looks at the dagger, which he realizes is identical to the one that he had used. As he starts to buckle at the knees, Morris's transformation from the werewolf begins. He looks at Coach Bloom, who is still 100 percent transformed as a werewolf, and utters, "My son," and drops the dagger, falling dead on the ground.

Coach Bloom backs up and looks to see that Jason, the other werewolf, has disappeared. He looks over at the girls who are still hysterically crying out of control, huddled in the corner of the tent. He takes a long glance at the two boys who both appear to be dead.

He hears the sirens of the sheriff's cars coming up the hill. He looks back at the girls and turns and looks at Morris one more time before exiting swiftly into the woods. As he is running through the woods back toward the bed and breakfast, he starts to transform back to his human self.

The sheriff's car is the first one at the scene. The sheriff hops out of his car and runs to what's left of the shredded tent. The girls are totally in shock, crying, rocking back and forth. He looks over and sees Donovan and then Donnie, lying on the ground bleeding.

The other deputies come rushing up to the scene; Deputy Cooper stands frozen looking at the remains of Beth's body. He turns and looks at the sheriff who has tears in his eyes, standing and looking down at the remains of Sammy.

"Jesus Christ, Cooper, I want every deputy we have up here as quickly as they can get up here. This is a mass kill, Cooper."

"Yes, sir, Sheriff, right away. Why did these kids come back up here? Sheriff, what the hell were they thinking?"

"I don't know, Cooper, I wish I did."

One of the deputies comes over to the sheriff

informing him and escorting him over to show him the mangled body parts of Billy, who has been torn apart into many pieces after Morris had finished feeding on him.

As he is standing there stunned, looking over Billy's body parts, another deputy comes running over to the sheriff, "Sheriff, come with me, it looks like the Gray boy may still be alive."

The sheriff turns and runs quickly toward Donovan. "Donovan?" As the sheriff rolls him over he sees that Donovan is definitely alive. "Cooper, call and tell 'em we need a couple more ambulances up here, NOW!"

The sheriff runs over to where Donnie is and looks at his body. Rolling him over gently, he sees that Donnie is breathing, but very shallowly. "Cooper, get your first aid kit out of the car and tell those ambulances to get up here fast!"

Various authorities, medical personnel and investigators arrive at the scene, one by one. Hours later, after getting all the kids out of the campground and sent to the hospital, the sheriff is ready to head back home. Wondering if each of the survivors would live or die, the sheriff is overwhelmingly devastated. He blames these events all on himself, and as he is driving along, he is listening to soft music on the radio.

Unexpectedly, tears start to stream down his face as he is overwhelmed with sadness. He can barely continue to drive he is so plagued with sadness; his tears are uncontrollable. He can barely see through all the tears in his eyes. Out of the blue, Brittany appears in the seat next to him.

"Daddy, it wasn't your fault. You did everything you could just like the night that Zach, Jeremy and I were taken."

He looks over at the passenger seat and sees Brittany sitting there through a blur of tears.

"Brittany, that can't really be you. I must be dreaming this."

"No, Daddy, it's me. We all get one chance, if we want, to come back one time for one visit, and this is mine. I wanted to come back and tell you that it's not your fault. You are a good dad and you took really good care of me and Jordan. Jordan's going to be okay, too. He is going to be different, but he is going to be okay."

Okay, wait a minute. I need to pull over; I'm hallucinating, the sheriff says to himself as he pulls over the car and stops.

"No, daddy, you're not. I'm really here."

"Can I touch you? Can I hold you?"

"No, I'm sorry. You can't, but I can sit here with you for a minute because I want to let you know how important you were to me."

With tears in his eyes, he says, "How important I was to you? You were everything to me. You were the light of my day. When we lost your mother, if it would not have been for you, I would've gone crazy. You took care of Jordan, God, how I miss you."

"I know you do. And, I miss you and Jordan," Brittany added. "You just have to know what you don't understand right now, that is okay and someday you will understand it all."

"Understand what?"

"That none of this is your fault, especially what happened tonight."

"How do you know about tonight?"

"That's why I'm here, for you, to make you understand that it's all out of your control. I love you, Daddy! My time is up, and I have to go now. I miss you and I miss Jordan."

Brittany starts to fade away.

"No! Don't go! Please, don't go! I love you

Brittany."

The sheriff sits back in the car seat, dropping his head into his hands and starts to cry uncontrollably, trying so hard to understand what he doesn't understand. Trying to understand what has happened not only to his daughter, Jeremy and Zach, but to the kids tonight up at the campground behind the old Hidden Valley Bed & Breakfast. The sheriff sits there staring out into the darkness, trying to figure out what Brittany has told him . . . that someday he will understand what he doesn't understand now.

CHAPTER 30

It's a dark bedroom and all you see is the silhouette of the nightstand next to the bed. The phone rings and the man rolls over, still asleep as he fumbles for the phone. "Yes, what is it?"

On the other end of the phone is an undistinguished voice, "Do you know what just happened in Hidden Valley? I thought you told me you had things under control."

"What are you talking about? I do have things under control. Everything is fine."

"I think you better make a phone call, because everything is not fine. What the hell has happened? There is no way we can keep things quiet with this type of mass murder going on. Now get it fucking taken care of, do you understand me, or I will have you taken care of."

"You better remember something if you want that land, you need me. Don't you fucking threaten me, do you understand? Because I have been told from the very beginning that I am safe and no one is to know anything. I'll make a phone call and I'll find out what's going on and I'll get back to you. But don't you ever fucking threaten me again!" He slams down the phone.

The man throws the covers back and gets out of bed. In the dark you can't see his face, but in the shadows you can see that he is naked as he walks over to the dresser and picks up a pack of cigarettes and a lighter.

From the other side of the bed you hear a female voice that calls out to him, "Honey, what's wrong? It's three o'clock in the fucking morning, come to bed."

He looks over at her, "It's okay, it's work related." As he lights a cigarette and takes a long drawn-out puff and then looks back at her and says, "I got to think about something and I got to make a couple phone calls. You go back to sleep."

He takes his cigarette and phone and walks out onto the balcony where he can oversee the entire city down below him with the lights, the traffic and all the hustle and bustle, even though it's only 3 a.m. He sits down and starts to make a phone call. It's answered by a younger male voice that is obviously still asleep. "Yeah who is this? Why are you calling at this time of the night?"

"It's me," says the man.

The younger male voice perks up, "Oh, what's wrong?"

"What the fuck is going on in Hidden Valley? I thought you told me the incident that happened up there six months ago was just a fuck up and that it would not happen again. Well you were obviously wrong, because I just got a phone call and I was told there was another mass murder done tonight. I want to know who's behind it. You better get on the phone and call Morris and find out what the fuck is going on up there, do you understand me?"

The younger voice answers, "Yes I understand and I'll take care of it right now."

The man hangs up the phone.

The younger male is sitting in bed wiping his eyes. He looks over at the clock, 3:45 a.m. He immediately dials Morris's number and only gets Morris's voice message. He hangs up the phone and immediately calls another number. The voice on that phone answers immediately and says, "What the fuck is going on?"

The younger male says, "I don't know that's what I'm calling you about."

The other voice says, "Morris is dead and it was a bloodbath."

The younger male looks horrified, "Morris is dead? Are you sure?"

"I am very sure, yeah. They better do something, because it's all coming apart and I don't know what the fuck is happening."

"Who killed Morris?"

"I have no fucking idea. The better question is why Morris went after the fucking kids and why did he go for the kill - but he accomplished his goal from the looks of what he was doing, anyway. Holy fuck . . . holy fuck, what the fuck did you guys get me into?"

"You aren't into anything that you aren't being very well paid for, so get things taken care of now!"

To be continued . . .

Hidden Valley Game On

Chapter 1: Understanding

The same old pile of cars that were surrounded by
other piles of junk such as loose tires mixed in with a
bunch of cardboard boxes is still there from the first day
he came in to town. Curt pushes his way through. The
dogs start to bark as he walks over towards the office -
the little square box in the middle of the junkyard that
Jason refers to as his office. All the dogs are snarling and
growling as Curt opens the door slowly and sees Jason
sitting at his desk writing in a notebook. Jason turns
slowly and sees Curt Bloom standing there with a smile
on his face.

"I was wondering how long it would take you to
figure it out," said Jason.

Curt looks at Jason and asks, "So it was you that
saved my life?"

"Well, you saved my life, too."

Curt sees an old chair by the window; he grabs it and
pushes it over to the desk.

Jason smiles and nods, "Sit down."

"Okay, tell me what's going on."

Jason sits back in his chair and looks at Curt. He shakes his head yes and starts to fill him in, "It's a very long story, do you have the time?"

The Sheriff is at the hospital in Jordan's room. Jordan is sitting up in bed with a smile on his face, looking much better than when his dad last saw him.

"It's amazing, are you sure you're really feeling better already?" asks the Sheriff.

Jordan looks at his dad, "Yeah, dad, I feel great. I actually feel really good. It's kind of crazy, you know, I feel strong and okay."

The Sheriff shakes his head in wonder, "The doctor said you slept really well all night."

Jordan smiles and shakes his head, "Yeah, thanks to Coach Bloom, I did."

"What the hell did Coach Bloom have to do with your sleeping?"

Jordan is caught off guard by this question and is a little bit surprised, "Well nothing really, other than he made me understand something."

"What did he make you understand?"

"Well, dad, I decided I want to play some sports."

The Sheriff looks at him in disbelief, "You all of a sudden want to play sports? When the hell did this happen?"

"Coach thinks that next year I might be able to be the quarterback on the JV football team."

"What?" the Sheriff is mystified; this is the kid that hated football. "You're going to be the quarterback? What the hell is going on here?"

Curt Bloom is back at the bed-and-breakfast with Judy. They are sitting at the table having a bite to eat. Tristan has his eyes focused on Curt who is looking deep into Judy's eyes. Judy has a big smile on her face.

"You know, you are one special woman," said Curt.

Judy nods her head in appreciation, "Well thank you, you are pretty special yourself."

Tristan had returned to eating when he hears his mom's response to Curt's statement he looks up from his plate and asks, "What's so special about him, he's just the Coach?"

Judy looks over at Tristan, "Oh no, he's more than just the Coach," with a big smile on her face. She asks Curt, "So you think you have this pretty well figured out?"

Curt looks at Tristan, gives him a little smile and looks back at Judy, "I have a pretty good idea of what has happened. I have a meeting with Dr. Marcus, the Sheriff and Jason at Mr. Fuller's diner in about two hours. I think we'll get some answers that'll make everybody happy."

"Well, I'll be very happy as long as you stay here," said Judy.

Tristan looks up again, "You want him to stay here?"

Curt smiles at Tristan, "Werewolves couldn't drag me away."

Tristan glances at his mother and returns his attention to Curt, "I keep telling you there are no werewolves; it's a myth, and it's a lie. But maybe there should be one, and maybe he could drag you out of here." Tristan glares at the Coach with steely eyes.

Curt ponders Tristan's statement for a moment and thinks to himself, "Nope, no way."

At the hospital, Dr. Marcus is in the room with Donovan, Donnie and the Sheriff.

Dr. Marcus is examining the boys, "This is the damnedest thing I've ever seen, Donovan's doing great. I almost feel guilty keeping both boys here in the hospital any longer. But, after those injuries they sustained last night, it's hard for me to believe they are almost ready to go home. And, Donnie, remember I said he would probably have to have some facial reconstruction. You can scratch that. That's about what it looks like on his face - nothing more than just a scratch. I'm telling you Sheriff it's the damnedest thing I've ever seen."

The Sheriff is standing and looking in amazement at both of the boys who are a hundred percent better than they were last night when he found them up behind the old bed-and-breakfast in a bloody mess. He can't believe what he is seeing, "Does this mean I can talk to them now?" asked the Sheriff.

Coach Bloom walks into the room just then, "Hey, Sheriff, why don't you wait until after we have our meeting at the diner."

The Sheriff glances up at the Coach with a questioning look on his face, "Why wait?"

Curt makes eye contact with Dr. Marcus then focuses back on the Sheriff, "Let's just do it for the kids, what do you say, Sheriff?"

The Sheriff shakes his head, "What the hell are you talking about Bloom?"

Curt has a worried look on his face knowing that he really has to push the Sheriff, he needs this extra time. Just a little more time so he can put things together, then he can talk to the Sheriff.

Curt shrugs, "What I'm saying, Sheriff, is let's give these kids a little more time to get over this. I told you, you will get all your answers tonight."

The Sheriff peers at Bloom. He is frustrated, tired, and worn-out. He thinks for a minute, nods his head, "Okay, Bloom, but if I don't get my answers, I'm coming right back here to talk to these kids. Do you understand me?"

Curt agrees, "Fair enough, Sheriff."

Donovan reaches over and grabs Curt's hand, catching Curt off guard. He looks at Donovan who has a sorry look in his eyes, "Thanks, Coach."

Curt smiles reassuringly, "Anytime Donovan, that's what I'm here for. Remember that."

Curt walks over and pats the Sheriff on the back as they walk out of the room.

Curt leaves the hospital and heads directly over to the high school looking for Danny. He finds Danny sitting on the hill up above the track. He walks up to him, "Danny, how are you doing?"

Danny looks up at the Coach with tears rolling down his cheeks. He immediately wipes the tears away trying to act as if it's no big deal, "I'm okay, Coach."

"Are you sure, Danny? That was your girl that was killed last night."

Danny looks over at the Coach, stands up and wipes himself off, "She wasn't my gal. I mean, I knew her, we went out a few times, but that's all, there was nothing there, nothing at all, Coach."

Curt takes a step back, he is shocked by Danny's statement, "Okay, so are you ready to be the next big thing when it comes to football that this school has seen in the last 35 years?"

Danny turns his head in Coach's direction, "Yeah, that's it. Coach Miller said I'd be the hottest rock star this football team has had in the last 35 years." He looks the Coach square in the eyes, "And, that's exactly what I plan on doing, do you understand me, Coach?"

"Okay, Danny, we will see."

Danny starts to walk away, turns and looks back at the Coach, "You will see." He turns and continues up the hill.

Curt stands there and thinks about him, "This kid scares the hell out of me; I'm going to have to keep a real close eye on him." He decides he needs to go back to the hospital and talk to Donovan about what just happened before he goes to the diner to speak with the Sheriff, Jason and Dr. Marcus.

Curt walks into the hospital room where Donnie and Donovan are recuperating, "Okay, you two, we all know what happened last night and it's going to stay between us. Danny's not going to talk. He's pretending like he didn't even know the girl, which has me very concerned and means that we have to keep a very close eye on him. I am depending on you two, to help me with that. Is that understood?"

Donnie and Donovan shake their heads in agreement. Donovan said, "Yeah, Danny is fucking crazy. He did say to me, 'Ask me if I want to control it?'"

Donovan looks up at the Coach, "I'm sorry, Coach, I should've listened to you and Donnie. I was really stupid; I thought I knew what I was doing. I thought I was ready, but it's obvious I wasn't."

The Coach reaches over and pats Donovan on the shoulder, "It's all taken care of. Hey, so we don't get that football title this year, nothing says we can't get one in baseball." The Coach winks at both Donovan and Donnie, who smile back at him.

"That's right, Coach, nothing says we can't get it in baseball," agrees Donovan.

Curt heads over to the diner thinking about how to handle this. He already filled Mr. Fuller in on what's going to happen and Mr. Fuller told him he's got it under control. He walks into the diner and sees Mr. Fuller, the Sheriff, Jason and Dr. Marcus sitting at one of the big tables. He walks up to the table, acknowledges everybody and goes over and pours himself a glass of water. Curt can see the Sheriff is starting to get antsy - he wants answers to his questions. Curt takes a drink of the water and looks at the Sheriff. "Okay, Sheriff, here it is, as crazy as it sounds." He looks at Mr. Fuller, "You want to tell him Mr. Fuller?"

Mr. Fuller shakes his head yes. He gets up, walks over and pours a glass of water for himself and takes a drink. He sits down next to the Sheriff. "Sheriff, this all started about a year and a half ago right here in this diner. One day Bob Miller came in, sat right there at the counter, and we were talking about how it was 35 years ago when we won our last, and our only, state championship. That was a great time, Sheriff; it was pretty out-of-control. I remember it as if it were yesterday. Miller decided that we were going to win one again and when he told me his plan, I told him I didn't want anything to do with his crazy idea. Morris had gotten some doctor to get a bunch of steroids that would work on these kids, giving them the strength of about 20 guys and making them able to do some unbelievable things. As you see, up until now, we've been pretty much unbeatable, Sheriff. Miller, he got crazy out-of-control. That kid, Billy that was killed last night, Sheriff, there were some things going on that were not right between Billy and Coach Miller, you know . . . in a sexual way. Well, Billy was going to talk to you; but Morris was afraid that if Billy did that it would all come out that he was getting the steroids for Miller to give to the boys, especially Billy. So Morris killed Bob Miller, but when he did, Katie and Bob Parker came along at the wrong time, so he killed them too. He made it look like a wild animal. He thought he could control Billy with the steroids, but they pretty much took over Billy. He became very strong and out-of-control. What Dr. Marcus says is that the steroids probably gave him a major sexual appetite."

The Sheriff looks over at Dr. Marcus who was shaking his head in agreement.

Mr. Fuller continues, "Morris came in here last night and told me everything. I told him this had to stop and I was going to go to you, Sheriff." With a shaky, emotional voice, Mr. Fuller looks right into the Sheriff's very sad eyes, "Morris told me that Billy killed Britney and the other two boys. So, last night, what we all figure is the kids decided to sneak back up to the bonfire and from what the doc says the evidence shows that Billy was having sex with the two girls, and ended up killing them both. From what we can tell, then Billy and Morris killed each other."

The Sheriff puts his hands up, looks around at the four men in the diner. He stands up and walks over to the pitcher of water, pours himself a glass turns around and takes a sip, "Do you really expect me to believe that B.S.?"

Jason gets up and walks over, gets himself a glass of water, looks at the Sheriff, Curt, Mr. Fuller, Dr. Marcus and then back at the Sheriff, "Well, Sheriff, that's the best we can come up with. Someday, Sheriff, you'll understand what you don't understand today."

The Sheriff steps back, drops his glass of water and it shatters on the floor. He looks at everybody in the room with a look of disbelief on his face and thinks to himself, "That's exactly what Britney said to me last night in the car when she came to visit me as a spirit." He stumbles over to the counter and picks up his hat.

Dr. Marcus is concerned, "Sheriff, are you okay?"

"Yeah, yeah, I'm okay except I'm not sure how much of this bullshit I can believe." He walks to the door, turns around and says to Curt, "Somebody else said that to me last night, 'That what I don't understand now, someday I'll understand.'" He turns and walks out the door.

Chapter 2:
It'll Never Be the Same

It's about 10 o'clock in the evening and Sheriff Thompson is sitting at his desk smoking a cigarette. As he sits there, the cigarette smoke billows around his face. With just the light from his desk illuminating it, it appears as if he is sitting in fog. The Sheriff's son, Jordan, comes up from behind his father and slowly places his hand upon his father's shoulder.

Jordan has his father's attention, "Daddy, it's not your fault; you did everything you possibly could. You warned everybody, daddy. You told them it was way too dangerous to have that bonfire. Nobody knew for sure what really killed Britney, Zach and Jeremy."

"Well, we do now, don't we? And, tomorrow is going to be one hell of a day, Jordan, having to deal with all those funerals. Having to look each of those parents in the eyes and knowing how each one of them feels."

Jordan sits down on the corner of the desk in front of his father, "Daddy, I understand. I understand more than I ever thought I could. Knowing how and why Britney was killed. That Billy did it because of the steroids that Coach Miller had given to so many of the kids. It all makes sense to me now, dad."

233

"Did that son of a bitch Miller try to get you to take those steroids too?" The Sheriff has such anger in his eyes it scares Jordan beyond belief.

"No, no, dad, I didn't take the steroids," Jordan is very uncomfortable. He gets up off the desk and starts to move away from his father.

The Sheriff grabs Jordan by the hand, "Look me in the eyes. Did you take those steroids Jordan?"

Jordan is frozen. He doesn't know what to say. He knows his life has changed forever, he will never be the same and he has to cover it up. He has to keep his dad from knowing; but at the same time, he can't let his dad go on feeling that it's all his fault, that's not fair.

He looks at his dad with tears in his eyes, "I had just started taking them. I wanted you to be proud of me. Coach Miller told me if I took the steroids and became strong, I could play sports and make you proud of me. They would make me the son that you wanted."

BIOGRAPHY
Jon Morgan Woodward, Writer and Producer

Jon Morgan Woodward has proven himself as an accomplished producer and director both on stage and in the area of television commercials. He has been acting since he was a child, going on to star in films such as: *"One Hour Fantasy Girl," "The Day The Music Died,"* and *"IJE The Journey."*

In the 1970s Jon was creating some of the very best in off-Broadway theater. He directed the outstanding comedy drama *"Overtown,"* which was reinvented and rewritten as a musical, as well as the very popular *"I'll be Home for Christmas."* He also directed *"Mr. Scrooge finds Christmas,"* starring Patti Page as Mrs. Cratchit, and Neil Simon's incredible play *"Plaza Suite."*

Continuing forward with some of the best theater production companies, Jon was the co-producer and director of the incredible old-time favorite *"Curse You Jack Daulton,"* for which the musical score was written and directed by David Lee. Jon also helped produce the off-Broadway production of "*Catch-22*," an incredible theatrical success. Many of the plays that he directed or help produce received incredible reviews.

Although Jon was a very popular character actor in the 70s, some of his most well-known performances are those that were done through television commercials. It was during this time that he appeared in a featured role in Paul Newman's critically acclaimed motion picture "*Sometimes a Great Notion*."

Jon was the national spokesman for The National Glass Company for 2 1/2 years. He was on television selling energy saving ceiling mirrors for bedrooms and living rooms created to reflect the ambient light from large cities at night.
In the 80s Jon became very involved with both the "Just Say No to Drugs" campaign and with the White House Conference for Drug-free America. He did television commercials with Nancy Reagan and the like, telling us to "Just Say No to Drugs." With Drug-free America and their team they created the commercial, "This is your brain on drugs."

In the 90s Jon continued his work in television commercials and then in 1999, he appeared in the Hallmark Hall of Fame movie "*Night Ride Home*." This was the 200th feature length production from Hallmark, starring Rebecca De Mornay, Keith Carradine and Thora Birch.

Taking time out to marry, raise a family and earn his Ph.D., Jon has returned to Los Angeles to resume his acting career. Jon lives by the motto, "no part too small, and no character too large."

HIDDEN VALLEY

THE

AWAKENING

Additional Copies or e-Copies of *Hidden Valley: The Awakening*
Available through:
www.HiddenValleyTheMovie.com
*Discounts offered for multiple book orders.

Audiobook Copies of *Hidden Valley: The Awakening*
Also available!

As read by Jon Morgan Woodward, the author of *Hidden Valley: The Awakening* and the author of the original screenplay *Hidden Valley: The Awakening*. Woodward adds the mystery, intrigue, and dramatic climaxes throughout the twisted tale that promise to keep you in suspense.

Also on www.HiddenValleyTheMovie.com

- Information on book signings

- Information on upcoming opportunities to meet the cast

- Recent news of book, movie, cast, and celebrities associated with the movie

- Updates on future releases within the *Hidden Valley Saga*

More on the author, Jon Morgan Woodward

For further information about Hidden Valley: The Awakening, The Hidden Valley Saga Series, or Hidden Valley The Movie, visit
www.JonMorganWoodward.com

Stay current with Social Media

www.Twitter.com/HiddenValleyMOV
www.Facebook.com/HiddenValleyTheMovie